ROMANCES OF THE METAPHYSICALS

BOOK III:

THE
FINAL FORTNIGHT
OF YEARS:
THE DARKENING

LARRY RINEHART

Cover Art: From Gustav Dore's illustration for
                    Revelation 12:1.

Cover Design: Shelley Savoy, Savoy Designs.

TABLE OF CONTENTS

AUTHOR'S PREFACE

This third Book of my *Romances of the Metaphysicals* completes the narrative course of seventeen years, from the college graduation of the titular characters until the End of Time. Along the way it picks up two more Metaphysicals, born of the original four, and follows their developing romance, not to mention their artistic accomplishments, into their thirteenth year. The characters of the elder Eckharts and Losskys are also fleshed out a bit more, in the usual idealizing style of these Books. Overall, the narrative focus for the Darkening Years is more on the inner lives of the characters as they anticipate the approach of the End. In Book II, households were established, environments and occupations were described, and the Quest for the Glorious Synthesis preoccupied the principal characters, while the children lived their early childhood. In Book III, although plenty of outward adventure remains, the adults grow more introspective while the children develop into romantic lovers—within the bounds of courtly celibacy, of course.

The era of the Antichrist is depicted here within the broad framework of biblical prophecy, and scriptural signs are cited along the way, but much imagination is deployed in the details of the plot, as well as in the insertion of the theme of an American Restoration into the history of the apocalyptic war. This latter operation necessitated the description of certain events dating from 2017 through the author's contemporary moment, placing him in an interesting position to comment upon occurrences current and recent. It is, therefore, the most political of the three Books, despite my repeated insistence that the political aspect of their narrative be considered a *mythos*—a fictive construct. I write as a romancer, not a prophet.

Given that the target audience, or better said, the ideal Reader of these *Romances* is an intellectually insatiable Christian, who loves not only Holy Scripture but the tradition of the Church of All Time, some explanation is due of several theological peculiarities in our tale. To begin with, not only does Christ repeatedly appear to our Metaphysicals, He consistently appears as the Christ Child, either or both of which contingencies may appear questionable to some readers. To this I plead the precedent that our Lord has appeared to spiritual Christians periodically in the history of the Church, and sometimes in His form as a Child—both St. Anthony of Padua and St. Rose of Lima are examples. Then there are the two children, David and Magdalena, born at the express direction of the Child (that their parents marry and bear children), and drawn into an ongoing relationship with Him which culminated in "playing a game" together. The suggestion here is that God has a playful side, even as the Greek philosopher Heraclitus, who spoke of the Logos, likened the Creator to a child at play, and that therefore the Christian romancer be allowed the license to imagine a non-biblical side plot to the great biblical narratives of the End.

Another matter deserving of a word of explanation is

the ecumenical ambience of these *Romances*, specifically the displacement of the See of Rome by the Patriarchate of Moscow, and the rapprochement of the latter with orthodox Lutherans. To the former point, I believe that Vatican II was a disaster for the Roman church and for all of what was once Christendom; and that the arrival of Francis marks the end of papal authority, although individual bishops and priests, and societies thereof, will maintain the Roman tradition. Of the other five ancient Sees, only Moscow is free of Muslim governance, wherefore I offer the fictive hypothesis that Orthodoxy, rather than Catholicism in the Roman sense would offer the solidest ecclesiastical anchor in chaos preceding the End. As for the turning of orthodox Lutherans to Orthodoxy (leaving aside the prominent example of Jaroslav Pelikan), even that staunch champion of the Lutherans, Hermann Sasse, reflecting on Vatican II in 1976, expressed the hope that "the Eastern Orthodox Church ... will prove itself the guardian of Orthodoxy." (*The Lonely Way*, V. 2, 433) Once again, the reader is reminded that these Books are apocalyptic romance, not prophecy.

It should perhaps be pointed out that two specific theological errors are called out for anathema in the course of the narrative: the notion that rapture of I Thessalonians precedes the great Tribulation rather than coinciding with the return of Christ *after* that dire period; and the idea of a peaceful earthly millennium under the rule of Christ, before the End of Time. The former error is perhaps more prominent among Evangelicals and the latter among Roman Catholics, but neither is founded on the traditional interpretation of Scripture.

Northrop Frye, in his magisterial *Anatomy of Criticism*, describes an "archetypal criticism" or "theory of myths," on the premise that "in myth we see the structural principles of literature isolated." Frye defines "four narrative elements of literature which (he calls) *mythoi* or generic plots." He explains: "If we are told that what we are about to read is tragic or comic, we expect a certain kind of structure and mood, but not necessarily a certain genre. The same is true of the word romance, and also of the words irony and satire." The four *mythoi* just mentioned—comedy, romance, tragedy, and irony/satire—correspond in turn to four seasons of the year—spring, summer, fall and winter, respectively—as learnedly elaborated by Frye. The point of all this is to identify, in the optic of archetypal criticism, the literary *mythos* of these *Romances*, the *genre* of which has been discussed in the previous two Prefaces. Besides being romances by genre, it seems to me, these Books bear also the *mythos* of romance, where "the essential element of plot is adventure (culminating in) the quest." But just as each of the four seasons borders on those preceding and following it, such that the seasons intermingle at their extremities, an analogous mingling of *mythoi* is described by Frye. For example, as early summer may still wear shades of spring, so the *mythos* of *romance* may be mingled with a *tinge of comedy*—which is exactly how I would classify these Books in the cycle of *mythoi*, given the invincibly comic plot of the Christian revelation, to which these narratives aspire to be faithful.

The Preface to Book II quotes Hawthorne to the effect that what the American romancer needs is an "atmosphere" akin to a "Faery Land" in order to ply his art on American soil, to which my response was that "these *Romances* seek to suggest an Angelic Land, ontologically overlapping the earthly habitats of our characters and rigorously grounded in Christian metaphysics." That intention has remained in play throughout the composition of the Book in hand, dear reader, and on that note I conclude my literary comments by quoting from the Frontispiece of William Blake's *America a Prophecy*:

> **But tho' obscur'd, this is the form of the Angelic land.**

Consider it a motto for these Books, of which now only the Paradise remains to be written.

Finally, heartfelt thanks to my editorial staff: my wife Donna, who does the first read-through with markups, and Jim Henderson, whose critical adeptness adds a second layer of corrections and rewordings, which are invaluable in producing the final MS. In addition to their inestimable help in the production of these *Romances*, Donna has been a wonderful partner, companion and lover for more than thirty years, and Jim, a steadfast friend since our college days, has consistently supported my adventures into literature.

With all of that said, my Metaphysicals have promised me a tour of Paradise, where I shall now attempt to follow them, presumably not literally, just yet. I'll write when I can.

June 2023

PROLOGUE:
SILENT AND STILL

Having closed the previous Book of these *Romances* on Christmas Day, 2050, we open the present one just two weeks later, on January 8, 2051, the Sunday after Epiphany. Christopher Eckhart, as we join him after supper that evening, has retreated to the hayloft study he shares with his wife and is alone there. His intention is to meditate on one of the sermons composed for that Sunday by his namesake the Meister—the one on the text where the boy Jesus tells His earthly parents that He must be about His Father's business. But the events of the past week, on top of the Global Quake in December and the disastrous elections in November, are presently preoccupying his cogitations, and the book of Eckhart's sermons is still lying unopened on his desk. The events in question began with another election, worldwide in scope, in which hundreds of delegates from all over Earth convened in the ruins of Jerusalem, voted a Declaration establishing a Global Emergency Council (GEC) and, on Tuesday, January 3, elected a Chairman.

The stated mission of the GEC was to coordinate provision of disaster relief and oversee reconstruction of the areas most devastated by the Quake, and the organization was very well funded to address that mission. In fact, the sufficiency of the funding extended to a modest military force under GEC authority, and mention was made of a possible expansion of this force with troops from designated nation-states. Moreover, the governments of the sovereign nations were requested to ratify the GEC Charter, subordinating the nation-states politically to the GEC. Russia had immediately refused, but the American situation was complicated by the destruction of the District of Columbia, and the consequent dispersion of the Senate, putting in doubt the ability of that august body to convene a quorum in order to give consent (or not) to the Charter. After four days of tense uncertainty, the President just yesterday, Saturday, had invoked Article IV, Section 3, declared an "extraordinary Occasion," and dissolved Congress, promptly replying to the GEC that the United States would not be signatory to the Charter. Given the recent Socialist takeover of Congress, and the globalist sympathies of the new majority, this executive action was likely to be contested—how vigorously remained to be seen—raising the question of what stance would be taken by the military. The year ahead would doubtless be an "interesting" one.

Another, related theme on Christopher's mind that evening pertained to the participation of his family in local food relief efforts, as Rosa's farm-to-table network had dipped into their winter reserves for delivery to harder-hit areas around Pittsburgh. The participating farmers were also making plans to produce enough in the season ahead, God willing, for regular shipments of vegetables, eggs and meat to designated areas, until the normal supply chains could be restored. Then there was the new gas well that he and John had been planning since they discovered that the Quake, having left their buildings undamaged, had opened a seam of natural gas in the Carboniferous Absaroka sediments they farmed, with a vent in one of their grass fields. This was an almost unbelievable Godsend, but much thought was required in figuring out the best way—and the cheapest—to cap and contain the gas for running tractors and heating. Meanwhile, he and Sophie had assured Killgower that they would keep their shoulders to the wheel of polemical counterattack in defense of the Glorious Synthesis, against the critical attacks of those who sought to refute or discredit its theoretical claims, or its empirical evidence.

Christopher's study is steeped in the silence of the January night—no cattle are lowing below in the barn, not even a mouse is stirring—as he stares at the book on his desk by the light of two candles, pondering still upon current concerns. The Sheriff has already been in touch, and was calling up the Posse to convene in Clarion on the Ides of January, for the purpose of organizing regular patrols within the county and along its borders. In addition, there were likely to be a couple of weekend training sessions, all of which would involve a commitment of time by himself and his dad, but after all, it was for emergencies like this that they had signed on to the Posse in the first place. They and their neighbors were going to have to navigate their way through a political battlefield where the President, having dissolved Congress to save the sovereignty of the Republic, would be embattled both by members of that

Congress and by the Global Emergency Council, to which the sovereignty of the Republic was to have been ceded. Vigilance would have to become their watchword.

Then there were the ominous theological implications of the so-called election of the globalist Chairman, to whom Pastor Cornelius referred this very morning as the leading candidate for the Antichrist, the Son of Perdition himself. The Chairman's initial pronouncements have portrayed him almost as an angel of light, so beneficent and reassuring has been his rhetoric, replete with promises of abundant relief and future prosperity. In addition to restoring supplies and services, the GEC would undertake titanic projects of reconstruction in major urban areas devastated by the Quake, including a massive restoration of the Temple Mount in Jerusalem and construction of the third Temple. The pastor had probably nailed it, and if so, his sermon had just announced the beginning of the seven-year reign of Antichrist foretold in biblical prophecy.

As these distracting cogitations arrive at the sermon of Pastor Cornelius, our hero is recalled to the sermon of Meister Eckhart, for the Sunday after Epiphany, upon which it has been his intention to meditate. With a deep sigh, he leans toward his desk and opens the book. Having studied the sermon before, Christopher proceeds by perusing the whole of it while taking special note of the passages marked from earlier readings, thoughtfully recalling the overall shape of the discourse. The Meister's main subject is "the eternal birth ... which occurs every day in the innermost recess of the soul," and he says that "to know this birth ... one should be about his Father's business," like the boy Jesus in the sermon's text. The knowledge of this innermost, eternal birth is conceptualized in terms of a theory of intellectual operations, as involving the agent intellect and the possible intellect in relation to divine Intellect. Ordinarily, the agent intellect abstracted intelligible form from knowable objects while the possible intellect received the abstracted forms, completing the act of knowledge. In knowing the eternal birth, however, the agent intellect became passive to divine Intellect, "so that God may undertake the work at hand, and then the mind must hold still and let God do it," and what is received by the possible intellect is the Word of God.

> God begets His Son or the Word in the soul
> and, receiving it, the soul passes it on in many
> forms, through its agents, now as desire, now
> as good intentions, now in loving deeds, now
> in gratitude and whatever concerns it. These
> are all His and not yours at all.

A philosophical smile tugs at the corners of Christopher's mouth. Here is a welcome counterweight to the maelstrom of disquiet that has surrounded him in the refuge of his study. This teaching of the Meister reminds him of Luther's understanding of faith and works, whereby Christ and the Holy Spirit, actually indwelling the spiritual heart by faith, actively perform the good works accomplished by the believer. The sermon continues:

> Above all, claim nothing for yourself. Relax

and let God operate you and do what He will
with you. The deed is His; the Word is His;
this birth is His; and all you are is His, for you
have surrendered self to Him, with all your
soul's agents and their functions and even your
personal nature.

Here was the counsel he needed to cope with the coming
years, which he now had every reason to believe would
bring to pass the great tribulation, culminating in the fiery
End of Time. There would be words to be spoken, actions
to be taken, deeds to be done; but God would do it all if
one only "surrendered self."

Then, at once, God comes into your being and
faculties, for you are like a desert, despoiled of
all that was peculiarly your own. The Scripture
speaks of "the voice of one crying in the
wilderness." Let this voice cry in you at will.
Be like a desert as far as self and the things of
this world are concerned.

This is no doubt the right counsel for the times, but it
is *hard* counsel, Christopher Eckhart murmurs to himself.
I'm a Lutheran farmer, not a Dominican friar like the
Meister. Can I surrender self, and even personal nature, to
be despoiled of everything peculiarly my own? Can I let
God operate me?

Breathing deeply, he turns to the final

paragraphs of the sermon, where he is brought to a halt by this sentence:

Let your spirit be uplifted and not downcast, burning and yet pure, silent and still.

Leaning back in his chair, Christopher closes his eyes, as the aforesaid philosophical smile spreads across his bearded visage.

YEAR EIGHT

(2051 A.D.)

I.

Looking back over the first six months of the Year of Our Lord twenty fifty-one, Father Maxim Lossky-Mendes was at a loss to tell where they had gone, leaving behind such a blur that only the liturgical regularity of the weeks lent order to his recollection of them. After the successful conclusion of the Quest for the Glorious Synthesis, followed by the Global Quake with its apocalyptic overtones, our theologian had taken a pronounced inward turn, intellectually, increasing his already regular practice of the Jesus Prayer, fingering more frequently the knots of his *tschotki*. *Lord Jesus Christ, Son of God, have mercy on us sinners*. Maxim preferred the first-person plural, *us sinners*, to the singular *me a sinner*, for thus he was praying for the whole Church, himself included, as in the fifth article of the Lord's Prayer, *Forgive us our trespasses*, and not for himself alone. At heart, however, the practice of the Jesus Prayer was not simply a plea for mercy, let alone a pious devotion, but also an alignment of the human intellect with divine Intellect, the Logos of God in the *perichoresis* of the Holy Trinity, which provided spiritual stability amidst the mental stresses associated with the apocalyptic atmosphere.

Still, those six months remained mostly a blur—with two notable exceptions. The first occurred on January 6, the Feast of Epiphany, when several parishioners of St. Michael and All Angels Russian Orthodox Church, as they approached the nave doors for the Divine Liturgy, were astute enough to notice a slight but startling alteration in the icon of the Archangel above the doors. The reader of Book II of these *Romances* may recall that Maxim's mother Manuela had donated this icon to the church in the fall of 2044, where it had guarded the entrance to the nave for nearly seven years: St. Michael resplendent in celestial armor, standing upon a recumbent red dragon, the point of his lance piercing the beast's crimson scales. At least, that was its original form. Now, it seemed that the feet of the Archangel had shifted just enough that he no longer stood *on* the beast but just beside it, and that the point of his lance, while poised above the writhing red body, no longer penetrated the latter. The prophetic implication of this apparently miraculous alteration of the icon was not lost on the astute parishioners who reported it to the priest, any more than on Maxim himself. Divine restraint of the Adversary, which had made possible the Age of the Church and, more recently, the Eliatic Restoration, was being loosed *for a little while*, according to the *Revelation* to St. John, *to deceive the nations which are at the far corners of the Earth*. Given the nature of the times, the miraculous alteration was in one sense hardly surprising, yet a miracle was a miracle, and this one afforded a somewhat startling diagnostic of the *zeitgeist*.

The other notable exception to the general blur of that half-year was the appearance of two visitors at the door of St. Michael's parsonage one chilly winter night. Maria and

Magdalena had been reading a storybook about the prophet Elijah—how God had used him to oppose a wicked king and queen, how an angel had given him bread and water in the desert, how he had been taken straight to heaven in a chariot of fire amidst a whirlwind, and how he would come back before Jesus did. Maxim, who had been listening quietly, rose to answer a knock at the door and found, as he opened it, two venerable old men clothed in the manner of the ancients, both wearing robes and mantles. Frozen at first with astonishment, the priest quickly recovered his composure and, with a reverent bow, invited Enoch and Elijah in from the cold. He and Maria had met these venerable ancients only once before—by the Great Lake on the planet Sadronia, more than seven years earlier—but their identities were unmistakable once the shock of surprise subsided. The visitors immediately wanted to meet Magdalena, upon whom they both pronounced the warmest of blessings while she, for her part, could hardly believe that here was the holy prophet she had just been reading about, and a friend of his that God had also taken directly to heaven! Maria quickly brewed a pot of tea, and over steaming mugs the venerable pair imparted the import of their visit. Their itinerary would take them to Jerusalem, where the Lawless One would establish his capital—yes, this new "Chairman" was indeed he—and their mission was to denounce him unflinchingly and to defy him with supernatural powers. The two ancients had stopped by on their way, as they also would visit the Eckharts, to meet and to bless the two children as well as to encourage their parents to stand firm in the coming years. Declining to stay the night, Enoch and Elijah then departed as abruptly as they had appeared. Thanking Maria for the warming refreshment, they put down their empty mugs, raised their hands in blessing, and disappeared into thin air.

Especially interesting to Maria was their confirmation of the apocalyptic identity of the global Chairman, who had become an object of her own studies in current history. There was a certain obscurity surrounding his origins, but he presented himself as being Jewish, and though several early references mentioned the tribe of Dan as his lineage, from the time of his entry into public life he had claimed to be of the tribe of Judah. Since the latter was the royal tribe of David, Solomon, Josiah, Hezekiah and Jesus, this claim would be crucial for his appeal to the Jewish people to be their long-awaited Messiah, who would make Jerusalem the capital of the world and rebuild the Temple. Indeed, the first half-year of his tenure suggested that that was exactly his plan, although he was proceeding cautiously, biding his time and building his image as a fascinating, intelligent and merciful man who was interested only in alleviated the suffering of the billions of people impacted by the Global Quake. At his disposal was an enormous reservoir of private wealth, accumulated in networks of trust funds and nonprofit foundations, for financing massive reconstruction projects along with visionary agricultural initiatives to feed the hungry. Regarding his appeal to Jews, the picture was not yet clear. His appearance seemed to have stirred up a ferment among the varieties of Jewish people, generating speculation, discussion and controversy, with polling results that fluctuated inconclusively. But then, after all, he had not yet made any explicitly messianic claims.

Maria was finding the transition from geometer to historian an enjoyable one, occasionally amusing herself by comparing the two disciplines, the abstract and the concrete, mathematical necessity and historical contingency, all the while loving them both. As an historian, our pert, blue-eyed blond had taken on the epic project of portraying the American Restoration as prelude to the last seven years of time, and simultaneously portraying those last seven years *as they happened.* In relation to this project she liked to think of herself, half-ironically, as the "Thucydides of the Apocalypse," a moniker that always made her smile and her bright blue eyes twinkle. She considered the Restoration as having started c. 2017, when an intelligence memo entitled "Political Warfare" was presented to the providential President, detailing an array of tactics already in play by networks of domestic operatives in league with several foreign adversaries. The election of 2016 had disrupted a long-term, bi-partisan plan to subordinate the American Republic to globalist governance, and thereby to destroy the liberty and plunder the wealth of the American people. The Chinese Communist Party, along with certain globalist foundations, reacted to the disruption of their operation by colluding with their agents in political, media and social media circles to launch a multi-pronged attack on the duly elected President.

The 2017 memo also outlined a broad counter-attack, including the use of military intelligence and cybercommand resources to mount defensive actions, and to gather evidence for presentation to military tribunals, should the corruption of the civil judiciary prove incapable of justice. Later that year, a cadre of military intelligence officers began dropping crumbs of information on a dark-web message board, including pictures and time-stamp correlations proving beyond statistical doubt that they were working with, and at the direction of the President. The drops also described a covert military counterinsurgency operation to counter the globalist gambit, with particular mention of the Special Forces and the Marines, and presented a staggering volume of damning evidence implicating prominent public figures in criminal activities, including human trafficking and the sexual abuse of children. As our Thucydides considered the remarkable results that eventually came to pass from that covert operation, she felt confident in assigning the origin of the American Restoration to that seminal year.

Theologically viewed, that marvelous period appeared as an Eleatic interlude in the final formation of the system of the Antichrist—Eleatic as occurring just prior to the return of Christ—which currently looked to be no more than seven years away. Politically, it was simply too soon to draw comparisons between the continuity-of-government operation in 2021-22, which she had not yet fully chronicled, and the current situation of the Republic, which she had not yet entirely sorted out. With the Capital destroyed and the Senators and Representatives dispersed, the President had dissolved Congress under the "extraordinary Occasion" clause, triggering a rash of lawsuits that were bogged down in the courts, on top of which only six justices of the Supreme Court had survived the Quake. So far as she and Max could discern, neither the City of San Angelo nor local law enforcement had heard anything about a devolved military command in the region—not even the Sheriff of Tom Green County. The arrival of spring brought a sudden upsurge of illegal border crossings, just like in the early twenties, and the Lucky M was barely sixty miles north of Del Rio.

Ah the Lucky M! What a joy it remained for the three of them! Maria and Magdalena drove down to the ranch twice a week for equestrian purposes, on one of which excursions Maxim would generally accompany them. The little girl was delighted to be riding between her parents, comfortably astride her little red burro, among the lovely and melodious ridges and valleys she had known from infancy. There had been some discussion of moving Thunder, Sable and Dancer to a boarding stable on the outskirts of San Angelo, for convenience and economy, but Magdalena argued vehemently for keeping their mounts in the Hill Country. Her journal writing at that time drew much of its material from the little ranchero where her grampa had been a cowboy, and she and David had ridden sheep, and where they now had to ride around several landslides from the big Quake. For the time being her pleas prevailed, but with conditions at the border deteriorating the discussion was far from closed—and for that matter, a young girl's fancy is prone to wander.

The other principal theme of Magdalena's writing was her cousin David, who knew such things, and did such valiant deeds, and sang her such songs to his lute, that he left her almost breathless at times—even over her i-screen. She liked to write about adventures she and David would have as they got older, and one of the interesting points about those adventures was that they were centered around the Eckhart farm in western Pennsylvania, not the Texas Hill Country—a point which her parents quickly discovered to have nonfictional implications. The reader may recall that David and Magdalena had earlier discussed (not to say conspired about) her family moving to Pennsylvania, and the girl was now gradually introducing the idea to her parents, using her adventure stories as conversation starters. Given her love for the little ranchero in the Hill Country, it was not without a twinge of attachment that Magdalena found fancy diverting her desire northward, closer to David and to Dancer as well. Her parents initially dismissed the proposition with smiles; however, it may have lingered in the backs of their minds.

In St. Petersburg, meanwhile, Sergei and Manuela were getting pretty well settled into their new situation, as repair work got underway on the relatively minor damage to bridges and other infrastructure wrought by the Quake. Sergei was enjoying his teaching post in the Russian Language Program for international students, especially for the opportunity it gave him to meet intelligent and interesting young people from a variety of countries and cultures. In conversation with several Chinese students, for example, he learned much about the revival of traditional Chinese civilization that had followed the collapse of the Communist Party in the mid-twenties, as well as about the recent reappearance of troubling agitation and propaganda by

underground Communist cells. He also had the opportunity to question a couple of bright young Palestinian
Arabs with family in Jerusalem regarding the rumors about
the reconstruction of the Temple Mount and the possible
erection of the third Temple. The word on the ground was
that this was actually under negotiation with Arab Muslim
leaders, who were considering alternative sites for reconstructing the mosque of Omar, destroyed in the tectonic
collapse of the Temple Mount during the Quake. It seemed
that the majority of Israeli Jews, cheered on by certain
American Evangelicals, were fairly enthusiastic about the
project, although a number of orthodox rabbis and their
synagogues remained skeptical of the messianic credentials
implied by the Chairman's proposal.

Another interesting thing Sergei was learning in the
Russian academic milieu was how highly regarded, and how
widely discussed in those circles, was the Glorious Synthesis. Creation science research had been underway in Russia
since the beginning of the century, and science in this key
had been taught in public schools alongside standard scientific theories, educating cadres of scientists who had in turn
contributed significantly to the Quest. Sergei's colleagues
were delighted to discover that here was the father of two
of the legendary Metaphysicals—and father-in-law of the
other two—making him something of a minor celebrity in
their midst. The visiting professor happily conveyed this
wave of positive response to the aforementioned four, sup-
plementing his messages to Chris and Sophie with specific
references, as he knew it was they who were tasked with
monitoring responses and mounting polemics.

By the arrival of spring Manuela had found, and been accepted by, a master iconographer and Hieromonk at a nearby monastery, the Holy Trinity Alexander Nevskiy Lavra, to study the sacred art more deeply under his tutelage. They would meet twice a month at the monastery, and in between she would work (and pray) on a miniature icon of a subject he would assign. Manuela set up a small studio in the cottage with just enough room and light for her icon work, as well as an easel or two upon which she intended to dabble in watercolors. She also was able to acquire a couple of dairy goats and a local supply of fodder—her available grazing area being but minimal even in the best grass-growing weather—and Sergei had helped her build stalls in one of the outbuildings, along with another stall large enough for a horse. They had agreed that two goats and a horse were about all the livestock they could keep in their reduced circumstances, having confirmed that they could occasionally rent Manuela a mount from a neighbor. Sergei therefore proceeded to purchase a handsome grey stallion, somewhat elderly but still in prime condition (just like himself, he mused ironically), which he promptly christened "Whitman" after the "Good Grey" poet. It seemed to him fitting that having named his American horse after a Russian literatus, he should name his Russian horse for an American one—and besides, "Hi Ho, Whitman!" didn't sound half bad at all.

Those same six months passed over Pennsylvania with equal eventfulness, and with equal alacrity, to the manner in which we have narrated their passage in Texas and in Russia. We begin with the visit of Enoch and Elijah to the

Eckhart farm, which occurred immediately upon their sudden disappearance from St. Michael's parsonage, when they appeared on the veranda joining the farmhouse and the cottage, knocking on the door of the latter. Sophie, who was finishing up in the kitchen, opened the door to find the venerable pair standing there. Recognizing them at once, she reverently invited them in as she called out to Chris, who was tussling with David on the living room floor and showing him a few wrestling holds. The two old men beamed at the father and son as they rose from the floor, Christopher bowing slightly and David following suit. Sophie's offer of hot chocolate was gladly accepted, and as she returned to the kitchen to prepare it, Enoch and Elijah each laid a hand on the boy's head and blessed him. David of course, whose big brown eyes were now about as wide as they could get, wanted to know who these awesome fellows were, and how they knew his mom and dad, upon which Christopher reminded him of the tales he'd been told about the starship *Synaxis*, and the Great Lake on the planet Sadronia, and what had happened there. A look of comprehension crossed David's face. "Wow! Enoch and Elijah!" Smiling solemnly, the venerable ancients then repeated to the young Eckharts what they had revealed to the Texans regarding the eschatological identity of the global Chairman, his plans for Jerusalem, and their mission to oppose him there. With that said, they drained their mugs of hot chocolate, admonished David and his parents to stand firm in the faith, and departed in the same fashion as before.

The visit of the ancients, impressive as it was brief,

left David eager to hear again the tale of how Enoch and Elijah had been waiting for his mom and dad, and Uncle Max and Aunt Maria, when they arrived on the backs of unicorns at the shore of the Sadronian Lake. They had landed on that planet in the starship *Synaxis*, ridden on golden-horned white unicorns, and after being greeted by the two venerable men had seen the Christ Child fly in on a giant swan, and had taken Communion from Him, and as the Lake had turned all golden, a shining City had risen out of the water! Then the two had told his mom and dad and aunt and uncle to go home and get married and have him and Magdalena. On this score David felt thankful to them. Indeed, they quickly became his new heroes, which entailed two new action figures plus a Christ Child figurine for good measure (his other Jesus figure being grownup). These new figures, along with those of Noah and his family, David and Goliath, and the grownup Jesus with the Twelve and Mary Magdalene, brought his total cast of characters to twenty-seven, which allowed him to man the *Synaxis*, the Ark and the fishing boat perfectly for the high adventures he dreamed up in his fantasy play. The latter, meanwhile, assumed a somewhat more combative tone, for while David did not possess a parallel collection of villains, he did have Goliath, who was well qualified to lead the enemy forces, as well as an impressive cadre of dinosaur figures, including several fearsome renderings of *T. Rex*.

With this array of toys on hand, our boy genius was well positioned for hours of creative theater, with the figures of David and Magdalena always in the thick of the action and never far from the Christ Child, as the forces of light fought with the forces of darkness. There were also, of course, both musical and literary aspects of David's play, and not infrequently, songs were introduced into the action—songs in the sweet new style inspired by the mysterious *white stone*. Taking the seven enigmatic characters engraved on the stone as the seven tones of the octave scale, and systematically changing the order of the tones in seven-note phrases written out on music paper, David had developed a method for stringing these musical phrases together into melodies. The corresponding lyrics were scanned as seven-syllable lines matching the melodic phrases, and the very simplest accompaniment on the lute rendered the result utterly enchanting—a sweet new style indeed—especially with Magdalena chiming in over the i-screen.

The silver-grey mule colt named Samson, in the meantime, was growing to be a full year old, already a stalwart fellow and mostly obedient to his young master—mostly, because he did after all exhibit a certain mulishness from time to time. With the expert instruction of his mom, David was becoming a capable rider, and he and Samson were beginning to explore the farm on their own, in between books, chores, and theatrics in which the yearling mule could not participate. One day when he and Samson were out for a ride, David thought to himself what a fantastic birthday present the noble beast had been, which naturally turned his thoughts to the question of what he might ask for this year. It shouldn't be anything too big, for he knew Samson had cost pretty much, and he had enough toys at the moment to keep him occupied at play, but there was one thing he had thought of while fighting Goliath—a slingshot! Not the kind of sling David used in the Bible but the Y-shaped kind, a real one that he could use for hunting squirrels and rabbits after he practiced up. Chris and Sophie gave much halting thought to the matter, but in the end they decided to follow the precedent they had set, that so long as he continued to live up to the standards they had set for him they would honor his birthday request.

Sophia found herself devoting extra time during that period to her collaboration with Rosa on farm-to-table affairs, specifically the retooling of their network of farms and workers for provision of emergency food aid to the metropolitan Pittsburgh area, which had sustained heavy damage from the Quake. Then there was the supervision of David's education, shared with her husband, which she found to be sheer joy, so eager was the boy to learn everything he could, and so self-directed that their oversight was fairly minimal. Intellectually, she was more or less resting on her laurels vis-à-vis the kind of theoretical work that had culminated in the Glorious Synthesis, although on the astronomical front she continued to follow avidly the ongoing observations of the startling celestial blueshift first observed in the aftermath of the Quake. The more the astronomers looked, rotating their titanic telescopes back and forth across the sky, the more it appeared that the blueshift was *universal*, in that all of the formerly red-shifted celestial objects now had their elemental spectra shifted to the blue side of normal. On top of that, it appeared that the *degree* of blueshift was more or less uniform across all latitudes and longitudes of the celestial sphere, which implied that the stars and galaxies were now converging upon Earth from all directions, and at more or less the same velocity. The sky was falling! "Chicken Little" jokes proliferated in astronomical circles and in the popular press, but beneath the humor it was evident that the gravity of the situation called for further study, especially regarding the time-scale of the apparent cosmic collapse.

Wednesdays at the Institute added a welcome element of variety to the weekly routine, almost a sort of getaway for her and Chris, when they could hole up in a conference room and work together on their new assignment from the Director. The Reverend Doctor Killgower, having turned seventy the previous year, had retired as Dean of the College while remaining Director of the Institute, where he was responsible for curating the voluminous archives of the Glorious Synthesis, and for promoting public recognition of its achievement. In the latter capacity he had tasked our two Metaphysicals with monitoring public response to, and discussion of, the massive scientific presentation to the 14th International Conference on Creationism the previous summer. Those welcome Wednesdays, then, were the primary time for the two of them to confer closely and without distraction on their assignment: pulling together any notable statements or claims published in the past week, analyzing and classifying the major matters requiring response, and formulating those responses.

One of the tactics employed in the media campaign against the Glorious Synthesis was blunt, outright ridicule—"Uproarious Synthesis Unveiled by Creationists," for example—and it seemed to Sophia and Christopher that the only apt response to such an attack would be an equally blunt and ridiculous *meme* of some kind, something to which they would have to give further thought. Another tactic they frequently encountered was misrepresentation, such as, "Scientific Proof Straight from the Bible," which implied that the scientific findings coordinated in the Synthesis could not stand on scientific merit, but had to be supported by biblical data accepted on faith. But this was either a misunderstanding or a deliberate misstatement of the whole biblical-creation paradigm upon which the Synthesis was based, for under that paradigm, scientists drew upon biblical data only in the formulation of theories, which were then tested empirically against the natural data in their subject domains—just like all scientific theories! Another twist on this confusion about the role of biblical data in the Synthesis, and its corresponding Christocentric character, was the concern whether scientists of other religious traditions, or none at all, would be justified in dismissing it as a "Christian thing." But here again, it was the overwhelming evidential support of the natural data that gave scientific credence to the biblically-derived theories, and not the fact that they were biblically-derived. Thus, competent scientists could judge for themselves, whether the formulated theories fit the natural data, or not. Should scientists of another religious tradition wish to replace the Christian description of the uncreated origin of substantial forms with different theological symbolism, there was in principle no reason this could not be done, though the fact would remain that the theoretical structures were biblically-derived.

Christopher found himself taking to the polemical part

of the assignment like a duck—or perhaps an amphibious assault vehicle—to water. In one sense it surprised him, how readily his dander was aroused as he wrote furiously in response to critiques and attacks, ranging in tenor from naïve incomprehension to disingenuous distortion to vicious calumny—after all, he was a philosopher who studied detachment from the passions! On the other hand, it was simply a fact that anger was his characteristic vice, and while the Holy Spirit was working on him as he grew in wisdom, part of that working was to sublimate the emotion to a sort of intellectual fire, "to forge the golden armor of Science for intellectual war," as William Blake had it somewhere, "with long-winged arrows of thought." Whether our philosopher was directing disputants to files of natural data, correcting misstated or distorted data, or counterattacking paradigmatic theories, he and the angelic genius inspiring him made good use of his irascible temperament.

But other thoughts, and more than thoughts, were at work in Christopher over those six months as well. Of the former, for example, ever since Enoch and Elijah had appeared (and disappeared) so suddenly, he couldn't stop wondering what sort of bodies they had. He remembered that Wolfgang Smith had speculated on a "celestial corporeality," in relation first of all to the resurrection body of Christ, which had appeared and disappeared suddenly, and several times had eaten with the disciples, just as Enoch and Elijah had drunk hot beverages. Pulling out Smith's *Wisdom of Ancient Cosmology*, Christopher reviewed the Christian sage's pursuit of the notion from Tertullian (who ascribed corporeality to God), through Scotus Erigena (who applied the dogmatic logic of Chalcedon to cosmology and held that corporeal substance will not perish but be ontologically elevated), to the Lutheran shoemaker and *philosophus teutonicus*, Jacob Boehme. The general idea was that the world of corporeal matter as we know it formed a kind of outer shell enveloping the inner kernel of our eternal nature (our *logoi* and substantial forms), and that this inner kernel consisted of the substance of heaven, best conceived as a pure radiance, a celestial light which was none other than the glory of God. In other words, the substance or flesh of this celestial corporeality was the archetypal or primordial Light.

Christopher had every intention of pursuing these thoughts further, including the connection that Boehme had seen between celestial corporeality (*himmlische Leiblichkeit*) and the birth of Christ in the faithful, the inner birth proclaimed in the sermons of the Meister, his patronymic namesake. It was this particular thought, of all that were at work in him that winter and spring, which began to blossom into something more than thoughts in his inner life—something that tended to silence the voices of thought. In truth, it was not yet a blossom—more like a sprout—but something was stirring in Christopher's soul that occasionally gave him glimpses of a spiritual outlook so detached from the world of time and matter that his intellect seemed inverted, or reflected, into the Intellect of God. This was all the Lord's doing, an effect of pure grace, not a power he could claim as his own to exercise at will— for the operative will was God's.

We have already referred to the retooling of farm-to-table operations undertaken by Rosa and Sophie in light of anticipated food shortages in the urban region to their south. A series of meetings were held in the parish hall at Jerusalem Lutheran, Rosa presiding, to work out the issues and difficulties attendant upon this charitable effort, beginning with the economic ones. Although their farm-to-table work had not been a major source of income for the participating farmers, neither had it been an insignificant one in the working economy of the farms, and what they were contemplating now was the sacrifice of that income, possibly even with a modest expansion of production. The general consensus of the farmers, many of whom were members of the parish, was that since the past two or three seasons had been so beneficent of weather and so bountiful in harvest, they should forego any farm-to-table revenue for the present season, and see if they could manage a little extra produce.

For John Eckhart, these plans involved considerations such as: how much produce could they donate on the current scale of their operations, while still supplying their CSA clients (who also had to eat), and keep the farm accounts out of the red; and which items of their production could they feasibly increase? He and Rosa agreed that vegetables, eggs and beef were the items most suitable for the urban relief effort, and starting from there John figured they could increase their vegetable output by fifteen to twenty percent, if they could get volunteer help for harvesting and preparation. There was nothing they could do about increasing egg production but start extra pullets in the spring, but they wouldn't start laying until fall. Likewise they could donate two or three steers, but not until they'd grazed into September. So that's what they would try for starters, and see how things developed.

John and Chris both attended the gathering of the Posse up in Clarion on the Ides of January, where the Sheriff briefed about 500 of his deputized civilian backup on the state of the county in the wake of the global emergency precipitated by the Quake. After conferring with law enforcement and miliary intelligence contacts, the Sheriff's assessment pictured a twofold hazard: incursion of migrants into the county, both urban refugees and foreign illegals; and military or paramilitary incursions of globalist forces, should the GEC attempt to subjugate areas standing up for the constitutional Republic. The migrant issue depended largely on how the urban relief efforts worked out, and on whether globalist operatives were transporting illegals from the border into the heartland. As for the blue helmets, there were presently no indications of immediate threat. Although the Sheriff did not at that time establish a schedule of patrols by the Posse, he admonished everyone to keep their eyes open, and to report monthly for a half-day of training.

Over the course of that winter, John worked out the design and materials list for the gas well, which he planned to keep simple and cheap, basically capping the narrow fissure from which the natural gas was venting, and using a solar-powered pump to fill the tractor tanks. During a dry spell in early spring, when the field was firm enough to get equipment and concrete to the site, the structure was installed as planned. The well promptly began functioning more or less as expected—with only a few minor instances of what John liked to call the geological application of Murphy's Law. Another geological matter much on his mind was the question of the Quake, specifically the analysis of tectonic formations underlying the global pattern of the major temblors, with an eye for detecting any signals of supernatural intervention. In whatever time he could find for the project, he meticulously collected seismic data and plugged it into the $\mathcal{G}$-field model he could access on a cloud supercomputer, so that he and Maria could run regression analyses to infer underlying tectonics. This work was ongoing.

Pastor Cornelius Chen and his fair wife Evangeline celebrated their second wedding anniversary in late winter, a happy couple and a dual blessing to the congregation of Jerusalem Lutheran. Evy's background as a farm girl made her a real asset in the farm-to-table work in which so many parishioners participated, and her musical skills availed in the enhancement of the choir and in the private instruction of others, with the promising possibility that an ensemble might develop out of this. Her husband the pastor kept in close touch with the other six pastors of the "Illumination Seven," whose congregations had received apparitions of the New Jerusalem in the wake of the original vision in New Bethlehem, now seven years ago. The latest result of their contact was that each of the seven churches had started a study group to explore the Glorious Synthesis as foundational for a Christian worldview.

II.

If Father Maxim's recollection of the first half of that year had been something of a blur, the remainder of 2051 came sharply into focus around a single event, which will be narrated momentarily. The cognitive background or atmosphere in which Maxim learned of this event was constellated, or generated by the new intensity of his prayer life, his increasing recourse to the *tschotki* and to the interior invocation of Jesus. In time with his breath and the beating of his heart, the repetitive invocation became condensed into one present instance, one abiding moment of time filling his consciousness, while persons and matters demanding his attention clustered quietly around its margins. In this mode, for example, he remembered the Irradiation at St. Michael and All Angels, seven years ago now, when the icon of Christ Pantokrator in the dome overhead had irradiated the congregation with quasi-visible rays of a subtle-intellectual nature and influence. This visionary occurrence had been followed by a surge of new members into the congregation, many of them converts to Orthodoxy, as well as a deepening of the *sobornost* or liturgical fellowship in which the congregation worshiped, and in which they lived.

Maxim's remembrance of the Irradiation included several additional results that had followed it, like energizing his mother's iconographic practice to produce beautiful and eye-catching sacred images for display all over San

Angelo, as well as a brilliant series of Creation icons featuring the Christ Child. There was also the icon of St. Michael that hung above the doors into the nave, the one that had changed at the time of the Quake—a change so evidently miraculous that it vied with the Irradiation itself in magnitude. Then there was the computer scientist from the congregation who had stepped up to become a linchpin of the team that formulated and presented the Glorious Synthesis, adeptly digitizing the mathematical models and the operating system of the Holotron display. Not least, an upper school language teacher had been inspired to attempt a Christian romance of the End Times, had succeeded in the attempt, and was forging ahead with a sequel set in the final Tribulation. *Lord Jesus Christ, Son of God, have mercy on us sinners.* Still in the background (or atmosphere) of these remembrances flowed the current of prayer, ebbing in toward the center of his heart as the memories emerged on its margins.

The Glorious Synthesis, in the formation of which Maxim had been so deeply involved, could hardly have failed to remain among the themes of his meditation. He was not so much concerned with the outward ramifications of that monumental achievement (which he always pictured as the great, radiant sapphire in Manuela's painting); Chris and Sophie were more than capable of covering that angle. When the Glorious Synthesis entered Maxim's contemplation it was as if it enveloped him, situating him in its very midst as an intelligent being subsisting in direct derivation from an uncreated *logos* in the divine Intellect (*Logos*). It was as if he were inside the great, multifaceted sapphire, at its very center, illuminated by a single, bright ray of the rising sun and witnessing through its crystalline blue the refraction of that ray through the facets of the gigantic gem into forms of scientific knowledge reflecting the natural order of creation. *Lord Jesus Christ, Son of God, have mercy on us sinners.*

It was in this cognitive atmosphere, then, that Maxim learned of the singular event aforementioned, which was actually a double event in the sense that two things happened at once, together effecting a major change in the lives of our little family in San Angelo. As summer was turning into autumn, illegal border crossings at Del Rio surged to an all-time high, with migrants overwhelming the Border Patrol and Texas Rangers while National Guard resources were tied up with Quake relief, then pushing further northward on foot and horseback. Diaz and Mendes ranches in the Hill Country, including the Lucky M, suffered losses of livestock including horses. Gunfire had been exchanged, but none of the ranchers or raiders had been seriously injured, and though the rustlers made off with Tolstoy, Thunder, Sable and Dancer were safe. Less than an hour after Maxim learned of this raid, he received a letter from the Reverend Doctor Killgower, offering him the position of chaplain at the Institute of Biblical Creation Science on the campus of Luther-Aquinas. Although the College already had a chaplain, the Institute was becoming something of a pilgrimage site, being the principal repository of the archives of data and theoretical formulations comprised in the Glorious Synthesis. Accordingly, the Board had agreed to establish a chapel on site,

and Killgower had persuaded them that the young Orthodox priest would make a more than fitting chaplain, given
that he was versed in the Western Rites of St. Gregory (a
traditional Roman Mass) and St. Tikhon (based on the
Anglican Book of Common Prayer). The Director had also
made use of his connections in the Moscow Patriarchate
to facilitate Maxim's transfer, should he agree to the offer,
and the Bishop of Lubbock would see to his replacement at
St. Michael's. With the news of the raid on the ranch fresh
in his mind, the reader may perchance surmise how our
theologian received the Reverend Doctor's offer.

Maria, in the meantime, pursued her parallel studies
of the early phase of the Restoration and of the Endtime
situation thirty years later, finding a trove of material on
the former period in a set of bound manuscript books
entitled, *The Journal of Jeremiah Jefferson*. On the title page
of the first volume of this set was an epigraph attributed to
the President to whom her grandfather had liked to refer as
"my illustrious ancestor."

> *If we are to guard against ignorance and remain*
> *free, it is the responsibility of every American to*
> *be informed.*

A major theme in what followed was the documented collusion of the media networks, including social media, in
the operations of the insurgent global left ranging from
the continuous campaign to remove the providential President from office, to the mass terror over a treatable virus
to justify draconian social control measures and facilitate

election fraud, to the theft of the 2020 election. The government installed in that election had immediately opened the southwest border, indiscriminately allowing caravans of migrants to enter the country, while the mass media either applauded or looked the other way. The usurpers had also shut down energy production so that the nation, seemingly overnight, had gone from energy independence to an increasingly desperate dependence upon foreign supplies, whereupon they blamed the situation on foreign powers, which the media promptly and in lockstep demonized. On top of everything—and here her grandfather's prose approached a true jeremiad—several figures in the installed government, including its president and speaker of the House, were deeply involved in corrupt energy transactions in the Ukraine, a region they also utilized in order to station armaments and bioweapons laboratories right on the border of Russia. And yet again it was the media that provided cover, by glossing over or ignoring outright the blatant evidence of this corruption, so that the glaring facts available in public records remained largely invisible to the masses. Meanwhile, as Grampa Jeremiah's memoir made clear, those Americans who knew the facts about the election and who believed the elected President had initiated a continuity-of-government operation before departing Washington, were wondering intensely *what red lines* remained to be crossed before the Space Force would override the propaganda networks and begin broadcasting incontrovertible facts and disclosures.

As for contemporary parallels, it was becoming pretty clear that major election fraud was a factor in the Socialist sweep of Congress, although this time the President had retained office and, in the chaos following the Quake, had adjourned Congress under Article II, Section 3, "to such time as he shall think proper." He had also devolved the Executive authority to regional military commands which, in cooperation with county Sheriffs, were tasked with keeping the peace and assisting in Quake relief efforts. Perhaps it was the scale of the latter that explained the obvious failure of the military to defend the border against GEC-sponsored caravans like those deployed by globalist operatives back in the twenties. Maria found it fascinating that, whereas the national emergency of '21 and '22 had been precipitated by the installed government, the current one was caused by the Global Quake—though God only knew how much damage the Socialist Congress might have done. As for the media, never again since the early twenties had a monopoly of the communication networks been allowed to develop, but rather a broad and diverse web of viewer-supported channels had been fostered, allowing access to a wide range of news coverage and opinion. Of course, nothing prevented individuals and groups from limiting their access only to information they found agreeable in one way or another, but at least every American had the *opportunity* to be informed, so on the whole, she thought Grampa Jefferson would be pleased with the improvement.

More concretely, she and Max had been concerned all year with the border situation, and their conversation with the Sheriff of Tom Green County did nothing to allay their concern. As was often the case with university towns, the electorate in San Angelo was sufficiently leftward-leaning to overrule the residents of the rest of the county and elect a Sheriff with Socialist sentiments. Thus, not only was the chief law enforcement officer in the county *not* going to call up a Posse for the defense of the citizenry, he was looking forward to welcoming an unspecified number of undocumented illegal immigrants into the county. As the reader may well imagine, this information became a factor affecting the decision that Maxim and Maria had to make regarding a move to Pennsylvania, where John Eckhart had assured them that folks in the counties on the Appalachian Plateau were pretty particular about their Sheriffs. Then too, if she would be collaborating with her dad on the $\mathcal{G}$-field analysis of the Global Quake, what could be better than working side by side now and then?

Magdalena, of course, was ecstatic at the turn her discussions with her parents had taken, on the subject of moving to Pennsylvania. Though she knew she would miss her beloved Hill Country, the shock of having nearly lost Dancer to rustlers overrode her attachment to the ranch. Right after the raid, her parents had quickly found a boarding stable just outside the city limits, and moved their three mounts off the ranch to a place barely ten minutes from the parsonage, so that already she was able to spend more time on Dancer. But at the Eckhart farm she could spend whole weekends, and even longer, not only with Dancer but with David and Samson too. What fun they could have, and what daring adventures! Not surprisingly, this turn of events was richly reflected in her writing—in which, by the way, her spelling was beginning to converge upon standard orthography. After a couple of tales about the raid on the Lucky M, and how brave Dancer had been, she turned her imagination entirely to Pennsylvania.

She remembered lots of trees there, but since she had visited mostly in the fall their leaves had been either yellow, orange, red, brown, or already fallen to the ground. Only last summer, when they'd gone for the college reunion and the creationism conference, had Magdalena seen the awesome green of all those trees and grasses and wild plants with flowers, and now her girlish heart imagined that enveloping verdure as a fitting habitat for romance. The reader may smile at the notion of a girl of seven entertaining fancies of a romantic nature, and regarding her cousin, no less. And yet the affections of the heart are mysterious, and the context of the Final Years unique, whence a sort of courtly love between children might be deemed plausible—at least in romantic fiction. In any case, there could be no doubt whatsoever about the mutuality of warm affection between Magdalena and David, as their relationship blossomed over the Web that allowed them to see one another's faces so frequently. In the adventures devised by David, she was always cast as a noble and heroic girl, and she in turn would aways describe with romantic exaggeration the dramatic moves and countermoves made by the boy, when she recorded the action tales in her composition book. To say that they both were looking forward to her family's move would be an understatement.

Sergei and Manuela were alarmed and saddened by the news of the raid on their ranchero—alarmed for the safety of Maxim's family as well as the that of the Diaz and

Mendes relatives, and saddened by the loss of property, including good old Tolstoy. Beyond the immediate loss of livestock, the question of the future security of their property rights loomed large, in view of the perilous condition of the federal and state governments in America. The situation in the Russian Federation appeared much more stable, as neither Moscow nor the republican capitals had sustained major damage, and the independent oblasts had maintained a robust self-sufficiency. Depending upon how things developed over the next year, Sergei told Manuela, it might behoove them to consider extending their stay an extra year. His two-year contract would expire the following year, but he was sure the university would extend it if he asked, especially since his family relations with the renowned Metaphysicals had rendered him genuinely popular among the faculty and administration.

His Palestinian students, Muslim and Christian, were telling him now that two old men had assumed the mantle of prophets and were preaching in Jerusalem, against the reconstruction of the Temple Mount—preaching at the very site where the massive project was already underway. So far, the authorities were ignoring them and relying on the media to lampoon and ridicule them as harmless cranks, but the word was that many orthodox Jews were hailing them as prophets. Shortly thereafter, the presiding priest at Divine Liturgy announced in his homily that Enoch and Elijah had indeed appeared in Jerusalem, and that this signified the beginning of the reign of Antichrist. A student from northern India reported that a Maharishi of the Kashmiri Saivites had seen a vision of the Kalki Avatar, the rider on the white horse who comes at the End of Time. He had seen this Avatar on a faraway mountaintop, looking back over a landscape of dark, parallel valleys—six or seven valleys, the Maharishi had reported. Interpretation of the latter vision is left to the reader.

Manuela's iconographic study, meanwhile, was proceeding happily. Every other Wednesday she would drive to the Holy Trinity Alexander Nevskiy Lavra, just off of route P21 on the way to St. Petersburg from the cottage in Ozerki, and meet with Hieromonk Amvrosy. After a period of silent prayer, she would show her teacher what she had done since their last meeting, and he would take the small icon in his hands and lovingly trace the colored lineaments of its sacred image. Sometimes he would comment laconically on some particular, or on the overall design, but other times he would only smile, or even frown ever so slightly, as Manuela watched him with careful reverence. Under Amvrosy's tutelage, she had written by the end of that year several renderings each of the Theotokos and Child, the Christ Child Himself, and Christ the Teacher, bearing the traditional inscription (in Cyrillic): *I am the light of the world; he who follows me will not walk in darkness, but will have the light of life.*

Sergei and Whitman were making frequent forays into the countryside around Ozerki, which they found to be fairly flat with broad expanses of grass, and groves or copses of trees clustered near the water, of which there was a great deal. Besides Ozerki Lake, which was massive, smaller lakes and ponds dotted the region, some of them connected by streams and creeks; yet the most marvelous thing about all

47

that water was the way it reflected the sky. Manuela would sometimes accompany her husband and his good grey horse on a rented steed, and in this way the two of them came to have favorite places to stop and enjoy the landscape, including one on the shore of Ozerki Lake, looking out over the wide sheet of water. The rental arrangement for Manuela's mount was quite economical, being a simple barter of goat cheese from her little dairy for time on a neighbor's horse; thus, she could ride with her husband as they had done in the Hill Country. The latter analogy was a double-edged one, for while it offered a sense of continuity with their former life in Texas, it also raised the question of whether they would ever return to that life, given the current collapse of civil authority in the States. For the time being, our cowboy-professor and goatherd-painter were finding happiness in Russia, gradually growing accustomed to their new environment and making themselves at home there.

David Eckhart was every bit as excited to learn that his cousin Magdalena would be moving to Pennsylvania, as was the dear girl herself. Nor was the boy's animation regarding this prospect any less romantic than hers, in the sense of strong feelings of affection that somehow depended upon the fact that she was a girl and he was a boy—indeed depended specifically upon the fact that she was *this* girl and he was *this* boy. As David went about his daily chores, studies and play, he liked to pretend that Magdalena was watching him lift that heavy water bucket, or solve that hard set of arithmetic problems, or gallop Samson across the pasture, almost as if he were performing for her. An analytical psychologist might say that the boy's *anima* was projected on his cousin, and her *animus* upon him, constellating their relationship under the archetype of the Sacred Marriage, although marriage in the earthly sense was to be denied them. In any case, as David and Magdalena celebrated their seventh birthdays at the end of that summer, entering upon the prime of childhood, as it were, their eyes and their hearts were fixed upon each other as they both awaited joyfully the coming move.

David's fantasy play formed another apt arena for the budding romance, by the way he deployed the David and Magdalena figures in the action scenarios he was imagining, which were increasingly evoking an apocalyptic atmosphere. Pastor Cornelius had been preaching of late on St. John's *Revelation*, so David had adopted that apocalyptic book as a reader for his required reading time and was working his way through it chapter by chapter. Accordingly, the mythos of his fantasy play arrayed the ultimate forces of evil, played by Goliath and the dinosaurs, in stark opposition to the forces of the Light of God, played by the two Jesus figures (grownup and child), the Twelve, Noah's family, Enoch and Elijah, and of course David and Magdalena. Goliath was now the Antichrist, and *T. Rex* the Great Beast (now marked on each side with the numeral 666), while the remainder of the saurians formed a mutable horde or legion of various agents of evil in league with the Antichrist. As if war-gaming the Apocalypse, David was dreaming up and acting out dramatic variations on the simple theme of the final defeat of the forces of darkness by God and the forces of Light. Throughout the variations of this play the figures of David and Magdalena remained integral to the action, always side by side, usually in the company of the Christ Child, and invariably conducting themselves with the utmost courtesy, and with unfailing loyalty, toward one another.

Then there was Samson. David rode the silver-grey yearling nearly every day, putting him through his gaits across the fields or along tractor trails between them, although the two of them were not yet qualified to take the Olean Trail to the knoll northeast of the farm. This restriction was fine with David, for plenty of adventure could be found within the confines of a 250-acre farm, if you knew where to look for it, and especially if you had a brand-new slingshot with a sight, and were practicing your aim on muleback as well as on foot. Thus, when our boy hero would reign Samson to a halt and tell him, "Stand!", the mule would hold perfectly still, solid as a rock, while David took aim at a tree, or an ear of corn, which momentarily assumed the role of an agent of the Adversary. Naturally, being a mule, Samson's performance in this maneuver was not *always* precisely as just described, but frequently enough it was, being a goal toward which both of them were striving.

As 2051 hastened toward its end, Sophia also found herself spending more time in the saddle sometimes in company with Chris and Alba or David and Samson, but often by herself, on Honeysuckle. The gentle palomino mare had a calming effect on the young woman, whose experience ever since the Quake had been anything *but* calming, indeed frankly upsetting. Although she was glad that her parents were currently safe and content in Russia, she had no idea when she would see them again—or the ranch where she had grown up, even if it remained in the hands of family. The creative intellectual work she had done in the Quest for the Glorious Synthesis was largely accomplished, and the methods she and the others had developed were now in the hands of their students, as well as published and archived for investigation by other researchers. In her current assignment at the Institute she was responsible for intercepting the weekly barrage of communications, critical or negative, responding to the robust scientific claims published at the ICC. She classified as *critical* those responses that articulated a rational critique of some theoretical proposal or evidential claim, and could thus be rationally countered by arguing in support of the theory or adducing the evidence in question. It was the other category, the simply *negative* reactions, that began to burden her soul, for most of these were undisguised, or poorly disguised expressions of pure hatred toward God, and toward anyone who believed in Him. Sophia knew, of course, that the prophecy was apparently being fulfilled, that the Darkening Years had begun, and that the final concentration of evil would now be in the ascendant. But the weekly barrage of sheer negativity unsettled her, causing her to question whether her courage would be sufficient for what lay ahead.

Then there was the one bit of astronomy—a rather large bit, in fact—that still preoccupied her, namely the universal blueshift of the starlight and other electromagnetic radiation arriving at Earth, from all directions and apparently from all observable celestial objects, although the full-sky survey was still underway. Another pattern had also emerged from deep-space observations: there was a correlation between the degree of blueshift and the distance of the source from Earth, such that the further the object from Earth the greater its blueshift. On the face of it, all of this implied that the whole universe was beginning to collapse concentrically upon Earth, with more distant objects approaching at higher velocities as though trying to overtake those closer in. At current velocities the collapse would take centuries, but there was no reason to believe those velocities would remain constant, for gravitational attraction would increase as the cosmos contracted, and since the sudden blueshift was likely of supernatural origin, nothing ruled out acceleration by the same divine energy.

So even the starry heavens bore tidings, these days, of the End that was coming upon the world—not just the world of the worldly-wise and the wicked but *her* world, the world of her family and her farm and her church and the people she loved, the *whole* world. Sophia believed with all her heart in the life of the world to come, and earnestly trusted that all would be well *there*. It was the thought of the intervening years that frankly frightened her, threatening at times her emotional balance as fear struggled with trust and love with envy—envy above all, of those who seemed impervious to the fear. The farm-to-table work she shared with Rosa kept her grounded, the deep and abiding love she shared with Christopher and with David helped stabilize her emotions, and Divine Service on Sunday mornings lifted up her heart to the Lord and gave her peace, at least for the rest of the day. Finally, the prospect of more time with Maria cheered her, and gave her something to look forward to in the near term—and riding Honeysuckle almost always helped.

Christopher, with his somewhat more choleric temperament, was taking the polemics provoked by the Glorious Synthesis well in stride, using clear evidence and plain reason to parry the rationally-articulated critical thrusts, and responding to the merely negative sallies with satirical broadsides and graphic memes. As an example of the latter, in response to a circle of journalists who had used the "Uproarious Synthesis" label, our philosopher produced a cartoon in which the center was occupied by the great, multifaceted sapphire of Manuela's painting, radiant with signs of all the sciences. Surrounding the gigantic blue gemstone mantled with emblems of knowledge, a ring of circus clowns in customary costume and makeup stood in various postures of mockery or doubled over in laughter, each clown clearly labeled as one of the offending journalists. The cartoon was captioned: The Eyes of the Beholders. The rhetoric of pure negativity, driven by hatred, was largely confined to ridicule of the "everybody knows" variety, e.g., "Everybody knows that Darwin (or Copernicus, or Einstein) was right." Such rhetoric laid itself wide open for satirical broadsides lampooning, by comparing with actual evidence, the paradigmatic sacred cows of modern scientism, and pointedly overturning the hypothetical bases upon which such ridicule of the Glorious Synthesis was founded.

Alongside this intellectual warfare, Christopher continued to think and to ponder on the notion of *celestial corporeality*, the mode of bodily existence of which the resurrection body of Christ was archetypal, and in which Enoch and Elijah had appeared to his family and to Maxim's. It was also the mode in which the blessed would be embodied in the general Resurrection, as the Apostle Paul wrote to the Corinthians: *There are celestial bodies (somata epourania) and there are terrestrial bodies (somata epigeia). It is sown a physical body (soma psychicon), it is raised a spiritual body (soma pneumaticon).* And St. John the Evangelist, the Theologian, wrote in a letter that *we know that when He appears we shall be like him*, meaning that when Christ returns in His resurrection body, not only He, but each of His human members will be as John went on to describe Him in *Revelation*, with *His face like the sun shining in full strength*, and *His eyes like a flame of fire.* What fascinated Christopher above all was the metaphysics of this celestial, or spiritual mode of embodiment—its ontological anatomy, as it were. The resurrected human being would still be ontologically distinct from an angel, for the angels were bodiless by nature, while the human beings of the eschatological New Creation would have resurrection bodies, celestial and spiritual physiques *like His.*

It is not without interest that much of our philosopher's profoundest cogitation on the foregoing theme transpired while he was engaged in agricultural exertions, like cultivating vegetables with a hoe while collecting the weeds for the chickenyard in the heat of the summer morning sun. The rhythm of his body as he drew the blade of the hoe through the soil tended to fall into synchrony with his breathing, moving the blade forward for a fresh bite while deeply inhaling, then drawing it toward him with a vigorous exhalation. There was more of this work to be done in the current season because of the effort to expand production for the urban relief project, and Christopher was glad to be able to do it, even as his well-trained muscles toiled under the sun and perspiration streamed down his body. Is it not interesting then, that these were the times when our philosopher most often found reflections on the celestial body flickering in his mind, and along with these reflections an inward detachment from his terrestrial body and its work, as if a new spiritual perspective were *being born* in him?

Outwardly, nevertheless, more was afoot that summer and fall than extra farm work. On the first Saturday of every month, for example, John and Chris would drive up to Clarion, where the Sheriff provided a variety of training options for members of the Posse, ranging from constitutional principles including the doctrine of the lesser magistrates, to standard operating procedures while on patrol, to handling and marksmanship drills with pistols and rifles, both semiautomatic and automatic. The two men enjoyed the time together away from the farm, and even though the drive was barely twelve miles it gave them twenty minutes or so, each way, to talk over whatever was on their minds. They both found the Posse training meaningful, not only tactically with regard to the political situation but meaningful for their sense of manhood, as protectors of their family. They regularly reviewed the status of the farm's participation in the urban relief effort, which over the period in question was rather successful, for though the weather was not as amiable as in recent years, a bit of extra labor at strategic times and a couple of absolutely essential showers saved the season. In addition to the extra vegetables, the Eckhart farm was able to donate two Angus beeves and a steady stream of eggs to the program. What they did not yet know was whether the combined contributions of the farms in Rosa's network would amount to more than a drop in the proverbial bucket of the needs of the Quake-ravaged region just south of them.

John would listen in silent wonder as his son shared some of his thoughts on the spiritual-celestial body, and then would report on his own investigations concerning the seismic tectonics of the Quake, in which he and Maria were collaborating. Using the supercomputer model of the $\mathcal{G}$-field which they had developed for the Synthesis, John had meticulously entered the global temblor data gleaned from several seismic databases, including geographic epicenters and corresponding depths. By late fall, they were evaluating several approaches to parameterizing the tectonics, in order to run regressive analyses targeting the underlying dynamics of the Global Quake. John's geological intuition told him it was unlikely that this had been a purely natural event, especially in light of its coincidence with the onset of the universal blueshift, a synchronicity he'd been discussing a bit with Sophia. He wanted her help in studying Quake tectonics in the $\mathcal{G}$-field as coupled with the cosmological $\mathcal{C}$-field parameterized for the Blueshift, hoping to detect a signature of supernatural intervention.

Rosa was a very busy woman those days, taking care of her home and her husband, which meant managing the complex affairs of the farmstead plus putting in extra time on the urban relief endeavor, helping look after David (which was delightful), and singing in Evangeline's choir. Reflecting on the fruition to which her farm-to-table work had come, it seemed to Rosa that the hand of Providence was evident in the preparations that she, Sophie and others had made over the years, forming a reliable network for local distribution of farm produce. Her group had slightly exceeded the agreed-upon goals in their first season, despite challenging weather, and hopefully could repeat the performance next year, but only time would tell how much of a difference they would make in the plight of the urban population. Currently, however, most of her thinking (and feeling) about the following year had much to do with her daughter, granddaughter, and son-in-law—who would soon be practically neighbors, and of whom she would be seeing so very much more that it prompted tears of joy when she thought of it.

The Reverend Cornelius Chen and his lovely wife Evangeline were by now well settled into a happily married life—life in a parsonage at that, for the pastor had long been lonely, and she had wanted to be a pastor's wife since girlhood. Evy, as she liked to be called, not only reveled in running a proper parsonage, playing hostess to parishioners and others as occasion demanded; she had also brought new energy to the Christian Education program at Jerusalem, and had taken over direction of the choir from an older member happy to hand it on. In addition, she was giving music lessons in several instruments with the hope of putting together a youth ensemble from the congregation, as well as helping to coordinate the collection and shipment of food donated by local farmers, many of whom were members of the church.

Her husband the pastor felt himself blest by the partnership of so energetic a wife, for while he tried to do his part around the parsonage, and exercised a prudent oversight of parish affairs, Cornelius was now primarily preoccupied with the signs of the times. Setting aside the prescribed lectionary for a time, he was preaching from the book of Revelation in parallel with Old Testament prophecies of the Day of the Lord, and with apocalyptic portions of the Gospels and the Epistles. One Sunday, for example, he reflected upon Ezekiel's vision of the eschatological Temple, the part in Hebrews about the uncreated heavenly Tabernacle, and St. John's vision of *the holy city, New Jerusalem, coming down out of heaven from God.* The latter, of course, was the biblical archetype of the illuminating apparition that had thrice visited the congregation in worship, and subsequently had visited six other Lutheran churches, most recently providing protection during the Quake. The preacher admonished the assembly to pray for guidance and protection, to the end that they might not only see, but also enter, that golden City filled with the Light of God.

YEAR NINE

(2052 A.D.)

I.

The winter and spring of 2052, overall, was a period of transition for Maxim and his family. Once he had informed the Director of the Institute and the Bishop of Lubbock of his desire to accept the chaplaincy, several ecclesiastical matters demanded attention, not least of which was the question of his successor at St. Michael's. Killgower's prior contact with Moscow had smoothed the way marvelously through the church hierarchy, so that Maxim's bishop readily acquiesced to the move, although he did not refrain from expressing his sorrow to be losing this particular priest from his diocese. Eight years had passed since the latter had commenced his pastorate at St. Michael's, and the mission congregation had thrived under his ministry—not only outwardly in visible ways but inwardly as well, both the priest and the bishop agreed. Maxim made it a point to visit as many of his parishioners as possible during the months that remained, and these pastoral visits reassured him that he was leaving the flock in reasonably good condition for their new shepherd.

The selection of the latter turned out, by providential serendipity, to be almost as obvious in hindsight as it was unexpected beforehand. What happened was that the Vatican, upon the announcement of the Third Temple construction initiative by the global Chairman, not only voiced the Roman church's approval in the heartiest of terms but offered unspecified assistance. The Society of St. Pius X (SSPX) and other traditional Catholic orders, no longer acknowledging the authority of Rome, promptly published denunciations of the Vatican's stance, resulting in renewed attacks on those orders by Jesuit agents and institutions. The bishops of the SSPX, convening an emergency online conclave, after long and prayerful deliberation and debate, drafted a formal declaration "that the See of Rome, in these unprecedented times, has forfeited both its primacy and its apostolic authority; and further, that the most reliable seat of apostolic authority is presently the Patriarchate of Moscow." Many of these bishops immediately converted to Orthodoxy, and priests in the order were advised to consider the option, which Padre Pablo Sanchez, for one, was more than happy to do. When the latter learned that his friend Father Maxim would be vacating the pastorate at St. Michael and All Angels, he took the news as a sign and a call that he should indeed convert, and then seek to succeed Maxim at St. Michael's. He knew that most of his congregation at Holy Angels would go with him to that parish, given the joint Liturgy they had already celebrated using the Mass of St. Gregory, and he hoped the Bishop of Lubbock would take this into account. And so did the matter turn out, resolving the question of succession.

Among the more interesting pastoral visits conducted by the departing priest was the hour he spent with the romancer whose literary efforts we have been following. His first book, *Arts of Love in the Endtime*, had found a small but intensely engaged readership while drawing what seemed a disproportionate volume of critical fire, consisting largely of negative reactions to his Christian premises and their ethical applications or else, from Christian quarters, to his correction of certain errors that had crept into the eschatological imagination. Laboring now over the sequel, *Before the Rapture*, which was to chronicle the great Tribulation, he was finding a unique set of challenges in the fictive narration of that period. For example, how literally should he take the prophetic indications that the Tribulation would last three and a half years? And since the tale would *terminate* with the Rapture, coinciding with the Resurrection of the dead, the End of Time and the return of Christ in glory, how on Earth would he narrate all *that*? On top of such questions, he confided to the priest, he had the uncanny sensation, those days, that historical events were overtaking his fictional ones, and that if he lingered overlong in his labors he might find himself narrating current events!

Then there was the melancholy business of bidding farewell to his cousin Diego Mendes, his wife and their new baby, who were holding the fort at the Lucky M, at least for the time being. Diego was visibly upset at the loss of Sergei's Tolstoy, but losses from the flocks were not crippling and it looked to be a good lambing season, so overall he was hopeful. As for security, the ranchers had met with the Sheriff of Crockett County, the Posse was activated, patrols were being organized, and everyone was well armed. It was not that local landowners were unsympathetic to the plight of the women and children being trafficked in the globalist caravans, he explained. The problem was that many of the migrants were military-age males, some of them armed: these were the rustlers, the horse thieves and the traffickers of the women and children. "And we!" Diego exclaimed, "We too have women and children, and we will defend them!" Maxim placed his hands on his cousin's shoulders and blessed him, invoking the protection of St. Michael on his family and on the ranch, to which the young couple responded with warm embraces, wishing the priest and his own family a safe and happy transition to their new life.

Another key element in that transition, to say the least, was to locate a residence to house that new life—ideally something modest on a small patch of land, roughly half-way between the Institute and the Eckhart farm. What they found was a brick rancher, built in the 1960s but well maintained, on a three-acre plot just south of Pinecreek, about sixteen miles northeast of the farm by the crows' reck-oning and less than half an hour's commute to the campus. Once they had decided on the move, Maria had taken the initiative in searching the real estate listings online for the desired area, with much advice and counsel from Magda-lena. When they found what looked like a perfect fit, Maria had Chris and Sophie look over the property on their way back from the Institute one afternoon, and confirm its suitability. Magdalena and her mother then presented the proposed property to Maxim, who was more than happy to accede to their proposal. The rancher was surrounded by about an acre of lawn, part of which could be tilled for a garden; the balance of the property was wooded, which especially pleased Maria and Magdalena, respectively. Also ideal was the agreement they secured with the current owner, to simply lease the property, renewable annually, with an option to purchase it later. Given their present lack of equity for down payment—having lived only in a parsonage—and their general uncertainty about the future, this arrangement suited them perfectly.

Besides finding a new nesting place for her family, our geometer-cum-historian had much else on her mind during those months of winter and early spring. On the mathematical front, her father had asked her to help him develop a regression analysis of the seismic data he had entered in their $\mathcal{G}$-field model, that would converge upon the tectonic parameters governing the Global Quake. She found this an enjoyable technical challenge, and patiently worked through a series of different approaches until she found a methodology that resolved the pattern of the temblors into two distinct tectonic profiles. This in itself surprised her, but still more surprising was the difference in geographic scale of their seismic expressions, one of which was expressed worldwide *except* for the *single region* expressing the other. Moreover, the anomaly was not only spatial but temporal as well, for the seismic expressions of the predominant profile occurred simultaneously to within a half of a second, while the temblor that struck Jerusalem came nearly three minutes later. In the confusion following the Quake, these anomalous circumstances had gone unnoticed, but the careful analysis caried out by John and Maria clearly showed that both the tectonics and the timing were different at the Temple Mount. This, in turn, called for further study.

As a small bust of Euclid on one corner of her desk had long kept watch over Maria's geometric studies, now a similar bust of Thucydides, a Christmas gift from Maxim, observed from another corner her studies in history. She was fascinated by the overlapping details her Grampa Jeremiah had documented in his Journal, especially for the year 2022, as more and more evidence came to light regarding the rampant election fraud by which the left had seized power. As the state and federal judiciaries continued refusing to hear electoral cases being brought to court, or to review the evidence on which they were predicated, while the media reliably denounced the litigators as liars, a Justice Department special counsel who had been working quietly for several years began to issue criminal indictments. The first few of these, by way of indicting several individuals, clearly laid out the structure of a criminal conspiracy involving numerous other individuals and organizations, including the national committee of the party of the left and its 2016 presidential candidate. At the same time, major media outlets were forced to admit that a laptop computer containing evidence incriminating the fraudulent president really did belong to the latter's son, and was not Russian disinformation as had been previously claimed. The evidence in question pertained to lucrative business deals between the president's family and the Chinese Communist Party, as well as certain other companies operating in the Ukraine, including a company involved with biowarfare laboratories. Yet another overlapping turn of events was afforded by the Russian invasion of Ukraine in March of the same year, whereby Russia was able to seize both documents and materials proving that the aforementioned laboratories were operating right across their border with Ukraine.

Then, with a wry glance at Thucydides, Maria would turn her attention to current events, in which a major difference from the early twenties was the apparently successful power play on the part of the Global Emergency Council in setting itself up as a de facto world government. The globalist operatives of thirty years ago had been thwarted in their attempted consolidation of effective hegemony by the Restoration's onset, but now the Quake had turned the tide, the Restoration was essentially over, and the stage was set for the final worldwide tyranny. The word from St. Petersburg was that Sergei's Chinese students feared a Maoist revolution in their homeland, which would effectively make China a GEC asset, and his Palestinians were telling of religious turmoil in Jerusalem. Apparently the Chairman was quietly preparing to unveil an artificial intelligence network called *Therion*, which was to have sweeping powers of surveillance comprising all electronic communications, geographic data on personal movement and, especially in urban areas, video observations. In the Greek of the New Testament, it so happened, *Therion* meant "beast."

By the middle of May the move to Pennsylvania was behind them, and as the adults settled into their new situation the romance of David and Magdalena blossomed like the woods and fields of that proverbially merry month. The new house was so close to the farm that they would have hours and hours together every week, including frequent sleepovers, when they could ride Samson and Dancer and work on their music, dance and drama. It was especially upon the latter arts that their courtly play quickly focused, for here they could synthesize the telling of noble tales, the sweetest of songs, the most graceful choreography and the mellowing tones of the lute. And here they could express most directly their affection and respect for one another, dignified by the developing elegance of their arts. Even their rides on the silver-grey mule and the rusty-red burro became impromptu occasions of operatic inspiration—whether David was packing his slingshot or his lute!

Besides being utterly bemused by the budding rhapsody of the "kissin' cousins," their parents and grandparents were enjoying the new opportunities for time together, afforded by the migration of the younger Losskys. Christopher and Maxim, for example, who had been best friends in college, had found their friendship stifled somewhat by separation. Neither had been very good at finding time for any substantive voice or video communication, and their written correspondence had been brief and sporadic, except for matters relating to the Quest for the Synthesis. Now, at the very least they could meet at the Institute every Wednesday, over lunch or otherwise, sometimes with Sophie present and sometimes not, for sustained conversation and general camaraderie. They found it singular that both of them had taken an inward turn in their intellectual lives, not so much to psychological introspection as to spiritual contemplation—Christopher by his studies in celestial corporeality and the inner birth, and Maxim by his practice of invocative prayer, meditation on the Glorious Synthesis, and reading St. Gregory Palamas. The latter theologian, a 14th-century Greek Orthodox monastic and intellectual heir to St. Maximus Confessor, had only recently come into focus in Maxim's reading, although of course he had learned something of Gregory's thought in seminary.

As Maxim related the Palamite's teachings to his friend, Christopher was especially taken with the theory of the uncreated divine Light as a divine energy (Greek *energeia*)—a truly uncreated and fully divine property of God's nature or essence (Greek *ousia*) and yet really distinct from it. In other words this uncreated Light, while inseparable from God's nature as one of its natural properties, was not identical with the divine nature. What struck our philosopher almost at once was that here was the metaphysical divide separating the Christian East and West, the elementary difference in understanding that underlay the Great Schism. Augustine, followed by Aquinas, had taught that nothing except the divine nature (essence) was uncreated, or conversely, that the only uncreated divine reality was God's essence itself. In this view, not only created substances but their energies and activities could only be seen as created realities, including spiritual energies operating within human beings. But this understanding made it impossible to conceive of real divine activity—that of the Holy Spirit, for example—within the created order, including the spiritual experience of human beings. Gregory Palamas, synthesizing the thought of the Fathers preceding him, argued on the basis of a distinction-without-separation of God's essence and His energies, that divine energies like the uncreated Light can and do operate within creation. Scripturally, Palamas identified this Light with the radiance of Christ transfigured on Mt. Tabor, arguing that this was the Light of glory proper to

His divine nature, and was therefore uncreated. In terms of spiritual practice, this illustrious theologian also identified that same uncreated Light with that experienced by certain practitioners of the Prayer of Jesus, who had been known to perceive a luminosity originating in the region of the heart, which was so intense it imparted a radiance to the body perceivable to others. Turning to eschatology, the Palamite maintained that the same uncreated Light—manifested in Christ on Tabor and, sporadically, in the saints on Earth at prayer—would also transfigure the resurrection bodies of the saints in light on the Last Day.

Christopher found all this enormously fascinating, not least because of the light it could shed on his thinking about celestial corporeality. After all, if the biblically-attested radiance of Christ in the Transfiguration and in the Apocalypse, by which *His face shone like the sun* in both cases, was the uncreated Light of His divine nature; and if in the Resurrection *we know that we shall be like Him*, what conclusion did this imply? Was it not that the "matter" given personal form in each of the risen saints would be nothing other than that very Light? Gregory Palamas clearly thought so, as well as that the bodily luminosity sometimes experienced in prayer was also that same Light, given hypostatic existence in the personal substance of the one who was praying. Christopher confessed to Maxim that this perspective was new to him, and thanked him for sharing it. He had not previously considered the metaphysical possibility that the celestial body could be composed of uncreated Light in the form of a created person, specifically a human being—although he had verged on this thought in his meditations on the Meister. On a personal note, he wondered whether his friend, whom he knew had been doubling down on the Jesus Prayer, had observed any luminous phenomena.

Maxim immediately replied that he had not, adding that the monastic masters of the practice unanimously emphasized that experience of the Light was not a goal to be sought—least of all by novices like himself—but a gift of pure grace at the Lord's discretion. Personally, the priest confided, he sought only the forgiveness of his sins, which were legion, and of the sins of others whom he held in his heart and remembered in the time of prayer. But there was another benefit, Maxim admitted, which he treasured very highly, and that was the profound inward stability, the spiritual anchorage in the midst of outward demands and difficulties, which he found that the practice was producing in his soul. If the Lord chose to show him the uncreated Light while he was still in the flesh, he would accept the gift as graciously as he could, but he was so arrantly imperfect, so utterly impure compared to the monastic saints, that he very much doubted he would see the Light until his death.

What Maxim especially wanted to talk over with Christopher were reports from Jerusalem, first routed through Sergei but now in public channels, regarding the activities of the global Chairman and the resistance to his plans mounted by Enoch and Elijah. Besides forging ahead with the Temple Mount project, the Adversary had approached the Orthodox Patriarch of Jerusalem and its Roman Catholic Bishop with a proposal to build each of them a new cathedral. Present indications were that the proposal was taken kindly by both parties. This was despite an appeal by the Patriarch of Moscow to his peer in Jerusalem, that he should have no truck with the Chairman. Then there were the reports of the massive AI surveillance system the Adversary had been planning to implement, and which he had the affrontery to name by the biblical Greek for the Beast of the Apocalypse. Christopher agreed that the signs were grim, if not unexpected, and went on to express concern over the tilt toward apostasy by the two Jerusalem prelates, before observing that they would all need to give some thought to possible ways and means of evading observation by *Therion*.

When their conversation turned to the initiative of Enoch and Elijah, both interlocutors were amazed at what they were hearing, not only about the vociferous public denunciations of the Son of Perdition's plans but also about the miraculous misfortunes invoked upon him by the venerable ancients. Clad in biblical cloaks and mantles, the lean and wiry old men had repeatedly prophesied at the site of the Temple Mount project, denouncing it as a counterfeit of the true Temple, and had confronted the Chairman himself as well as the two aforementioned prelates, accusing them of perverting their churches. The venerable ancients evaded all attempts to restrain them, seemingly appearing and disappearing at will, and had more than once caused extreme weather to spoil outdoor appearances scheduled by the Man of Sin. It was nothing short of uncanny to see history actually playing out, and fleshing in, the prophetic script supplied by Holy Scripture—and yet, from the standpoint of faith, what could be more natural?

Maxim also explained to Christopher the bit of ecclesiastical mechanics involved in his transfer from St. Michael
and All Angels in San Angelo, Texas, to a presently non-
existent chapel at the Institute of Biblical Creation Science
in Jefferson County, Pennsylvania. Formerly, our priest had
been in the Diocese of Lubbock, of the Russian Orthodox
Church Outside Russia (ROCOR), a self-governing part of
the Russian Orthodox Church since its reconciliation with
Moscow after the fall of Communism. His new mission
was under the aegis of the Archdiocese of Pittsburgh and
Western Pennsylvania, part of the autocephalous Orthodox
Church in America (OCA), which had been granted self-
governance by Moscow. Primary oversight of the chapel's
establishment, however, would be exercised by an elder or
hieromonk from the monastery of St. Tikhon of Zadonsk,
in the northeastern corner of the Quaker Commonwealth,
by agreement of the OCA hierarchy. There would be a
meeting with Killgower in early summer to finalize plans,
after which any necessary construction would commence.
By mid-fall the new chapel would hopefully be ready for
liturgical consecration.

Christopher made a point of briefing his friend and
brother-in-law, whose departure from Texas had partly
involved concerns about border security, on that very subject in relation to western Pennsylvania. He explained to
Maxim that a cluster of rural counties surrounding them had
formed a working coalition, coordinated primarily by their
respective sheriffs, to maintain vigilant reconnaissance for
groups of undocumented migrants and organize responses
to any incursions as necessary. He described some of the

training he and John had been reporting for, and suggested that Maxim check in with the Jefferson County Sheriff, even if he didn't feel called to enlist in the Posse. Just as Maxim had heard from his cousin Diego, Christopher was at pains to point out that security concerns related to illegal migrants were not directed at women and children, provided their numbers did not overwhelm local resources, for in fact many of these were being trafficked and needed rescue. The security concerns arose from intelligence reports of military-age males in substantial numbers, some of them armed, traveling in company with the women and children and often actually trafficking them.

Sophia and Maria were equally glad to be closer together and able to meet more frequently. For years now so much of their conversation had been technical, and so infrequently had they found time for a friendly chat, that they quickly made a solemn pact to be sure to make time for the kind of heart-to-hearts they had enjoyed in college and grad school. Now, as they opened their hearts to one another again, they found there were two major themes on both of their minds: the brevity of time and the romance of their children. As for the former, from the time they had returned from outer space and the prophecy of the Final Fortnight had become known to them, they had decided to take it as a hypothesis, act as if it were true, and see how the years unfolded. Well, their monumental Synthesis to the glory of the Creator had been published in the summer of the seventh year. Six months later, the Global Quake heralded the ascendancy of the Antichrist. To a historian's eye, Maria observed sardonically, the facts seemed so far to fit the hypothesis. But if the prophecy were true, then only five years and change remained until the End of Time—a prospect which, though hardly new to them, kept reasserting its relevance as the years fell into place, one by one. If the prophecy were true, Maria and Sophia had already lived more than half of their married lives, and their children had arrived at roughly the midpoint of theirs.

The latter realization brought a new perspective to the second of their major themes, for if David and Magdalena had already lived half of their mortal lives, it somehow made sense that the emotional maturity implicit in romantic love would develop as prodigiously as their intelligence and their talents. If the prophecy were true the kids would only live to be twelve or thirteen, depending upon how late in the last year time was terminated, so the question of a genetically impossible marriage could not arise, although they would all soon need to have the "birds-and-bees" conversation. But ruling out adult sexuality took nothing away from the possibility of romantic love in its highest register—however much the two wives and mothers had enjoyed the fullness of its marital expression. After all, many a knight in the chivalric service of his lady never once lay with her—however he adored her in his heart, or she him. Likewise Dante and Beatrice. Sophia and Maria, pondering these things in their hearts, shared with each other the wonderment of watching what the Lord was doing with their children, and of awaiting what He would do next.

Sophia also confessed to her friend the frustration of dealing with the negativity of so many responses to the Glorious Synthesis. Perhaps she had been naïve, she admitted, to expect a certain standard of intellectual integrity in those who presumed to speak as scientists or as reporters of scientific results. As it was, she was ready to move on, let Chris wage his intellectual war, and see if Killgower had anything else she could do. Maria remarked that her brother's mind was well-tempered for such an enterprise, provoking them both to laughter. Maria suggested that her friend prioritize their collaboration with John in analyzing possible correlations between the cosmological $\mathcal{C}$-field as parameterized by the Blueshift, and the geological $\mathcal{G}$-field as parameterized by the Quake. Since their visiting time was divided between the rancher south of Pinecreek and the farm north of New Bethlehem, it would be easy enough to set up some three-way conversations at the latter.

Late spring that year presented plenty of pleasant days for sitting outside at either of their homes, whether on the small patio at Max and Maria's or on the veranda joining Chris and Sophie's cottage to the farmhouse. At the former location they looked across a verdant lawn to the wall of trees that bordered it, surrounding the low brick house at a distance of perhaps forty yards, and from here they could sometimes watch the children at play. On the veranda their view was more limited, taking in part of the vegetable patch on one side and a sizable grass field on the other, and the kids would most likely be playing elsewhere around the farmstead. It was here that they sat several times with John Eckhart, comparing notes on possible formal correspondences between tectonic morphologies underlying the seismic patterns of the Global Quake, and celestial morphologies manifested in the spatial display of the Universal

Blueshift. The approach they envisioned would bypass the problem of the time required for causal transmissions to reach Earth from deep space, and vice versa, by employing the aeviternal mechanics developed for the Synthesis to explore connections at the level of substantial forms. John also emphasized the need for further study of the Jerusalem anomaly, to see what further details they could discern regarding the dynamics of that surprising outlier.

Maria was also glad to be able to spend more time with her mother, a sentiment that was heartily reciprocated by Rosa. The young woman arranged to spend at least a full day each week at the farm, helping with the harvesting, preparation and preservation of vegetables for the extended family, the CSA clientele, or the urban relief program. Rather than till up a garden at the rancher and do her own food production, canning and freezing, Maria decided instead to pitch in at the farm and then share in the yield. Besides giving David and Magdalena a full day together every week, this arrangement offered Rosa and her daughter numerous opportunities, some more lengthy and others more abbreviated, for a good, chatty talk. The objective melancholy of their historical period was not a mood they entirely avoided in their conversations, but neither was it something on which they chose to dwell. Rosa recalled a saying attributed to Martin Luther: when asked what he would do if he knew the world would end the following day, Luther replied that he would plant an apple tree. Life went on. There was work to be done, mouths to be fed, prayers to be said. There was worship to be offered, with praise and thanksgiving for all that the Creator had given, and for His promise that when He takes it all away, we shall be with Him. Thus spake the daughter of Jeremiah Jefferson to her own daughter Maria.

Rosa's farm-to-table co-op decided to strive for the same production goals as the previous year, but by early of June an extended dry spell was already putting those expectations in jeopardy. The Eckharts had an extra well for irrigation, but not all of the other farms were so equipped, and much would hinge on how the summer weather played out. Their expansion of the poultry flock had allowed them to donate roughly thirty dozen eggs per month over winter, so they added the same number of extra pullets in the spring to ensure a continuing supply. The level of volunteer support remained strong, and now—with Maria pitching in, the kids old enough to help a little, and Evangeline overseeing the collection and shipment of goods at the parish—Rosa was thankful to see her dream coming to pass, even against the backdrop of disaster.

John's new gas well was also operating splendidly, with its solar-powered compressor keeping the tractor tanks and the bottles that supplied the farmhouse and cottage refilled as needed, without challenging the production capacity of the well. With this in mind, he decided to donate fuel for the truck used by the co-op to transport produce to the city, a twenty-foot van converted to run on natural gas, as did the Eckharts' equipment. While waiting for the compressor to fill one tank or another, John would often think to himself that here was precisely the kind of application that called for photovoltaic solar cells. A moderate demand for electrical power in a relatively isolated location—in this case a small but powerful motor in the middle of a field a quarter-mile from the farmstead—not acres and acres of solar farms whose construction consumed massive amounts of carbon-based fuel, rare earth minerals, and toxic heavy metals.

Pastor Cornelius Chen counted himself among the beneficiaries of the relocation of Father Maxim Lossky-Mendes and his family, for he had felt a spiritual kinship with the Orthodox priest since the first of their several previous conversations. In times like those, spiritual bonds were a boon to be sought, and the Lutheran pastor looked forward to poring over the prophetic books with his fellow clergyman, seeking consensus on what foretellings and fulfillments were to be found in their current situation. He knew that Moscow had identified the global Chairman as the Son of Perdition, the eschatological Adversary, while many other hierarchs of the Church, East and West, had displayed an appalling tendency to collaborate with his proposals. The bishop to whom Cornelius himself was subordinate had not yet taken a clear stand, although he had expressed reservations about the increasingly utopian dimensions of the New Dawn that was being touted. His ministerium, the Society of the Holy Trinity, was to take up the question at its general retreat in the fall, leaving Cornelius without Lutheran guidance and, thus, all the more eager to talk with his Orthodox friend.

His wife Evangeline, meanwhile, was beginning to believe she had the makings of a four-piece ensemble, for starters, amongst the youngsters taking instrumental lessons. Given David's increasing facility with the lute, and a promising student each in violin and French horn, the arrival of an aspiring flautist, highly motivated and musically literate, put the final piece of the desired ensemble in place. It may amuse the reader to learn that the new arrival in question was none other than our Magdalena, who no sooner met "Miss Evy" than she asked if she could take flute lessons, having of course obtained her parents' permission beforehand. Our girl heroine had been wanting for some time to be able to play duets with David, as well as singing along with his lute, and erelong her fancy had focused on the flute—of all the instruments, perhaps the most birdlike in timbre. It was easy to schedule the lessons, with Maria helping at the farm at least once a week and Magdalena staying over on many weekends. Soon the girl was piping away at her practice.

Perhaps the most striking manifestation of the developing romance of David and Magdalena was what we might call the dramatic (or the theatrical, or the performing-arts) focus that formed so large a part of their play. This will come as no surprise to the reader who has witnessed this tendency in these two since they were barely three years old, and yet perhaps the moment has come to consider whether some sign of destiny lay here. In other words, was some providential design at work in their preference for this form of play? We shall have to see. In the meantime, however, let us look in on one of the episodes in the ongoing rhapsody of their play time.

It was a rainy day in the middle of June at the Losskys' rancher. Magdalena's room, unlike David's, was not equipped with an Ark, a fishing boat or a starship, let alone several dozen action figures, of which the boy had

brought along only the two corresponding to himself and
his cousin, in addition to his lute. What they both wanted
to play, on that particular day, was music, although Magdalena insisted on first setting up a miniature tableau on a
small table in one corner of her room, right under the icon
of the Synaxis of the Angels. First she set up her Jesus doll
on the table, with the icon directly behind and above Him,
removing the legendary white stone from a pocket in his
tunic and placing it on the table in front of him, engraved
side up. Then she asked David to position their action figures on opposite sides of the stone, facing the doll and the
icon. With these preparations complete, Magdalena curtsied and picked up her flute; David bowed, cradling his
lute, and strains of their sweet new style began, slowly and
cautiously at first, played in two-part harmony. The boy
had been practicing these on his lute, and once Magdalena
had learned her do-re-mis on the flute she could play either
part of a harmony, or switch from one part to the other.
Their music was measured in melodic phrases of seven
notes (doubled by the harmony), with each phrase containing all seven tones of the scale in different orders. It was
a rigorous method of composition, yet the form yielded
surprisingly beautiful results in performance. The source of
this elegant and enchanting sound, the reader may recall,
was the mysterious inscription in seven characters on the
white stone—the very one which rested, as the music filled
Magdalena's room that afternoon, at the feet of the Baby
Jesus, under the icon of the angels with golden halos, surrounding a circular nimbus of light in which the Christ
Child sat enthroned.

II.

That rainy day in the middle of June, which turned out to be a real soaker, commenced a meteorological turnaround in the prospects for the agricultural season, as regular showers throughout the summer promised a reasonably successful harvest. Among the more salient developments over the aestival months of that year was the design and construction of the new chapel where Maxim was to serve as chaplain. One day toward the end of June, Hieromonk Pyotr of St. Tikhon Monastery met with Director Killgower and Father Maxim at the Institute, where they sat together in a room roughly thirty feet square, which had formerly been used as a planetarium. The beauty of this space, as a possible Orthodox chapel, was the domed ceiling where the celestial motions had formerly been projected, as if readymade for the traditional icon of Christ Pantokrator. In addition, the walls of the room were parallel to the cardinal directions and its entrance was from the west, so the altar could stand by the eastern wall, as required. Pyotr observed with a smile that the fit appeared providential. Some of the seating would have to be removed to accommodate the standing style of Orthodox worship, and the lighting would need some alteration, but yes, this would indeed do nicely. All they needed was an iconographer, a movable altar, and a simple iconostasis to enframe it.

It was quickly decided that a set of folding wooden screens would suffice for the latter, to demarcate the sanctuary surrounding the altar from the rest of the nave and to display several large icons that would be supplied by the monastery. One of the monks at St. Tikhon was a gifted iconographer, and over three or four months would be able, God willing, to adorn both the dome and the iconostasis with appropriate divine images. The altar itself would not be of the *fixed* kind, which traditionally required a massive block of stone, but of the *movable* kind, in which a slab of stone formed part of the surface of a wooden table. Specifically, a square slab of white marble with small crosses engraved in its center and corners would be installed on the tabletop, to be liturgically consecrated by anointing with oil and placing incense on the five crosses. Thus consecrated, the stone would sacredly symbolize the stone anointed by Jacob at Bethel, where he saw the angels ascending and descending, and the apocalyptic stone of Nebuchadnezzar's dream interpreted by Daniel, as well as the Cornerstone, Jesus Christ Himself. It was upon this surface, or directly above it, that bread and wine would become the body and blood of the Lord in every celebration of the Divine Liturgy conducted by Father Maxim and other priests in the new chapel.

The question remained of what name this sacred room would thenceforth bear, and this, by consensus of the monks at St. Tikhon in conference, was to be *Philadelphia Chapel*—not after the city in the old Quaker Commonwealth where the Declaration of Independence was signed and the Constitution composed—but after the city in Asia Minor, where one of the seven churches addressed by Christ in *Revelation* was located. In St. John's narration, the apostolic church in Philadelphia was commended by the Lord as having *kept my word and not denied my name*, and then was rewarded with a promise: *Because you have kept my word of patient endurance, I will keep you from the hour of trial that is coming upon the whole world.* According to Orthodox tradition, the church in Philadelphia stood for the faithful Christians of the final epoch in history, the period immediately preceding the End of Time, and so it seemed good to the Holy Spirit and to the monks of St. Tikhon, Hieromonk Pyotr included, to call the new chapel by that name.

Thomas Killgower was gratified to see his dream of a chapel at the Institute being realized so splendidly, for it seemed to him that if the Glorious Synthesis was grounded intellectually in Divine Knowledge, and the Institute had become a sort of shrine of that scientific synthesis to the glory of God, then there ought to be a place of worship there. As for why a nominally Presbyterian Doctor of Divinity decided upon a Russian Orthodox chapel in particular, the answer lay in our Reverend Doctor's biography. Baptized and reared in the tradition of Calvin and Knox, Killgower had done his doctoral dissertation on Calvin's metaphysical presuppositions and then, in his early forties, had encountered the *philosophia perennis*. Perhaps the chief point of the latter was its insistence upon tradition, and the traditional, in all things philosophical and religious, as opposed to the various innovations and revisions introduced especially in the wake of the European "Enlightenment." Accordingly, the preferred forms of Christian practice were traditional Roman Catholic, or Eastern Orthodox, and though our subject did not convert to either but continued to worship as an orthodox Presbyterian, he long harbored an earnest fascination with the Eastern church. Thus, in his late fifties, while serving as Dean of Luther-Aquinas Evangelical College, our Reverend Doctor had been able to arrange a residency for an Elder of the Russian church, whom the reader of Book I of these *Romances* will remember as Elder Lavrenty. Killgower's friendship with Lavrenty, and his participation in many a Divine Liturgy celebrated by the Russian Elder, both cemented his love for Orthodoxy and afforded him contacts in the Patriarchate of Moscow. Finally, when he had the opportunity as Director of the Institute to establish the chapel and to call a chaplain, the way was already well paved.

And yet, as aforementioned, the Director remained a nominal Presbyterian, primarily for the reason that it facilitated his contacts with the circle of Evangelical prophets he called his Invisible College. This was the group from which originated the prophecy of the final fortnight of years—the last fourteen years of time—after having previously confirmed that divine intention supported the mission into outer space which provided the pretext of that prophecy. This group of prophets was also quite active in the discernment and disputation of erroneous teachings that arose in the ranks of the Protestant churches, given that the prophets themselves were situated in church bodies deriving from the Reformation. Killgower considered this circle an instrument of the Lord for the sifting of the latter-day churches, in addition to being a valuable asset for those seeking guidance, especially in light of recent developments. In short they were valuable contacts, and he believed he could communicate more effectively with them as a Presbyterian than, say, as a Russian Orthodox.

Killgower had another matter to attend to that summer, partly precipitated by Sophia Eckhart's appeal to be relieved of duty on the polemical front, but something he had been thinking about on his own as well. Dr. Eckhart and her husband had mounted such a spirited defense of the Synthesis, and so withering a barrage of counterpoints against the critical points and negative reactions brought forward against it, that the Director thought it was time for a change of tactics. The Eckharts had also analyzed and catalogued the range of responses along with their corresponding rebuttals, so why not automate the response process with a simple AI system capable of linking critical inquiries with appropriate responses? This would also free up the philosopher and his wife for another assignment, should they choose to accept it, namely to organize a Master's program in the Glorious Synthesis, a new degree to be issued by the Institute for equipping and edifying the saints. Chris and Sophie accepted the proposal gladly, provided they could keep to their one day a week on campus, and so was the matter decided.

Sophie was especially happy about the new assignment, and looked forward to working with Chris on something more overtly positive than fending off barrages of criticism, misinformation and invective. They would spend the fall term automating the polemics, designing the Master's program and setting up a schedule of courses for winter term, to be taught by a team of adjunct professors. On their days at the Institute, they would drop off Magdalena at Maria's on the way, unless the latter were heading down to the farm for some particular reason, though she almost always planned her days at the farm for when Sophie was there. And Sophie was there pretty much every day but the one day each week she and Chris were able to spend on campus, working creatively side by side—a welcome break from the routine of life on the farm. Besides, they delighted in dedicating their partnership to training a cadre of intellectual warriors for whatever final stand might be required, against those who not only denied the Creator but condemned whoever refused to.

Over that summer our Sophia also persevered in the endeavor she had undertaken with John and Maria, to determine whether some form of metaphysical coupling had occurred between the Quake and the Blueshift. On that front, by the onset of autumn, several startling discoveries had emerged. First, the aeviternal dynamics of the substantial forms governing the two massive phenomena showed such strong correlations that they could essentially be described as two facets of the same event. Second, this appeared to be a clear signal of direct divine action within the created natural order, although this conclusion was subject to theological review. Third, the correlations applied only to the predominant tectonic profile underlying all of the seismic patterns *except* for the Jerusalem anomaly, which implied that the latter was *not* the result of the divine action which had wrought both the Quake and the Blueshift. By early fall, John and Maria were at work on a detailed analysis of the Temple Mount temblor (TMT), which had effectively decapitated the holy site, destroying the Mosque of Omar and surrounding structures. What they found was at first surprising: the epicenter of the principal temblor was essentially the Mount itself, but the depth of its origin was unusually shallow, barely a quarter-mile underground. They also discovered seismic traces of several smaller shocks, apparently originating *inside* the Mount and located somewhat symmetrically relative to its central axis.

What was at first surprising soon took on a sinister aspect. For after Father Maxim, having consulted with Hieromonk Pyotr, affirmed the theological interpretation of the Quake-Blueshift coupling as signifying a divine action, it followed that the exclusion of the TMT from that signal meant that it was most likely of human origin. It was not the result of natural geological processes—of that, John was quite certain. He was also certain, moreover, that to plant a nuclear device a quarter-mile underground at a desired location was well within the capabilities of state-of-the-art drilling technology—not to mention placing a set of smaller nukes inside the Mount, perhaps under the cover of archeological work. Hypothetically, the devices had been planted well before the Quake, in anticipation of some climactic situation in which they could be detonated, with a team capable of doing so kept on constant alert for the command. When the Quake hit, the chief perpetrators immediately seized the moment, but the command took several minutes to be received and confirmed by the detonation team—hence the delta in time. This, at least, was John Eckhart's leading hypothesis, after he had carefully examined the data and talked it over with the Sheriff and several of the Posse who had backgrounds in military intelligence.

Forensically, the matter appeared almost transparent, for as soon as one asked the question of motive, a single figure stood out, namely the man with the monumental plan to build the Third Temple, after reconstructing the top of the Mount. The extremely delicate problem of removing the Mosque of Omar to make way for the new Temple had been deftly solved by the Quake—or at least that was what everyone was supposed to think. Moreover, moving on to the question of capability, there was no doubt that the Chairman and those who had backed his ascendancy would have possessed the financial and technical means to accomplish the hypothetical scenario. When Killgower was informed of these findings he decided to announce the technical analysis of the TMT, including its tectonic and temporal differences from the Quake but leaving aside the forensics, in the weekly webcast from the Institute. The criminal justice aspect of the matter was followed up by the Sheriff, who reported the Eckhart hypothesis to the constitutional sheriffs' network and to the regional special operations command.

Meanwhile, our Thucydides of the Apocalypse was closely following these remarkable developments, chronicling carefully the emerging manifestations of that terminal period, of which she aspired to be the historian. Biblical prophecy was pretty clear that the Antichrist would rebuild the Temple, but that he had first blown the top off the Mount was now, apparently, a matter of history. Likewise,

Revelation referred to a Beast (the Antichrist) that received power from a great red Dragon (the Devil), and also to *another beast* who *makes the Earth and its inhabitants worship the first beast*—and now the Chairman, assuming the role of the first beast, was going to roll out a global surveillance network run by artificial intelligence, and call it "Beast." Although there was no sign as yet of this ominous figure setting himself up to be worshipped, clearly the *Therion* system would be the perfect matrix in which to enforce compliance, and to detect noncompliance, with virtually any kind of edict, idolatrous worship included. In fact, the Son of Perdition had recently assumed a more religious mien in his public statements and pronouncements, never referring to God but only to vaguely spiritual values and powers, not to mention his financial diplomacy in relation to major church bodies.

It was not difficult to infer that the *Therion* system was intended to impose the most draconian control of information ever achieved on Earth, and on a global scale, dwarfing the degree of control that had been imposed in the early twenties. In those days, the globalist left had successfully suppressed information on a series of scandals, including collusion with foreign enemies to commit espionage on a sitting President, malfeasance in the handling of a pandemic, and theft of a presidential election. But that system of control had been based on consolidation of media and social media ownership, bordering on monopoly, and the arrangement proved vulnerable to circumvention by independent journalism on the worldwide web, and by changes in the social media landscape. As the degree of deception practiced by the corporate media became apparent to more and more people, the ratings of the networks plummeted as viewers stopped watching, while the dominant social media platform was purchased by an entrepreneurial free-speech advocate, and a brand-new platform was launched by none other than the providential President.

At that time, the latter was still waiting in the wings while the devolved Executive commands kept watch over certain *national essential functions* that were critical for the nation's survival, and the illegitimate government in Washington exhibited plainly its intention to destroy the country. Although there had been some degree of Marxist infiltration in the military, even up to the Joint Chiefs, the ranking commanders in the actual chains of command were running the continuity-of-government operation of devolution as defined in military doctrine and executive orders. The Marines and the Special Forces stood solidly with the President-in-waiting, whose security detail was composed of Army Delta Force operators, and here Maria could draw a parallel with the current situation, according to what Chris and John had learned from the Sheriff. In addition to a couple of his Posse having backgrounds in military intelligence, one of his deputies was on active reserve in that operation specialty, and they were informed by their contacts that the President was currently under the protection of the same two branches of the military. In stark contrast to the twenties, however—returning to the theme of *Therion*—the proponents of that draconian system planned to avoid the vulnerabilities exhibited three decades since, by capturing *all* electronic communications to be filtered by AI. It was a terrifying prospect, and Maria was glad that her brother was giving it some thought.

Christopher was indeed giving some thought to *Therion*, along with other matters—especially the new light that his encounter with Gregory Palamas had shed on the subject of celestial corporeality. The Palamite had steered him to several verses in St. Paul's second letter to the church in Corinth, which gave him much food for thought.

> *And we all, with unveiled face, beholding the glory of the Lord, are being changed into His likeness from one degree of glory to another, for this comes from the Lord who is the Spirit. … the god of this world has blinded the minds of the unbelievers, to keep them from seeing the light of the gospel of the glory of Christ. … For it is the God who said, 'Let light shine out of darkness,' who has shone in our hearts to give the light of the knowledge of the glory of God in the face of Christ.*

The *unveiled face*, implied by the Apostle to be prerequisite for *beholding the glory of the Lord*, was simply the human mind facing God in *faith*—"this true faith," as Palamas put it, "which comes about by the fulfilling of the commandments." It was this very faith that engendered a *knowledge* of God, but it did so "through that uncreated light which is the glory of God, of Christ our God, and of those who attain the supreme goal of being conformed to Christ." In this perspective, Christopher reflected, the last of the

Corinthian verses used the word *light* in two different ways: the light that shone out of darkness on Day One of Creation was obviously *created* light, while the *light of the knowledge of the glory of God*, according to Gregory, was an *uncreated* divine energy. Moreover, the latter's reference to "the supreme goal of being conformed to Christ" was right in line with the Apostle's assurance that the faithful *are being changed into His likeness from one degree of glory to another*.

It did not escape our philosopher that Palamas attributed the formation of true faith to "the fulfilling of the commandments," a tall order indeed considering the amendments added by Jesus, so that even desiring to break a commandment was to break it. Christopher knew from experience that the effort to keep the commandments, for most believers, was an ongoing struggle—spiritual warfare, in fact—by which the Holy Spirit gradually purified the soul that repented its transgressions. Thus, from one degree to another, the purified soul would approach that purity of heart which coincided, according to Jesus, with the vision of God, and which Palamas called "being conformed to Christ." This sanctifying process could also be described as an increasing participation in the *light of the knowledge of the glory of God*, implying the presence of this uncreated light in the intellectual heart of the believing soul, forming, as it were, an embryonic celestial body. Given the metaphysical conception of the celestial body as uncreated light in personal form, and given that a person being sanctified was more and more participant in that light—did that not imply the celestial body *in embryo*? This analogy, in turn, pointed to a birth, corresponding to a state of being conformed to Christ, which was surely none other than the *inner birth* predicated by the sermons of the Meister whose name Christopher bore, as for example, "God begets His Son or the Word in the soul." Naturally that logic brought to Christopher's mind the Christ Child.

By early fall, as it turned out, metaphysical farmer's thoughts on celestial corporeality had come to revolve around the figure of the Child, who seemed to incorporate the themes of his thinking on that subject—as uncreated light in personal form, indeed the very archetype of that composition, and as a young boy implying growth and development. Even when he turned his attention to the problem of *Therion*, and to the circumvention of the electronic dragnet that ominous name represented, the radiant Child was never far from his mind, and one night in October the two themes momentarily merged. Christopher was sitting in his barn-loft study, wondering how on Earth it might be possible to evade the capture of transmitted information by the minions of the Man of Sin. His reading light was switched off, and his half of the study he shared with his wife was dimly lit by a small lamp on the bookshelf behind him. As he stared out the window over his desk into the night, suddenly he became aware of a growing radiance from behind him reflected in the window. As he turned to see what it was, he heard a voice, as of a young boy, saying, "Peace be with you." The Child stood at the end of the bookshelf by the doorway to Sophia's study, a silver-white aureole surrounding His body and a golden halo around His head. His height was about like David's, but His build more slender, His face not quite so round nor His cheeks so full as when Christopher had seen Him before. On that occasion, as the reader of Book I of these *Romances* will recall, the Child had informed our hero of the design of the starship *Synaxis*, which not only navigated to the principal stars of the constellation Cygnus and back, but subsequently served as a time-sensor for research on the global Flood.

The luminous Child looked intently at Christopher, with a friendly though unsmiling mien, then turned and pointed to the wall above the bookshelf, where hung a framed blueprint of the double-polyhedral structure of *Synaxis*, including notations of the supercrystals installed at its vertices. With His right hand, He first pointed to the five upper squares of the inner polyhedron, and then traced a number of squares in the air around the blueprint. Turning again to Christopher, He repeated, "Peace be with you," and walking to the door that opened into the barn, He unlatched and opened it, walked through, and closed it behind Him. The first thought that came to our philosopher after the Child's departure was that *Synaxis* was now to find a third application, this time as some sort of aeviternal-routed communication system, powered by angelic intelligence as in its previous missions. The square panels to which the regal Child had pointed were the primary display screens for the representation of images and data during those missions, generated by the crew of angels and accessible to keyboard queries and input. The squares that He traced in the air, Christopher's thinking continued, could be mobile devices connected to *Synaxis* over the *aeviternum*, so any transmissions would be above time and undetectable. But much further thought would be required.

In Russia, meanwhile, the approaching expiration of Sergei's two-year contract at the university prompted him and Manuela to make a decision. The situation in southwest Texas remained tense, according to reports from Diego and others of the family, while the Russian Federation was still looking stable and secure. When the head of Sergei's program offered to extend the contract, they quickly decided to accept a one-year extension, renewable annually, which included an additional course along with the Russian language classes he had been teaching. The extra course was American Literature, which at first took Sergei by surprise since he had never taught the subject. But then he reflected that he was, after all, a professor of Literature, and that he had, as a matter of fact, delved a bit into its American strains during his thirty-year residence there. Moreover, he had named his good grey horse, Whitman, because he found in that poet not only the paradigm of an elan, an afflatus essential to the American character, but also a high estimation of Literature in the life of a nation. *In Democratic Vistas*, for example, the bard had written:

> Over all the arts, Literature dominates ... or
> at any rate, is capable of doing so. Including
> the literature of science, its scope is indeed
> unparalleled. To endow a Literature with
> grand archetypal models ... and to achieve
> spiritual meanings, and suggest the future—

these, and these only, satisfy the soul. The culmination and fruit of literary artistic expression, and its final fields of pleasure for the human soul, are in Metaphysics, including the mysteries of the spiritual world, the soul itself, and the question of the immortal continuation of our identity.

Sergei found such propositions exhilarating, and was soon at work planning his first Am Lit course.

Manuela's little dairy was doing nicely, as were her studies in iconography at the Lavra, where Hieromonk Amvrosy was pleased with her assigned work, and suggested she was ready to write an icon inspired by prayer. As Manuela prayerfully awaited such inspiration, she turned to her watercolors and began thinking about painting a few landscapes, various views of her new environs, her favorite being a certain perspective on Ozerki Lake. Sometimes she and Sergei would ride around to the eastern shore just before sunset, and watch the sun going down behind the trees across the lake, its reddening light trailing across the mirror of the lake toward them and tinting any clouds in its vicinity, both in the sky and in the lake below. This was the first landscape she wanted to paint, in at least two different renderings, one by means of a photograph and the other from a sketch of the scene. The sketch and the photograph were taken on different evenings, both notable for spectacular sunsets, and while Manuela strove for a fairly realistic painting from the photo, she applied colors to the somewhat abstract motifs of her sketch with a certain liberty of imagination. When the farmer who supplied hay for the goats happened to see the two paintings, he asked if the realist one was for sale, and when our *artista* expressed a preference for barter, he offered the load of hay he had just delivered—and the deal was sealed.

Back in Pennsylvania, David and Magdalena celebrated their eighth birthdays at the end of summer, and for their first-ever joint birthday party the dear duo performed a sort of operetta for the assembled celebrants. Present for the festivities were John and Rosa, the four parents and the Chens, all of whom were ushered excitedly into the living room of the farmhouse, more spacious than that in the cottage—before supper, so eager were the children to perform their piece. David's models of the Ark, the *Synaxis* and the apostolic fishing boat, all fully manned, were arranged in tableau at one end of the large coffee table, with Goliath and a cadre of carnivorous dinosaurs positioned at the other end. Taking up their instruments with a courtly bow, to one another and to their audience, the cousins played and sang a short overture summarizing the situation and the action, in seven-syllable verse according to the sweet new style inspired by the enigmatic white stone. The latter, it should be noted, was prominently on display on the roof of the Ark, flanked by the David and Magdalena figures with the Christ Child just in front, while the grownup Jesus with Peter, James and John stood ready to board *Synaxis*— apparently the command center for the imminent battle. Andrew commanded the fishing boat, with Enoch and Elijah joining the other apostles to fill in for the "sons of thunder." As the overture ended, David began narrating the action while Magdalena put aside her flute, gracefully swooped over to the table, placed Jesus and His crew inside *Synaxis*, and moved the fishing boat aggressively toward Goliath and the Dragons. Then retrieving her flute, she accompanied David's ongoing narration as he sprang into action, sliding the Ark directly toward the titanic figure that stood defiantly, surrounded by his horrible hoard, at the table's end. With the naval attack underway, the flute fell silent as David lifted *Synaxis* into the air above the forces of evil and Magdalena ceremoniously swept Goliath and the dinosaurs right off the table and onto the floor, then burst into a victory song that served for their finale, as David retrieved his lute to accompany her.

The pair were heartily commended for the artfulness of their act. Evy Chen, their music teacher, was especially expressive on that point, while her husband the pastor and Maxim the priest were more impressed by the prophetic mythos of the miniature drama. Apropos of their developing talent, our *wunderkinder* received after supper, for their birthdays, a simple recording system they could use to capture audio and video clips of their dramatic play, for the sake of critique and improvement. After that, they were allowed to take Samson and Dancer for a ride around the farm, a ride rendered especially felicitous by the obvious mutual affection of the silver-grey mule and the rusty-red burro, amplifying, as it were, the fondness shared by their young riders. All in all, it was the best birthday ever!

Perhaps the most significant development related to Jerusalem Lutheran during the second half of that year came about, oddly enough, as a result of a pronouncement by the titular Bishop of Rome, to the effect that he was prepared to bestow a blessing upon *Therion*. Now the *Societas Trinitatis Sanctae*, the orthodox Lutheran ministerium to which Pastor Cornelius belonged, was by its founding Rule "dedicated to … the Lutheran ecumenical destiny of reconciliation with the bishop and church of Rome." Previous papal nods of affirmation for the proposals of the global Chairman had already raised the question of the continuing propriety of that particular dedication, in light of the circumstances. The blessing of *Therion* was the last straw, and the order solemnly decided in conclave, at its general retreat in October, to replace the phrase "bishop and church of Rome" with "patriarch and church of Moscow, mediated by the Orthodox Church in America." This move more or less mirrored that of the Society of St. Pius X, Padre Pablo's order, earlier in the year, and could be likened to an ecclesiastical earthquake, though it would have no immediate effect on the teaching or worship at Jerusalem Lutheran.

The flow of parish life revolved much, in those days, around the farm-to-city relief project, although the center about which it revolved was the weekly Divine Service when the spiritual gifts of God were received with thanks returned to Him. The concentration on this project was not only because its de facto directors, Rosa and Sophie Eckhart, were members of the church, and Evangeline Chen, the pastor's wife, was pitching in on its administration, but also because many of the farm families supplying the produce were parishioners there. The other six churches of the Illumination—those congregations that had received apparitions of the New Jerusalem in the wake of the New Bethlehem event—were also actively involved in relief efforts, and the seven churches maintained regular communication regarding these undertakings. The Global Emergency Council (GEC) was by then supplying basic emergency rations, flown directly into the urban centers, on which their populations could subsist, but the farm-grown produce added invaluable variety and nutrition to the food supply. So far no trouble had emerged in coordinating with GEC personnel for the delivery and distribution of produce, but the truck from New Bethlehem was usually accompanied by a couple of the Posse, and the regional military command was always informed of the shipment.

The consecration of Philadelphia Chapel at the Institute of Biblical Creation Science did not take place until the first Sunday in Advent, when it was decided to proceed with the opening despite a few finishing touches still lacking on the iconography. The Pantokrator in the dome was perhaps nine-tenths complete, as was the Theotokos and Child behind the altar, while the two full-length icons on the iconostasis screen, flanking the entrance to the alter, were beautifully finished. To the left of the entrance stood St. John the Theologian, in whose book of Revelation the letter *to the angel of the church in Philadelphia* appears, and to its right St. David the Psalmist, holding a large golden key, because at the beginning of that letter Christ called Himself *the holy One, the true One, who has the Key of David.* Half a dozen monks had accompanied Hieromonk Pyotr from St. Tikhon to serve as a choir, and throughout the Liturgy the space of the new chapel was resonant with psalmody, and with Orthodox hymns of Advent, chanted and sung in an ancient choric mode. At the appropriate moment, the bishop of the diocese anointed the stone top of the altar with fragrant oil, and placed incense on the five crosses engraved in the white marble, chanting the richly symbolic phrases of the consecration rite.

The homily was delivered by Hieromonk Pyotr, who took for his text the part of the apocalyptic letter to Philadelphia where Christ said, *Because you have kept my word of patient endurance, I will keep you from the hour of trial that is coming on the whole world.* He pointed out that the Greek word for *trial* in that text was *peirasmou*, and that a plural form of the same word (*peirasmois*) appeared in St. Peter's first epistle, where the big fisherman was consoling *the exiles of the Dispersion* regarding the *various trials* which *for a little while you have had to suffer.* The consolation was that those *peirasmois* were suffered so that the *genuineness of your faith* could be *tested by fire,* and thus *result in praise and glory and honor when Jesus Christ is revealed*—in the general Resurrection at the End of Time. Pyotr then referred to yet a third use of the same word, in the sixth petition of the Lord's Prayer according to Matthew: *And do not bring us to the time of trial (peirasmon),* sometimes translated, *And lead us not into temptation.* In these three texts, the Hieromonk found succinct counsel for the present time: Christ bade us pray to be spared the *peirasmon*; St. Peter assured us that by suffering patiently such *peirasmois* as cannot be avoided, we refine our faith as by fire; and then Christ again, in the letter to Philadelphia, promised those who faithfully endured that he would keep them from the great *peirasmou* before

His return in glory. Under these holy auspices, Philadelphia Chapel came to be.

YEAR TEN
(2053 A.D.)

I.

It was midday, on the third Wednesday in January, as Sophia Eckhart settled into a chair in the reference section of the Institute library, with a stack of periodicals on the table before her. Chris and Max were having lunch at the Ox & Swan, and she had decided to give them some time for male bonding while she caught up on the recent journals. Winter term was well underway, the new Master's program had enrolled a dozen qualified candidates, and she was teaching a course on the metaphysical coupling of the Quake and the Blueshift as well as helping administer the program. Since she and Chris had committed just one day a week to this work, and her study time on the other six days was limited, it was easy to fall behind in keeping current. The latest *Creation Research Society Quarterly* was a real gem: one article corroborated John's and Maria's analysis of the Global Quake by a different mathematical methodology; another examined the metaphysical paradigm of the creation sciences as deployed in the Glorious Synthesis; and a third surveyed the accumulated data on the Universal Blueshift, illustrated in a variety of graphic forms.

Sophia remained intellectually engaged with these matters, and considered the scientific work a significant part of her Christian vocation—yet that day she found her mind beginning to wander as she looked quickly through the pile of periodicals she had assembled. One reflection that arose regarded the religious emotions awakened in her since she and Chris had attended Divine Liturgy in Philadelphia Chapel, with her brother the priest presiding. Not only had she been deeply moved by the consecration rite, as the monastic foursome filled the compact space of the former planetarium with ancient harmonies of sacred song, but she and Chris had returned on Epiphany Sunday with the same effect. Sunday services at the chapel were held at 2:30 in the afternoon, so they had been able to celebrate the Epiphany at Jerusalem Lutheran in the morning, have dinner at the farm, and drive to the campus in plenty of time for Divine Liturgy. This had afforded Sophie an intimate comparison of the Divine Service in New Bethlehem, in which the focus was on the visit of the Magi to the Christ Child, and the Divine Liturgy at Philadelphia, which commemorated the Baptism of Jesus by St. John the Forerunner. The spiritual intimacy with Christ which Sophia sought when she worshipped was fully afforded by both services that day—by the relatively attenuated rubrics of the Old Red Lutheran order of service as much as by the rite of St. Tikhon. But something like a resonance between these liturgical experiences had arrested our astronomer's attention, and lingered in the background of her consciousness, like a subtle emotional harmony enveloping her in the love of Christ—His for her and hers for Him.

This heightened sensibility of being loved by an infinite Intelligence with intimate knowledge of the very fibers of her being gave Sophia an entirely new perspective on her fears of the approaching Tribulation. Fleeting figurations of fearsome possibilities flickered still in her imagination—what about this! what about that!—but they merely flickered now, and flickered less alarmingly, in the enveloping emotional harmony of the love of Christ. The darkness foretold would be short—though it might not feel short at the time—and in the end the reward of endurance would be Paradise, the New Jerusalem, where the saints in light would be made *pillars in the temple of God*, as Jesus told the church in Philadelphia. This alteration in the spiritual life of our astronomer was apparently initiated, as noted earlier, by her dual experience of worship, in spirit and in truth, in the pews of Jerusalem Lutheran and beneath the dome of Philadelphia Chapel, on the First Sunday of Epiphany, the liturgical season of light.

Sophia looked wistfully at the stack of partly-perused periodicals, then sighed deeply as she closed her eyes and returned to the wanderings of her mind. The ambient love of God was becoming apparent to her not only in the background of her consciousness, but also as reflected in the relations of those who loved her, and whom she loved. Foremost among these was her husband, without a doubt. However much she loved their David, or her parents, or his parents, and however much they loved her, it was Christopher, next to God, who most made her feel herself beloved, and whom she did herself most deeply love. Only a few nights before, she had caught a glimpse of herself in the full-length mirror in their bedroom, already undressed for bed, and had paused to critique the condition of her womanly figure, now that she was nearly thirty-five. She knew it was vanity, but a distinct frown of disapproval had begun to form on her lovely face, when suddenly the offending figure was embraced from behind by a pair of strong arms and Christopher's bearded face appeared, his head on her left shoulder and their faces cheek to cheek. She had watched her husband's deep blue eyes direct their gaze, slowly and lovingly, over every inch of her nakedness, and then she had squirmed around in his embrace and thrown her arms around his neck, and …

"What are you blushing about, my beauty"? Christopher's voice broke the silence of the library. "Time we got back to work, my delicious daydreamer."

When he was not making love to his lovely wife, our rustic philosopher had plenty else to preoccupy him over the course of the winter and spring of 2053, not least of which were his continuing ruminations regarding the metaphysics of the spiritual or celestial body. Over the course of that period, Christopher's thinking on the subject crystalized into two distinct analyses: one in terms of *form* and *matter*, and the other in terms of *esse* and *essence*. Each model was structured as an analogy between the physical body and its celestial counterpart. In the first model, the created soul was considered to be the *substantial form* of the body, as derived from a corresponding uncreated *logos* in the *Logos* of God. When this substantial form acted upon chemical matter, it produced and sustained the physical body, whereas when it acted upon the uncreated Light it produced and sustained the spiritual body. Thus, the identity of the created person in possession of either body was anchored in the uncreated *logos* as expressed by the soul.

The other model, based on the distinction of *esse* and *essence*, considered the body—physical or celestial—as part of a *personal union* with its corresponding soul or substantial form. This personal union was taken to be an *essence*, specified by its uncreated *logos* within divine Intellect (*Logos*), and expressed as an existing person by the action of *esse* in one of the three modes defined by Luther. The act of *esse natura* upon such a *logos* (or the *essence* derived from it) produced a natural human being with a physical body. The act of *esse gratiae* corresponded to the spiritual conversion of the (fallen) natural soul and the ensuing process of sanctification; and *esse gloriae*, acting on the selfsame logos-essence, produced the soul of a purified saint in a body of uncreated Light.

The case of the body of Jesus was more complicated—to say the least—because in addition to an individual *logos* specifying His *human* essence He also possessed the *divine* essence, by dint of actually being the Second Person of the uncreated Trinity. Furthermore, Christopher realized, it was His divine Person that provided the personal union of His human body and soul with the eternal divine essence (or nature) He shared with the Father and the Holy Spirit. According to his human nature (or essence) Jesus had a physical body, while according to His divine nature, as Palamas pointed out, He possessed in His personal unity the uncreated Light which He displayed at the Transfiguration. One might say Jesus had a celestial body by birthright, with no further infusion of *esse gloriae* required. Truly a unique case!

These metaphysical ruminations ran in parallel, during

that period, with Christopher's thinking on the Aeviternal Communication Network (ACN), suggested to him by the recent visit of the Child to his study in the barn loft. That bodily visitation had been followed by a series of further instructions that entered his mind at opportune moments, instructions voiced in his mind almost audibly, in the very voice of the boy Jesus. The angelic crew assigned to the legendary starship would activate a morphic field within the vessel's interior, which could be modulated to receive input by audio, video or keyboard and display content on the square-panel screens overhead in the cabin. Visual images and written texts displayed on the screens, and audible sounds impacting them acoustically, could then be reproduced at remote locations. The remote display function was to be twofold: a limited number of handheld mobile devices, and a capacity for projecting largescale planar images, with sound, to any specified geolocation. The number of mobile devices would have to be limited both for security reasons (the ACN would have to be a secret operation), and for reasons of cost, because the design called for a square frame of carbon-fiber rods, covered with silicon-coated glass fabric and with supercrystals in the four corners. They would essentially be scale models of the display panels inside *Synaxis*, and would be capable both of receiving image, text, and voice transmissions *from* the vessel, and of sending the same *to* the erstwhile starship, or *through* the latter to one another. The large-scale remote display function would be keyed to the GPS grid (easily accessible to the angels) so the desired location could be pinpointed, and the size and compass orientation of the virtual screen could be specified. Lots of details remained to be worked out—not least being what sort of activation rites would be required—but by late spring the Aeviternal Communications Network was definitively on the drawing board.

A third preoccupation of Christopher's during that period was the ongoing matter of human migration, somewhat exacerbated by the Quake but primarily driven by GEC-sponsored caravans overrunning the southwest border and actually being transported in groups to the interior of the country. The word was that some of these were now arriving in Pittsburgh, adding to the number of mouths to be fed and threatening to further destabilize the vulnerable civil order of the Quake-ravaged metropolis. This meant an increasing pressure on the population to push out into the surrounding countryside, potentially past the suburban belt and into the rural counties—and the southern border of Clarion County was barely fifty miles from the city limits. The Sheriff had advised all citizens living within two miles of the county borders to be especially vigilant for any migrant activity, and had announced that upon the first such report he would institute regular patrols.

John Eckhart totally shared his son's concern over the latter situation, and was more than willing to take his turn on patrol, if it came to that, but his current conversations with Sheriff Jones were more concerned with implications of his analysis of the Temple Mount Temblor. The Institute had reported the anomalous tectonics of the TMT in several podcasts, and had issued a press release to the media, many of which treated the announcement with skepticism, although a sufficient number of news outlets handled it objectively. Networks funded by the GEC were completely silent on the matter, as were a surprising number of scientific periodicals and broadcasts. By way of the Sheriff, however, the forensic findings of John and Maria were placed in the hands of a military intelligence unit attached to the regional command of the devolved Federal Executive, and from there found their way to the President. When a special envoy from the latter delivered the evidence to a general session of the GEC, he was shouted down and ridiculed in a manner that reminded Maria of the way Russian reports to the UN, on American-sponsored biolabs in the Ukraine, had been treated back in 2022. At that time, the truth had eventually come out, but now it might remain largely concealed until the End, when *everything* would be revealed.

John was turning seventy that year—three score and ten—the biblical definition of a full human life. And he *had* lived a full life, and was *still* living to the fullest extent of his powers and energies, devoted to his Lord and Savior, his family, farm and church, and maintaining his mental acuity and physical condition the best he could. His beloved Rosa, five years younger than himself, was aging beautifully, and he felt privileged to help her realize her vision of farm-to-table, and now farm-to-city agriculture. The previous year had seen a slight shortfall in production for the latter project, due to challenging weather conditions, and they decided accordingly to trim back their delivery goals for the current season and see what the Lord would provide. Another developing aspect of their urban relief endeavor was a recent encounter with GEC personnel by the produce delivery truck at the usual drop-off point, when two armed and uniformed operatives had demanded to be shown credentials. One of the Posse was riding shotgun that day and quickly stood down the obtrusive pair, explaining that he and the driver were free citizens of the American Republic, delivering farm-grown food to fellow Americans in need, and that they would be unloading the produce as usual. Was this a harbinger of trouble to come?

Meanwhile, Magdalena's journal was bearing witness to a gradual metamorphosis of the image of David portrayed in its pages. The girl's earlier renderings of the character of her beloved cousin invariably bore tinges of the rambunctious and the brash in the style of bravery she ascribed to him. But since the move to Pennsylvania had so vastly increased the amount of time they could spend together, the vocabulary describing our boy hero was shifting from words like *swift, strong, bold, battling, charging* and such, toward such terms as *noble, courteous, gallant, gentle,* and even *chivalrous*. Magdalena loved to idealize their play in her writing, creating short narratives in which elements of order, not necessarily noticed at the time, were introduced by hindsight—much to the delight of her dearest playmate. Sometimes they would even repeat the episode of play using Magdalena's narrative as a sort of script, like the time they took a fantasy-laden walk in the pine woods surrounding the Losskys' rancher, and then a week later took the same walk. Except that for the second walk the two were in costume—she in a pale blue dress that draped her modestly from shoulders to shins, and David dressed up in a bright green tunic his mother had made, with the Eck-hart crest blazoned on its breast. And the walk itself became the most pleasant performance of a courtly adventure in which, to be sure, there were several adversaries—ogres and the like—to be dealt with by slingshot or staff; and yet the dramatic emphasis fell more on the scenes immediately following those mythic battles. These were the scenes where the girl expressed high admiration for the gallantry of her knight—once tying a ribbon from her hair to the tip of his staff—and the boy, in his most courteous manner, declared his undying devotion to her.

David was truly delighted with his cousin's fanciful narratives—a genre he was more than happy to leave to Magdalena since his own literary gift ran to poetry, especially song, like his biblical namesake the Psalmist. Their play at the farm, except when the weather kept them under roof, almost always included Samson and Dancer, and there were few if any spots around the Eckhart farm that the four of them had not traversed. The equestrian mode lent itself naturally to motifs of chivalry in the adventures they invented as they rode, talked and sang their way across fields and along logging trails in the woods, casting benign spells of enchantment upon the landscape. Indoors, their new audio-video recording setup claimed much of their attention. They were allowed to use the extra upstairs room in the cottage as a studio and, with a bit of guidance by David's parents, had arranged a couple of old quilts (courtesy of Rosa), a folding screen, two chairs and a small table there. In this congenial space, the cousins continued their collaboration in exploring the musical and poetic possibilities of their sweet new style—including variable durations of the individual notes in the seven-tone phrases of the form—whole notes, half notes and quarter notes. The ability to record their best efforts and play them back for self-critique helped them to reach new levels of excellence. Thematically, David's lyrics during that period were giving more prominence to Enoch and Elijah in the fight against Antichrist.

Manuela cried as she watched the video clips, forwarded by Sophie, of her grandchildren looking so poised in the performance, and sounding so sweet as they sang and played—not to mention so obviously fond of one another. As happy as she had been in Russia these past few years, there was no getting around the act that she missed her children and grandchildren, and that screen time and videos, although so much better than nothing, were no kind of substitute for hugs and kisses. Intercontinental travel was still sketchy, with major airports closed and the GEC imposing certain restrictions on flights between designated countries, two of which were Russia and America. For the time being, she would have to content herself with things as they were. Fortunately, things as they were included much that she was thankful for, and her study with Hieromonk Amvrosy was not least in this category. After more than a year of assigned subjects for the icons Manuela was writing, her teacher had declared her ready to write a holy image by personal inspiration, and she had accordingly occupied herself with while praying for a subject. It was late winter before it came to her, in a dream: *The Church in Philadelphia at the End of Time.* The obvious connection with Max's new chapel notwithstanding, this was decidedly the subject with which the Holy Spirit had answered her prayers. Turning to the third chapter of *Revelation*, Manuela meditated upon the Lord's letter to that church, searching for motifs that might be translated in paint.

> *I have set before you an open door. I will keep*
> *you from the hour of trial. Whoever conquers, I*
> *will make him a pillar in the temple of my God.*
> *And I will write on him the name of my God,*
> *and the name of the city of my God, the New*
> *Jerusalem which comes down from my God out*
> *of heaven, and my own new name.*

We shall revisit our iconographer later in the year, and see how she expresses these motifs in figure and color.

Sergei had decided to commence his lectures on American Literature with Nathaniel Hawthorne, specifically *The Blithedale Romance*, set in an experimental utopian community largely invented by the author, but somewhat analogous to an actual community of that kind (Brook Farm) which Hawthorne had experienced. What especially attracted Sergei to the book was its peripheral perspective on utopian Socialism, despite Hawthorne's denial in his Preface that he has "put forward the slightest pretensions to illustrate a theory, or elicit a conclusion, favorable or otherwise, in respect to Socialism. In short," he continued, "his present concern with the Socialist Community is merely to establish a theatre" for the development of his characters and their story. Yet Sergei found peripheral glimpses in the *Blithedale* of a critical perspective on that theatre. For example, soon after convening at the farm where they meant to realize their utopian ideal, the ardent seekers were informed by the resident farmer of certain economic prerequisites for their survival, evincing the following reflection from the principal character:

> It struck me as rather odd, that one of the first
> questions raised, after our separation from
> the greedy, struggling, self-seeking world,
> should relate to the possibility of getting the
> advantage over the outside barbarians, in their
> own field of labor. But, to own the truth, I
> very soon became sensible, that, as regarded
> society at large, we stood in a position of new
> hostility, not new brotherhood.

Hawthorne here encapsulated the tendency of utopian projects to end up denigrating and demonizing their competitors, as the history of the twentieth century proceeded to prove. Another ironic barb aimed at the rhetoric of utopian Socialism claimed Sergei's attention in the context of a discussion of Fourier's doctrine, that eliminating the repression of personal needs and desires would produce a harmonious society.

> He has committed the Unpardonable Sin! For
> what more monstrous iniquity could the Devil
> himself contrive, than to choose the selfish
> principle—the principle of all human wrong,

the very blackness of man's heart, the portion
of ourselves which we shudder at, and which
it is the whole aim of spiritual discipline
to eradicate—to choose it as the master-
workman of his system?

Of course, the encouragement of personal liberation, the
professor reflected, pertained only to the preparatory phase
of Socialist operations, when the goal was to bring down
the traditional society at hand and clear the way for the
people's dictatorship. For that matter, the same Sin for
which Fourier was excoriated in this passage could be
charged to Capitalism, to the extent that it was ungoverned
by any spiritual tradition. Then there was the passage near
the book's end, where the hero is looking back, later in life,
on his sojourn in the Blithedale community:

Often, however, in these years that are
darkening around me, I remember our
beautiful scheme of a noble and unselfish
life, and how fair, in that first summer,
appeared the prospect that it might endure
for generations, and be perfected, as the ages
rolled away, into the system of a people, and
a world.

The collision of utopian idealism with human nature in its
fallen state: this was the peripheral perspective on Socialism
glimpsed by Professor Lossky in *The Blithedale Romance*,
and subsequently pointed out to his Am Lit students.

Father Maxim was settling into his new situation amiably. He loved the new routine, was delighted with the beautiful little chapel, and found the campus environment an invigorating challenge. On one hand, he was priest of an Orthodox chapel on the campus of Luther-Aquinas Evangelical College, and subject as such to possible pastoral relations with such faculty or students as might approach him. On the other hand, he was chaplain at the Institute of Biblical Creation Science, home of the archives of the Glorious Synthesis (including the Holotron presentations), and in that capacity was responsible for answering theological questions on the Synthesis from visitors to the Institute. Questions pertaining to the sciences of nature were the province of the scientists on staff, but when it came to the spiritual meaning of this august *summa* of the sciences, the buck stopped with Father Maxim. Part of his weekday routine was to sit for half an hour or more in Philadelphia Chapel, pausing between prayer knots for contemplation of the mystery of Creation, and sometimes a psalm verse would come to him: *I remembered the works of the Lord; for I will remember Thy works from the beginning*, or *Who coverest Thyself with light as with a garment, Who stretchest out the heaven as it were a curtain*, or *He spake, and they came to be; He commanded, and they were created*. Infinite Intellect comprehending the possibilities intrinsic to His infinite essence in one eternal Word (*Logos*), accompanied by an uncreated Spirit! Particular possibilities comprehended in the eternal *Logos* (Christ), uncreated *logoi* of possible creatures, chosen by the Creator to be actualized, became created substantial forms in the *aeviternum* producing

actual creatures, which came to exist in the world at specified times and with specified matter. The human substantial
form (the soul) was intrinsically intellectual, its mental pole
proceeding directly from divine Intellect and its cognitive
process reflecting the trinitarian order—the image of God
in humanity. Any scientific description of the natural order
was true, to the degree that it mirrored the order of the
logoi in Christ.

One afternoon in late winter, Maxim sat in the chapel
with his friend Cornelius Chen, who had driven up from
New Bethlehem for a scheduled conversation regarding the
signs of the times, and the situation of the Church. The
two clerics sat on chairs facing one another, in the center of
the nave, with the large icon of Christ Pantokrator directly
overhead. Having begun with prayer, they were conversing
quietly on the global Chairman's latest move. With the projected completion of the Third Temple just one year away,
the Adversary had announced the revelation of a unified
world religion that would be formally founded at the opening of the new Temple. In the name of Peace, Love, Light
and Community, the new religion was to supercede all
traditional religions by blending them into one, dissolving
their doctrinal distinctions while allowing whoever wished
to continue identifying as Christian, or whatever, to do so.
The Vatican had warmly greeted the announcement and
pronounced its benediction on the world religion, effectively identifying the sitting Pope as the False Prophet of
Revelation—a sign of the last years if ever there was one.

Maxim shared an observation regarding certain subtle
changes in campus life at the College, subsequent to Kill-

gower's retirement as Dean. It was difficult to pin down, but the impression was unmistakable that a new type of student (for Luther-Aquinas, that is) was appearing among the freshmen and sophomores—a sprinkling of students who seemed unaware they were attending a Christian institution. Or else they were aware, but scornful, even contemptuous. When he and the other Metaphysicals had been undergraduates, back in the late thirties when the Restoration energies were on the upsurge, virtually all of the students were serious Christians consciously equipping themselves, among other things, for defending the faith. That had been the standard at Luther-Aquinas. What Max was seeing now was a different attitude emerging, even if only occasionally discerned: glances of contempt at the holy icons as a group of students visited the chapel, a rhetorical roughness incompatible with courtesy in some of the discourse he overheard, styles of dress bordering on slovenly, even lewd. It was tough to put his finger on, but something was changing, and not for the better: yet another sign of the general darkening.

Cornelius wanted to talk about their ecumenical relationship—he as a Lutheran pastor and Maxim as an Orthodox priest. Since his ministerium—the Society of the Holy Trinity—had redirected its confession of ecumenical destiny from the Bishop of Rome to the Patriarch of Moscow, Cornelius had been pondering the meaning of that momentous move. He and Evangeline had attended Divine Liturgy at the chapel a couple of times over winter—once during Epiphany and once during Lent—and they both had found the service deeply moving. Just as Maxim had formerly experienced, in the Divine Service at Jerusalem Lutheran, a worship in spirit and in truth that was valid sacramentally, so Cornelius found in the Divine Liturgy of the Western Rites the same ancient liturgical order that had entered Lutheran tradition by way of the Roman Mass. When the pastor expressed surprise at the priest's pronouncement on the sacramental validity of the Lutheran Mass, the latter explained that his ecumenical thinking was grounded in the counsel of Constantine Zaitsev, a 20th-century monastic Archimandrite. The venerable Constantine had taught that as the Antichrist rose to power, promoting the false ecumenism of all-religions-are-one, the Holy Spirit would inspire a reaction within all the genuine traditions and denominations of the Church—those which possessed the fullness of truth and those which lacked certain elements of the full Christian tradition. Within each of these would arise a remnant who would hold fast to the truth of Christ that each contained, forming a resistance to the dissolution of that truth in a mythical mishmash of all religions. These separate remnants, in turn, would be drawn toward one another, enacting an eschatological ecumenism in preparation for Christ's return, and the Orthodox should welcome this development—according to the venerable Archimandrite.

Cornelius warmly thanked his friend for this perspective, and the two of them vowed to continue this discussion at another time. Before heading back to New Bethlehem, the pastor related his wife's enthusiasm over the children's quartet she was rehearsing at the church, and especially over the superb flautistry of Maxim's daughter. Evangeline thought a recital would be possible by late summer, if the kids kept up their practice, and there was even a possibility they would play an original piece composed by the lutenist. The topic afforded a note of euphoria which concluded their somber, apocalyptic conversation in a tone that was almost light-hearted.

Maria loved their new home south of Pinecreek. She was, after all, a Pennsylvania girl, and however much she had learned to love Texas, it had never really felt just right. The brick rancher was surrounded by coniferous ever-greens which displayed year-round the signature verdancy of the sylvan Commonwealth, and the kids loved to play on the trails that traversed those woods. The birdsong in springtime was marvelous, and now often mingled with the melodious piping of her dear daughter, who carried her beloved flute wherever possible, and who not so much *practiced* as simply played, and played. Maria felt that she herself was really in her element here, so far as her earthly life was concerned: her marriage with Max was still won-derful and their daughter a delight; she saw her best friend Sophie once or twice every week; she got along great with her twin brother, adored her nephew, and loved seeing her parents regularly—though she felt sorry for Sophie on the latter score. Her earthly life! How happy she would have been to live another half-century, had she not been pre-destined to be born so near the End of Time. And yet, how else could she have chronicled this incredible epoch of which she would be the historian?

The first half of the third year of the Darkening con-tinued to display remarkable illustrations of apocalyptic prophecy, with Enoch and Elijah playing an ever more prominent role. As construction of the Temple proceeded apace, and propaganda promoting the world religion began to intensify, the two venerable ancients correspondingly increased the intensity of their denunciations of the Chairman and all his works. Miraculously evading the most intricate security arrangements, they would suddenly appear at the most awkward moments, rudely interrupting the Adversary's most exquisite utopian rhetoric with strong words, in the name of the Lord, contradicting his claims and promises. They also precipitated a drought in northern Palestine and parts of Syria, where the Chairman was sponsoring a massive program of collective agriculture—a drought which began right after they announced it and caused catastrophic failure of the program. On top of that, they called down a viral plague which only infected the Man of Sin, his staff, and those who supported him—a disease which passed quickly but left disfiguring scars on the faces and bodies of it victims. Those who rejected the Chairman remained unscathed.

After the plague—which became known as Devil Pox because no natural progenitor could be found—a new tone of impatience and anger appeared in the proclamations and press releases of the GEC, especially with regard to those nations and individuals who insisted on remaining sovereign with respect to any claims of global governance. As for nations, this was pretty much America and Russia—and even America's sovereignty hinged on a devolved Federal Executive operating through regional military commands and county sheriffs. But there were hundreds of millions, at least, of individuals scattered among the broken nations of Europe, Africa, South America and elsewhere—Christians and others who knew better than to follow this fake shepherd with his false prophet—and they would be the most vulnerable to the encroaching global tyranny. Maria was glad to be working with Chris on his secure network.

As for the early Restoration, the pivotal nature of 2022 in that penultimate epoch was evident by the spate of pages it occupied in the *Journal* of Grampa Jeremiah, and not just because of the midterm elections in November, but even more because of the six months leading up to them. The hallmark of the latter was a constantly increasing drip of information into the public sphere, revealing both financial corruption and treasonous collusion with foreign enemies on the part of prominent political figures. These nefarious activities included the development of lethal viruses in laboratories located in the Ukraine, which led to the Russians calling for an international tribunal for crimes against humanity, according to the Nuremburg protocols. The information drip also documented, bit by bit, the insurgency against the providential President during his first term of office, which culminated in the theft of his electoral victory in 2020. Meanwhile, a series of constitutional rulings by the Supreme Court elicited violent reactions by the left, including threats to the safety of the Justices; food and energy prices rose sharply due to leftist policies, and the invasion of illegal migrants across the southwest border approached crisis proportions. It seemed as if a storm was about to break.

II.

The summer of that year was of the sort to turn a farmer philosophical—unless he was already a philosopher. In Christopher Eckhart's case, it was more a matter of turning his philosophical mind to the mud and the sweat, the toil and the tiredness attendant upon his physical vocation. It was seasons like this, when the sheer wickedness of the weather displayed, to the full, the fallen state of nature— the curse on the ground and the sweat of the brow— seasons like this, that turned a farmer's thoughts to the substance of his trade. Wresting the human food supply from recalcitrant soil while relying on weather that was intrinsically unreliable, all the while subject to crop damage by emerging insects and diseases—was this not the essence of farming? The wickedness of the weather consisted that year of a wet, cold spring that lingered into late June, then suddenly turned hot and dry through July and August, delaying the spring planting and then stunting or even withering its yield. The excessive wetness also produced a plague of earwigs in the vegetable patch, as well as a horde of long, black bugs never seen before, which together took a serious toll on the chard, beet greens, lettuce and spinach. Still, in spite of it all, Chris could confirm his vocation to farming unflinchingly; in fact, he absolutely loved it—was this not the essence of a farmer?

Then too, what better place to bring up his son, how-ever few years such upbringing might amount to? If the prophecy continued to hold, David would only be twelve or thirteen at the End of Time—five or more years short of full manhood—yet a boy of that age could foreshadow the man he would be. Was it not the age at which Jesus amazed the rabbis in the Temple? As David's father, our philosophical farmer was firmly determined that self-discipline would stand tall among the traits he hoped to instill in his son, as his father had done for him. And there was no better place than a farm, with the variety of challenging tasks involved in running it, to hone the self-discipline required for the mastery of those tasks. Hoeing the row you were given to hoe, whether you felt like it or not; gaining the strength to heft heavy bales of hay, and learning how to stack them in the mow so they wouldn't topple over; working with Samson to drag saw logs out of the woods or help move the steers—these and other tasks offered challenges requiring efforts of will. And such training of the will was one prerequisite of self-discipline.

Yet the sheer power of the will, undirected by a spiritual perspective, was potentially menacing, hence the strong emphasis, in David's upbringing, on the presence of Jesus in his heart—the real presence of Jesus, by faith, in the spiritual intellect of the boy. Also, there was the emphasis on Wisdom. The book of *Proverbs* was part of David's curriculum, and Christopher had him memorize parts of it for occasional recital. For example:

> *Happy is the man who finds Wisdom, and the man*
> *who gets understanding,*

for the gain from it is better than gain from silver,
and its profit better than gold.
She is more precious than jewels, and nothing you
desire can compare with her.
The Lord by Wisdom founded the earth; by
understanding He established the heavens.

The boy had even made this text into a song to be sung to his lute (sometimes accompanied by flute), and then went around humming the tune. Christopher thought to himself: as a man destined to have just one child, this one suited him just fine.

Intellectually, our philosopher was provisionally satisfied with the metaphysical analysis of the human celestial body at which he had arrived, and was presently preoccupied with theorizing about the Aeviternal Communication Network. He was beginning to conceptualize the system in terms of the intellectual capture, by angelic intelligence, of specific spatio-temporal configurations in the electromagnetic field. The initial input to the network was electromagnetic in nature: stable or changing patterns of pixels on a planar screen, controlled by keyboard or by video transmission; and on the audio side, digitized streams of acoustic information, input by microphone. Angelic intelligence, according to Christopher's theory, would read the audio-visual forms directly from the electromagnetic field, and then transpose their knowledge of these forms onto morphic duplicates in the *aeviternum*. These in turn would function as quasi-substantial forms for the further reproduction—whether on one or more handheld devices, or on a large-scale virtual screen—of audio-visual displays originating inside *Synaxis*. The original displays would essentially be transcribed from the electronic field into the *aeviternum*, then copied back into the field at remote locations, manifesting as light and sound.

In tandem with his thinking on this subject, Christopher arranged for the fabrication of two handheld devices, supercrystals and all, by the same specialty manufacturer that had constructed *Synaxis*. By the time those prototypes were ready in early August, another key component of the new technology had fallen into place, compliments of the Reverend Doctor Killgower. Christopher had confided in the Director that he was still lacking an activation rite which would constellate the angelic network, recalling that Killgower had been instrumental in formulating the two previous rites—for the voyage to the stars and for the observation of the Global Flood. Once again, it was from a dream that the old man gleaned the key verses, the solemn incantation of which would activate angelic intelligence—the crew of angels—to deploy a morphic field for the capture and communication of information via the *aeviternum*.

> *O Lord, our Lord, how majestic is thy name in all*
>   *the Earth!*
> *There is no speech, nor are there words; their voice is*
>   *not heard;*
> *yet their voice goes out through all the earth, and*
>   *their words to the end of the world.*

We shall look in on the actual operations of what would come to be called AeviComNet, further along in our narrative. For now, let the following facts suffice: Operation of the ACN required only two of the Metaphysicals—one male and one female—to be present in the cabin of *Synaxis*. For the first trial of the handhelds, Chris and Sophie held that post while Max (at the Institute) and Maria (at the rancher) held the devices. Successful two-way communication was established between *Synaxis* and both devices, as well as between the two devices. Work was also ongoing, during that period, on the large-scale remote display option, with the help of Maria's geometric expertise.

Christopher's brilliant and beautiful wife, meanwhile, was giving a lot of attention to the Master's program at the Institute, which they were jointly directing, although she was pulling better than half of that particular load. Sophia didn't mind the disparity in the least, both because she was happy to prove her ability and because she knew her husband was burdened with other tasks at the time. The fall term marked the second year of the program, and all twelve of the original students returned to continue their studies while ten new students enrolled for their first year. By spring, the second-year students would be deciding what topics to pursue in a third year of independent research, culminating in a Master's thesis to fulfill requirements for the degree. Sophia had several excellent linguists in that class, whom she was hoping to steer toward certain details in the Babel paradigm that required, in her opinion, further development. There were also some superlative astronomers, and these she hoped would be persuaded to pursue theoretical modeling of the Universal Blueshift, and even to collaborate with geologists in the class to model the metaphysical coupling of the latter with the Global Quake. She and John had demonstrated this coupling (except for the Temple Mount Temblor), but as with the Babel linguistics, certain details remained to be filled in, and who better to do so than her Master's candidates?

Our astronomer also continued to monitor ongoing observations of the Blueshift, and was aware of the gradual acceleration of the sidereal bodies in their omnidirectional fall toward Earth, as manifested by the shifting of the starlight absorption spectra of key chemical elements toward the blue end of the electromagnetic spectrum. The media networks—except in select circles—had largely stopped covering this, perhaps because it was inherently so unsettling; yet Sophia, rapt in the love of Christ, found in it foremost a fascinating sign of the prophecy's truth—the approach of the End. The love of Christ did not render her invulnerable to pangs of anticipated loss—the loss of all those years with Chris that might have been, and with David—the loss of her ripe old age, and even high middle age—all gone, pulled right out from under her. Some moments, indeed, brought her to the brink of a burning envy—envy of all the generations of believers who had lived out their threescore and ten or fourscore, or at least had enjoyed the possibility thereof. But almost month by month now, Sophia was growing toward something approaching foreknowledge of the world to come, the new Heaven and the new Earth that would replace the loss of earthly life as she knew it, and replace it so superlatively as to utterly annul any pangs of loss. Still, even if only four years remained until the End, it was already three years since she had seen her mother and father—screentime aside—and she was missing them terribly.

Sophia's sentiment was heartily echoed by Sergei and Manuela, who nevertheless continued to make the most of their sojourn in Russia until such time as return to the States became possible. As the reader will recall, earlier that year Manuela had been inspired, after prolonged and earnest prayer, to write an icon on the subject, *The Church in Philadelphia at the End of Time*. By early autumn she had determined the design and written her first rendering, which brought a radiant smile to the face of her teacher, Amvrosy. Manuela had chosen a board two feet long (or tall) and a foot wide, which she demarcated into two square panels, one above the other when the board was vertical. The lower panel was bordered thickly on three sides (left, right and bottom) by the writhing coils of a great red dragon, among which could be counted ten heads and seven horns. The square area surrounded by the dragon was marked off by thick lines of gold tempera (left, right and bottom), leaving that area itself open to the upper panel. Inside this central area stood twelve human figures, almost shoulder to shoulder, facing the viewer—six men and six women, of varying skin color and differing attire, with faces earnest and unafraid. Behind each of these, receding into the background and visible by little more than their faces, stood a column of eleven others, making 144 human figures in all. The twelve in front stood with folded hands, their mouths open as if in song, or prayer, and likewise the mouths of all of those figures shown closely enough for facial detail.

The upper panel of the icon was dominated by a cubic structure outlined in gold, and surrounded by a field of celestial blue in which seven golden stars were symmetrically arranged. In the interior of the golden cube, at its very center, stood a sapphire throne supporting a golden cloud upon which was inscribed, in royal purple, a triangle-trefoil design signifying the Holy Trinity. The remainder of the cubic interior was filled, without crowding, by upright columns or pillars of the purest white surrounding the sapphire throne. Twelve of these columns stood side by side across the front of the golden cube facing the viewer. Legibly inscribed upon each one, in royal purple, were the sign of the Holy Trinity, below it the initials (in Cyrillic) of "New Jerusalem," and below that the Greek monogram of the name of Jesus (IHS). Between the upper and lower panels, and connecting each of the twelve foremost human figures with one of the frontal white pillars above, extended the most subtle of fine lines, suggesting invisible rays. Manuela had used this technique in her Flood and Babel icons to symbolize supernatural causality, but now she introduced a new twist: twelve strands of horsehair from the mane of Sergei's good grey stallion, artfully embedded in the tempera. We shall doubtless be hearing more of this icon.

The steed aforesaid had earned the love of his master over many hours of riding the countryside around Ozerki, and indeed Sergei had come to think there was no better place to ponder American Literature than on the back of old Whitman—in more ways than one. In planning his lectures, our professor tended toward Walt Whitman's concern with grand, archetypal models, and with spiritual meanings. Moreover, the authors who attracted him were those that had classically characterized some prominent trait in the American soul—like Hawthorne with his Puritan realism dressed in Gothic romance, or Longfellow or Cooper, with their sense of the primordial wilderness that faced the early white settlers of the American shores. He loved the stately hexameters of Longfellow's *Evangeline*:

> This is the forest primeval. The murmuring pines
>   and the hemlocks,
> Bearded with moss and in garments green,
>   indistinct in the twilight,
> Stand like Druids of eld, with voices sad and
>   prophetic,
> Stand like harpers hoar, with beards that rest on
>   their bosoms.

Cooper, too, was master of this archetype, as shown by these lines from near the beginning of *The Deerslayer*:

> Centuries of summers had warmed the tops
> of the same noble oaks and pines, sending
> their heats even to the tenacious roots, when
> voices were heard calling to each other, in the
> depths of a forest, of which the leafy surface
> lay bathed in the brilliant light of cloudless

day in June, while the trunks of the trees rose
in gloomy grandeur in the shades beneath.

One of those voices heard calling in the depths of the
primeval American forest was the hero of the romance, one
Nathaniel (Natty) Bumppo, among whose epithets was
"Deerslayer," and whose portrait appears a couple of pages
further on:

> His face would have had little to recommend
> it except youth, were it not for an expression
> that seldom failed to win upon those who
> had leisure to examine it, and to yield to
> the feeling of confidence it created. This
> expression was simply that of a guileless
> truth, sustained by an earnestness of purpose,
> and a sincerity of feeling, that rendered it
> remarkable.

Sergei had lived in the States for three decades, keenly
observing the character of the American people—whites,
blacks, browns, reds, the full epidermal spectrum—and
there was no doubt in his mind that Cooper had caught
here a national trait. The encounter with the *forest primeval*
had made an indelible imprint upon the American character and produced a prominent type, as immortalized in
this passage where Natty is gazing at the wilderness lake he
called the "Glimmerglass."

> The spot was very lovely, of a truth, and it

> was then seen in one of its most favorable
> moments, the surface of the lake being as
> smooth as glass and as limpid as pure air,
> throwing back the mountains, clothed in dark
> pines, along the whole of its eastern boundary,
> the points thrusting forward their trees even
> to nearly horizontal lines, while the bays were
> seen glittering through an occasional arch
> beneath, left by a vault fretted with branches
> and leaves. It was the air of deep repose—the
> solitudes that spoke of scenes and forests
> untouched by the hands of man—the reign
> of nature, in a word, that gave so much pure
> delight to one of his habits and turn of mind.

It seemed to Sergei that these "habits and turn of mind" lived on in the American soul, and indeed had served the Restoration well.

Returning now to Pennsylvania, we find David and Magdalena turning nine at the end of that summer, and so eventful was the day on which they did so that we shall describe it in some detail. As the reader of Book II of these *Romances* may recall, our romantic cousins had been born on the same day, September 14, which was the Feast of the Holy Cross. In 2053 the date fell on a Sunday—the very Sunday on which "Miss Evy" decided to debut the children's quartet she had been rehearsing. During Divine Service the four would play an anthem, after the Epistle lesson, and then perform a short recital during part of Christian Ed hour. The recital consisted of four hymn tunes, each arranged in a distinctive mood—one a rhapsody, others pastorale, nocturne, and fugue. David and Magdalena were joined by ten-year-old Roland Engleman on the French horn, and on the violin by Melody Shaeffer, who was eleven. The children played beautifully, bringing tears to the eyes of Evangeline Chen, as the ancient tunes she had chosen and arranged were created anew by these bright-eyed young musicians' plucking and strumming, blowing, piping and bowing. The congregation could hardly believe their ears, even after what they had just witnessed in the Divine Service.

For the anthem, Evy chose a composition of David's, in which he summarized several verses from *Proverbs* in a stanza of his seven-syllable lines:

> God by Wisdom made the Earth
> And by knowledge Heaven made.
> Happy is the Man whose mirth
> Comes from Wisdom; who has weighed
> Wisdom precious more than gold,
> More than rubies; who has stayed
> In the ways of Wisdom old.

The Epistle for Holy Cross, from I Corinthians, had just referred to Christ as the *wisdom of God*, setting the liturgical scene for David's theme, and the Psalm had enjoined, *Sing to the Lord a new song*, heralding the novelty of the sweet new style arranged for quartet, and paraphrasing passages of Scripture. The four musicians stood side by side in the front of the nave, between the congregation and the altar, and played in a slow tempo through four variations of the stanza, each with a different arrangement of the instruments and statement of the melody. David sang the first three of these while Magdalena, holding her flute in abeyance, voiced the final stanza of this *new song* to the Lord. But just as she sang the last line, *In the ways of Wisdom old*, a gasp ran through the rapt congregation at the sight of the now-familiar golden cube—or cubic space suffused with an aura of gold—suddenly superimposed on the four players! The children stood just inside the frontal face of the cubiform luminescence, which extended behind them into the chancel, as they played the last line of the anthem. Then the apparition vanished, as suddenly as it had appeared. Although the vision lasted less than five seconds, the gaze of the entire congregation had been glued to the ensemble, so that when they suddenly appeared to be frontal columns in a foursquare structure, everyone clearly saw them. And that was just the *morning* of the ninth birthday of David and Magdalena.

For the sake of preserving the dramatic unity of the day, we skip over the midday festivities at the Eckhart farm, where the family was joined by Pastor Cornelius and Evy, the former being happy to discuss with his friend Maxim the latest apparition at Jerusalem Lutheran, and the latter just as delighted to celebrate two of her proteges. It was all but 3:00 before the festivities had run their course—concluding with a huge, heart-shaped cake bearing nine candles on each lobe—and the birthday kids begged leave to go riding for an hour or so. Saddling Samson and Dancer, they headed out the tractor path to the woods, riding between fields of stunted corn and beans, and parched grass fields, until shortly they entered the shade of what Grampa John called the Guardian Oaks. The latter formed a sort of belt, perhaps a hundred yards deep, along one edge of the farm's fifty-acre woodland, guarding the main entrance to the woodlots and timber stands further in, as well as to the place Grampa called Christmas Tree Hill, the sylvan promontory to which our *wunderkinder* were headed. The hill had a southern slope covered with pines and cedars of various sizes, but on its top stood a small grove of tall pines which offered good shade and a thick carpet of needles. It was a favorite spot of the two.

As they rode, David had been listening to Magdalena's impressions of what had happened in church that morning, when, just as they entered the shady grove on the hilltop, her melodious voice fell silent, and both of their noble steeds drew to a halt. Not more than fifty or sixty feet ahead stood the largest pine in the grove. On both sides of its thick, grey trunk, up to four or five feet above ground, appeared vertical arcs of a white luminescence, as if some radiant object stood behind it. David and Magdalena dismounted and, tightly holding hands, advanced silently across the pine-needle carpet toward the towering tree. When they had covered about half the distance to the shining trunk, lo and behold, out from behind the great pine stepped the Christ Child, enveloped in a nimbus of white light and clad in a regal robe of pale blue with purple hems. The cousins immediately reverenced the Child in their most courtly manner—David with a deep bow and Magdalena with her most elegant curtsey—as He raised His right hand in blessing and spoke to them. "You are my White Stone, and you will be known among the nations for my name's sake. You shall help me crush the dragon's head. For you are my White Stone: sing, play and dance!" He looked both children directly in their eyes, smiled beatifically, and disappeared. This was the crowning event of their ninth birthday, as well as the seed of further developments of which we surely shall hear more.

As the fairly disastrous agricultural season drew to a close, Rosa Eckhart found herself growing more reflective than resentful regarding the temporary collapse of her farm-to-city relief program—the culmination of her thirty-eight-year career as an agricultural home economist. Scant fare could be trucked south that season, though they'd been able to keep up with the eggs and a couple of beeves—but after all, Rosa reflected, it was the Lord's work she was doing, and He controlled the rain. She was thankful to have kept up (barely) with her CSA clientele, and to have stocked the farmhouse larder, so she saw no cause for great resentment in the situation. Besides, her participation in the church choir had grown more engaging under Evangeline's direction, and even a source of spiritual energy. She had been gifted with more than one way to serve the Lord!

Aside from the drought, which was not the first he had seen in his years, John's cogitations at that time were largely political, in the broad sense of the word. The attempt to bring public attention to the Temple Mount Temblor anomaly was ongoing, and both American and Russian military intelligence had acquired documentation linking several close associates of the Chairman to purchases of materials and services such as would have been deployed in a large-scale detonation. The two countries were pushing for an international tribunal on the affair, but given the GEC's consolidation of power it was not at all certain anything would come of it. Meanwhile, the first encounter with a small band of undocumented migrants in Clarion County was reported in mid-autumn, whereupon the Sheriff duly instituted regular patrols by the Posse, which meant that John and Chris would be on the schedule. The first party of migrants had consisted of unarmed women and children fleeing their traffickers, and after being questioned about the identities of the latter and other pertinent information, were housed and fed by a Baptist congregation in Clarion—but the alarm had been sounded. On top of that, the Sheriff had heard from the regional military command about confrontations between U.S. military and GEC personnel—just on the brink of actual skirmishes—especially inside the urban zone.

No undocumented migrants had yet been reported in Jefferson County, where Father Maxim and his family resided, and even if there were, he would not be riding with the Posse—but the situation in Texas was far worse. The U.S military, insupportably strained by nationwide Quake-recovery operations and funding shortfalls, had pulled back a hundred miles and more from the southwest border, and the Hill Country ranches were irretrievably overrun. The Crockett County Sheriff and his Posse had held out for a while, but at last were overwhelmed by the surge of migrants, heavily accompanied now by squads of armed men, and Maxim's family, Mendes and Diaz, had fled north. The Lucky M was no more. Maxim also heard from Padre Pablo that San Angelo was completely overrun, with multitudes of homeless migrants covering the sidewalks and trash everywhere—not to mention that St. Michael's, along with other churches, had been requisitioned by the city government for use as a homeless shelter. The home of his youth and his first assigned parish, both gone!

Providentially, other concerns occupied the mind of our priest that autumn, and one of his favorite places to ponder them, besides under the dome in the chapel, was on the back of his buckskin, Son of Thunder, who had been rescued from the earlier raid on the Lucky M and was now stabled at the Eckhart farm. Even when accompanied by his beloved Maria on her palomino, Honeysuckle, or by the kids on their fabled steeds, Maxim's mind would tend to revolve around his conversation with Cornelius on the latest apparition of the New Jerusalem, at Jerusalem Lutheran; and around the new icon his mother had written, of which she had sent a digital copy; and additionally, around certain texts in *Revelation*. He and Maria had of course been present at the Sunday morning service where Magdalena played in the quartet, and they had witnessed with everyone else the astonishing appearance of the aureate cube in which the four musicians had appeared as frontal columns. Through Abbot Alexander at St. Tikhon's, Maxim had duly reported the phenomenon to the primates of the Orthodox Church in America, and they had shared the report with Moscow. An affirmative response had been received from the primates there. Maxim himself had congratulated Cornelius on his ministry at Jerusalem

Lutheran, for having been so richly blest with grace—an assessment that Cornelius heartily acknowledged, all the while confessing his own unworthiness.

But Maxim could never recall that remarkable morning without thinking immediately of Manuela's Philadelphia icon, the copy of which had arrived less than three weeks later. Besides the sheer beauty of the holy image, even in a digital representation, our priest had been surprised to recognize that the twelve foremost pillars in the icon, standing across the front of the golden cube in the upper panel, corresponded perfectly, at a ratio of three to one, to the four children standing just inside the frontal face of the cubiform luminescence that enveloped them. Moreover, Maxim's reflections on this juxtaposition of images brought into play the letter to the church in Philadelphia, according to St. John's *Revelation*, where the Lord said *whoever conquers, I will make to be a pillar in the temple of my God ... and I will write on him the name of my God, and the name of the city of my God, the New Jerusalem which comes down from my God out of heaven, and my own new name.* The icon represented this prophecy beautifully by linking the faithful of the earthly Church, holding out against the dragon, with the pillars of the Temple in heaven surrounding the throne of God, each one marked with the triple inscription described in the text. What this visual correspondence had done, in effect, was to place the four children in the icon—its upper, heavenly half—which also fit, as Maxim thought about it, with a certain celestial quality in the music they played that morning. The Holy Spirit was definitely on the move at Jerusalem

Lutheran. Another matter that was much on the mind, not only of Maxim but of his fair wife Maria, had to do with the developing aftermath of their daughter's most recent encounter, in David's company, with the Christ Child. The cousins had conferred with each other for a couple of days before telling their parents of the incident, and by then they had determined its meaning for themselves: David and Magdalena were to present themselves publicly as an *act* (in the sense of performance) to be known as "White Stone." Their mission was to celebrate the love of Christ, to praise His name *among the nations*, and to help Him *crush the serpent's head*. White Stone was to consist only of David and Magdalena, but they were hoping to call upon Roland and Melody as musical backup for some of their pieces. Now Maria and Max, no less than Sophie and Chris, were far from unfamiliar with the prodigious potential of these two children, as manifested in their creative play over the previous five years. But this announcement took matters to an entirely new level, and raised questions that would require some serious thinking, as the act to be known as White Stone began to take shape.

One such question that occurred to our Thucydides of the Apocalypse had to do with the eschatological identity of White Stone: was the act in any way prefigured in the prophetic books, especially *Revelation*? In His letter to the church in Pergamum (or rather to its angel) Christ promised: *To him who conquers I will give him a white stone, with a new name written on the stone*; which assuredly resonated with the actual white stone, enigmatically inscribed, with which the kids had long been playing. But there was no mention—she had confirmed this with Maxim—of any such pair as David and Magdalena, given that Enoch and Elijah already fulfilled the roles of the Two Witnesses, as Maria continued to document. Increased efforts of the Adversary to arrest those venerable ancients had provoked them to activate yet another of their prophesied powers: fire had issued from their mouths, incinerating several squads of operators dispatched to detain them. Meanwhile, the current year had seen a significant upsurge of religious conversions whereby orthodox Jews were accepting Jesus as the Messiah, even as the Chairman augmented the propaganda for his One World religion. But perhaps the most startling prophetic development that fall was the staged assassination of the Adversary by a gunshot wound to the head, when it was announced first that the wound was definitively fatal, and then, three days later, that he had miraculously recovered. The coherence of current history with the biblical script could hardly have been more plain, yet numerous Evangelicals kept denying the obvious because they hadn't yet been raptured out—just as some American patriots were hard put to realize that the Restoration had been an Eliatic interlude before the End, not the final victory of good over evil.

Grampa Jeremiah had commented at length in his *Journal*, on what he called a "post-millennialist utopianism" that formed one strand in the cultural fabric of the American Restoration, affecting both the emphasis on national greatness and the joint military-civilian operation signified by the capital letter Q. It was true that a great concentration of evil had come to a head during the first two decades of the twenty-first century, manifesting as a globalist insurgency aimed at subjugating the sovereign nations to a global government, and deeply involved in human trafficking operations including the sexual exploitation of children. Not to mention actual Satanism among the elite of the insurgency. It was also true that the movement led, at least symbolically, by the providential President, aimed at radically disrupting the entrenched networks of control established by globalist operatives, and at restoring the sovereignty of the American people. In that perspective, the success of the movement was a victory of good over evil. But it could not possibly have been the final victory, unless Christ returned at once and finished the job! Jeremiah Jefferson knew his Bible as well as his history, and as he read the signs of the times he could not envision the Restoration enduring more than half a century, maybe less, despite the utopian optimism of some.

Maria loved rereading the *Journal's* copious entries for the summer of 2022—what high drama! The same parties that had subjected Donald Trump to two failed impeachment trials and a failed special counsel investigation were attempting, in committee, to implicate him in a planned coup d'etat on January 6, 2021—when in fact it was he who had urged the deployment of troops to protect the Capitol, and his opponents who had refused. Then in August, the FBI raided Trump's private home on the pretext of seizing classified documents he had illicitly stored—when in fact as President he had lawfully declassified the documents in question, and moreover had shown the whole cache to the Bureau only a few months earlier. Maria found it interesting that her grandfather, who was no stranger to the Q-operation, took so detached a tone in recording such events as these, while occasionally interspersing, in capitals, such pithy propositions as PANIC BREEDS DESPERATION, and NOTHING CAN STOP WHAT IS COMING.

YEAR ELEVEN

(2054 A.D.)

I.

The winter of 2054 found Christopher Eckhart up to his ears (as he liked to put it) in technical work related to development of the Aeviternal Communication Network (AeviComNet): conducting further trials with the handheld devices, working with Maria on the remote planar display application, and even writing up documentation of this novel technology—although he had no plans to apply for a patent! In the initial trial with the handhelds, Chris and Sophie had activated the angelic field inside *Synaxis* by chanting the prescribed psalmody, and when the angelic icon appeared on the square screens overhead, they added the commands, "AeviCom One, over. AeviCom Two, over." At this, the faces of Max and Maria appeared on two of the screens as their voices were heard in the cabin, "Read you, *Synaxis*. Loud, bright and clear." Max and Maria were also able to see and speak with each other, by simply saying, "AeviCom One," or "AeviCom Two," whereupon the two mobiles connected with each other. Next to be worked out was how the handhelds could be activated by the users instead of by a human crew inside *Synaxis*, in order to contact one another—assuming this could even be done without a crew on board. As he prayed over this, Christopher conceived the notion of putting technical questions directly to the *angelic* crew of the vessel by typing them into the Network, and sure enough, he received a succinct reply: "Mobile Activation Code: *O Lord, our Lord!* Followed by AeviCom number of device to be contacted. ACN field, once activated, remains in virtual mode." Just like clockwork, the first trial of this feature also worked like a charm: when the specified psalmic phrase was spoken to the device, the angelic icon appeared onscreen; when the Aevicom number was spoken a soft but sonorous horn would sound from the device being called, and when answered with a simple reply the connection was perfect. Had the angels found a way around Murphy's Law?

Likewise, Chris's work with Maria on the remote planar display (RPD) application of the Network was progressing nicely toward their goal of a trial run by early May. The principle of sound and image replication via morphic duplication in the angelic realm was the same as for the handhelds, except that in RPD mode the aeviternal duplicates were transcribed, not onto the screen of a device but on a sort of virtual screen, demarcated out of thin air. The main technical problem to be worked out was how best to specify the location, screen size and orientation of the planar display, which would consist essentially of a sheet of electromagnetic energy malleable to morphic input from the *aeviternum*. The basics turned out to be remarkably simple: The size of a square screen was defined by a single side-length in any convenient unit of measure; its orientation by the compass direction of its top and bottom edges and the vertical inclination of its sides; and its visual height by the distance above ground level of its bottom edge. As for geographic location, it emerged that the angels had cognitive access to the GPS grid; thus, the geometric center of the virtual screen could be specified precisely. If the exact coordinates were unknown, the angelic crew could adjust them according to verbal description. We shall witness the trial run of this ingenious application further along in our narrative.

That winter was also a wet one, and cold. As a result most of the precipitation came as snow, which began to accumulate before the ground froze so that it could melt from the bottom and soak in, insuring at least good groundwater for the summer to come. As for what else they could expect from that summer, God only knew, but Christopher was hopeful that the weather would be more amenable to crop production than the previous year's withering drought. He and John were also concerned about the fertilizer supply, which was becoming unreliable, and so this year they decided to plant an acre of vetch to be harvested for seeds, which they would sow the next year for a cover crop. Tilling in that crop of vetch the following spring would add nitrogen to the soil, reducing the amount of that nutrient to be added chemically. If this approach proved out, they could increase their acreage—if there were any more *time* by then. He was often reminded, those days, of the anecdote of Luther's that his mother liked to recite, how the Reformer had supposedly said that if he knew the world was to end the following day, he would still plant an apple tree. As long as this beloved (though also accursed) soil was here to be farmed, our philosopher reflected, he would be farming it—and when its *elements dissolved in fire* (as St. Peter put it) he would see what use the *New Earth* might have for a farmer. After all, Adam had farmed in Paradise! Happily, that spring brought a season of beneficent weather to the region, putting the farm on a good footing as summer loomed.

Also developing that winter was the participation of Chris and John in the newly-instituted Posse patrols, driving one day a week over their assigned circuit: south from the farm to New Bethlehem, then west on 861 to Rimersburg, from which a series of state and local roads took them to the bend in the Allegheny above Hillville, whence they stayed more or less parallel to the river up to Parker's Landing, then took 368 east and headed back to the farm, passing through Callensburg and Sligo on the way. The circuit came to about forty-five miles and took and hour and a half to two hours to drive, depending upon conditions. Thus far their patrols had been uneventful. Perhaps the least that could be said of this development is that it offered a unique father-and-son experience!

Sophia, meanwhile, was happily shepherding her two classes of Master's candidates (and their professors) as they explored and developed the scientific riches enshrined in the Glorious Synthesis in its original, canonical exposition. The aim of the program was that each student acquire a comprehensive overview of the Synthesis by means of a solid grounding in each of the biblical creation sciences, and then specialize in one or two of these—multidisciplinary studies being welcome. Several of the second-year candidates, as spring drew near, decided to collaborate on a formal comparison of the Global Quake with Noah's Flood, using the geological field models of each catastrophe developed by John and Maria. Another group would be investigating an anomaly that had emerged from ongoing observations of the Universal Blueshift: the light of the five principal stars of the constellation Cygnus—the very stars visited by our Metaphysicals in Book I of these *Romances*—appeared to be shifting further to the blue than that of any other sidereal object. What this implied, of course, was that those five stars were approaching the earth at higher velocities— falling faster, as it were—than the rest of the heavenly bodies, and Sophia wanted a detailed examination of the data. She also had a couple of linguists who chose to reexamine the set of all existing languages, by the methods of comparative grammar and the semantic analysis of key meaning clusters, with the aim of confirming the number of linguistic phyla and their geographic distribution. Meanwhile and in tandem, a pair of molecular biologists would be compiling all available data on the three genetic haplotypes corresponding to the sons of Noah, traceable in post-Flood populations, and their subsequent geographic distribution, and then merging this data with the linguistic results, hopefully solidifying the evidence for the Babel para-digm. The Master's program was indeed up and running.

Also up and running was her nine-year-old son, an energetic and brilliant little boy with his father's build and hair but with her own big, brown eyes, who sometimes seemed to run circles around her, yet still, endearingly, came sometimes to her arms for a motherly hug. David's education was practically autonomous: Sophie and Chris set curricular guidelines and monitored his studies, but the boy was already mastering material at high school level. He said that Jesus showed him what the words meant, and how the ideas were related to each other, and that when he made songs, there was an angel that sort of whispered in his mind. And now there was White Stone—a development Sophia was slightly ambivalent about. On the one hand, what a marvelous way for the Lord to make use of these children, whose conception and birth had resulted from His instruction to their parents, once on a planet far away—though now apparently, along with its star, drawing nearer. On the other hand, according to the prophetic cycle they were apparently nearing the cusp of the great Tribulation, and these two children were being called to be *known among the nations*, and to *crush the serpent's head*. It was enough to give pause to any mother, and she knew Maria shared her feelings. But they also agreed that it had to be up to the Lord: they were gifts from Him, and they'd have to wait and see what He would do.

Sophia's desire to see her parents, and to spend some time with them, had continued to wax stronger as the months passed. Gradually the idea took shape in her yearning that perhaps she could persuade them to come live in Pennsylvania. After all, the Lucky M was lost, there was plenty of room for two more at the Eckhart farm—between farmhouse and cottage—and her folks had never planned to stay in Russia more than a couple of years. They could ride out the final phase of world history in the company of their children and grandchildren, they would have access to horses, her mom could keep goats and do her painting, and her dad could doubtless do some teaching at the College.

Christopher, John and Rosa thought the idea a splendid one. The guest rooms in the farmhouse, where Chris and Sophie had lived before building the cottage, could easily accommodate the couple, including a compact study for Sergei and a small studio for Manuela. With this consensus in hand, Sophie proceeded to present the proposal to her parents.

Manuela was practically beside herself at the prospect, for besides missing her children and grandchildren ever more poignantly, she had been stricken hard by the loss, not only of the Lucky M, but of her family's ranchlands as well. Not only had she lost the ranchero where she and her dear husband had lived and raised their children, but she had lost the Hill Country in which she grew up—lost not only property rights but free and secure access to territory that was no longer under the rule of law. She grieved over this for months, even knowing full well that the whole Earth's lease on time was running short—indeed it may be that her grief over the Hill Country was exacerbated and prolonged by an underswell of *eschatological* grieving, over the imminent loss of everything whatsoever. She also knew full well of the *gain* that would follow the End—immortal bodies in a New Heaven, on a New Earth—but that would be *then*, and she and her loved ones were *now* still living in time! Such was the mental stress Manuela was suffering when her daughter proposed the move to Pennsylvania. The reader may imagine her reaction.

Manuela had also been amazed to learn from Maxim of the striking visual correspondence between the celestial pillars in her *Philadelphia* icon, and the young musicians—

two of them her own grandchildren—in the apparition at the Lutheran church in New Bethlehem. Her icon had interpreted *the temple of my God* in the Lord's letter to Philadelphia, in which each of the faithful was to become a *pillar*, as the space inside the aureate cube of the New Jerusalem, essentially surrounding the *throne of the Almighty and of the Lamb*. The heavenly pillars within that space corresponded to the faithful on Earth, holding their own amidst the draconian encirclement of the Antichrist—and now the apparition of the celestial City, engulfing the four children in the manner described, had virtually enacted the icon in the nave of Jerusalem Lutheran! Whatever else the apparition might have been taken to mean, Manuela accepted it gratefully as a sign affirming her iconography, and with the permission of her teacher Amvrosy, began praying for another inspiration. She was also pleased that her son the priest had requested a copy of the icon for Philadelphia Chapel, and over the winter she produced a fine replica of the original, which she wrapped and packaged securely for shipment. The word was that the American and Russian military were opening up an air freight corridor between the two countries, with limited passenger service possibly to follow, so she was hoping to ship the icon in the spring, and then maybe, later on, fly back to America with Sergei.

The latter was also sympathetic, to say the least, with the notion of returning to the States and settling at the Eckhart farm, at least temporarily, given that the invitation had been extended. His contract at the university ran through the fall term—the end of the year—but after that, as soon as transportation became available, why not? Overall, security was still better in Russia, with the American government currently governed by a devolved Executive operating through regional military commands and supported by county Sheriffs, but rural Pennsylvania apparently stood in pretty good stead under these conditions. Sergei loved his native country, so long the butt of Western contempt, and yet he felt himself as much an American patriot as a Russian, and maybe America needed him more at this point—not to mentions his kids and grandkids! Nevertheless, while things were getting sorted out on that front, he had his lectures on American Literature to occupy him, and he was delighted with the occupation. Another of the authors examined by Professor Lossky in his quest for archetypal American characters was one he had known, and loved, in his youth—the author who had almost singlehandedly inspired in Sergei what he later had laughingly called his "cowboy complex." The novels of Louis L'Amour, from Sergei's archetypal perspective, were every bit as much Am Lit as the romances of Hawthorne and Cooper, and the characteristic archetype they displayed was a *certain kind* of cowboy.

L'Amour's heroic cowboy was, to begin with, a big, strong man, tall and muscular, a master of hand-to-hand combat, with a lightning draw and deadly aim with pistols—but such merely physical attributes also characterized the leading villains. The thing that made L'Amour's hero was his thinking, his philosophy, his ethics, the way he understood the world, as reflected in lines like these, from *The Man Called Noon*:

> Here in these western lands men were fighting
> again the age-old struggle for freedom and for
> civilization ... The weak, and those unwilling
> to make the struggle, soon resign their liberties
> for the protection of powerful men or paid
> armies; they begin by being protected, and
> end by being subjected.

Or again, in declarations like this, from *The Mountain Valley War*:

> This was a wild, new land and a place where a
> strong man had to stand for what he believed.
> One could not yield to the lawless and the
> ruthless, or there soon would be no freedom.
> It was among men as it was among nations.

This worldview had ethical implications, as portrayed in the thinking of the hero in *North to the Rails*:

> He was realizing how cheap are the principles
> for which we do not have to fight, how easy
> it is to establish codes when all the while
> our freedom to talk had been fought for and
> bled for by others. ... If a man would not
> put restrictions on himself, if he would not
> conform to the necessary limits that allow
> people to live together in peace, then he must
> not be allowed to infringe on the liberties of
> those who wanted to live in peace.

Here it was not the forest primeval that challenged the American spirit, but the primary evil, latent in the fallen nature of humankind, and the consequent need to establish and defend law and order, for the sake of preserving the peaceful enjoyment of liberty. In the words of the hero of *Fair Blows the Wind*, a 17th-century Irish immigrant and early ancestor of a dynasty of cowboy heroes:

> If we sit serene at this hour, this day, it
> is because the thin walls of the law stand
> between us and evil. A jolt of the Earth, a
> revolution, an invasion or even a violent
> upset in our own government can reduce all
> to chaos, leaving civilized man naked and
> exposed.

The cowboy novels of Louis L'Amour, in Sergei's professional opinion, presented a prominent trait in the American soul: a sharp awareness of the precariousness of liberty, and the necessity of law and order to its survival. In a fit of whimsy, the professor actually read several passages from his lecture to the good grey horse he had named Whitman, who vigorously whinnied his approval.

No one was any happier than Magdalena over the prospect of her grandparents returning from Russia. She had always adored Grampa Lossky especially—although she adored Gramma too—and occasional entries in her journal gave voice to how much she was missing them. Another theme in the girl's writing that winter was the encounter she and David had experienced at the giant pine on Christmas Tree Hill—an experience she was intent upon chronicling to the last detail she could remember. One thing she remembered was that, just as the Child was telling them they were His "White Stone," she had a crystal-clear impression of the costumes they were to wear for the act: simple white tunics, long-sleeved, with David's falling to just above his knees and hers to mid-calf. Her impression included qualities of the fabric: it must be light-weight, sheer, and with excellent drape, especially in motion—a bill that her mother and Aunt Sophie thought could be filled by either silk or muslin, depending upon availability. Their tunics were to be gathered at the waist by golden belts, and their brows girded with headbands of the same golden webbing, but on the front of Magdalena's headband a white rosebud was to be affixed, while on the front of David's the mysterious white stone itself—source of the sweet new style. Yet while these matters occupied significant space in our girl prodigy's journal, it is no exaggeration to say that her dominant theme was still David. Again, a subtle shift in her vocabulary became evident, as she began attempting to describe her feelings for him. In reference to her feelings themselves, we find such words as *fond*, *tender*, *devoted*; while *charming*, *lovable*, *enchanting* and the like are ascribed to the object of those feelings. He was the unchallenged hero of her girlish heart, and she was happy to be living so close to him.

As for her hero himself, the reader is well aware of David's affection for Magdalena. Developmentally, however, as David traversed the tenth year of his life, he found that affection beginning to complexify, with respect to the sexual side of his nature. As he continued reading the book of *Proverbs*, he encountered sayings like *the lips of a loose woman drip honey ... but in the end she is bitter as wormwood ... Keep your way far from her ... Why should you be infatuated, my son, with a loose woman and embrace the bosom of an adventuress?* The boy's attention was electrified by this language. Who was this *loose woman*, this *adventuress* whose *lips drip honey*, and what was this about *embracing her bosom*? Somehow, vaguely, this language made him think of Magdalena, who liked the adventures they shared, and whose lips he liked to kiss sometimes, but they didn't taste like honey. He mulled the matter over for some time before finally asking his dad about it, one morning in mid-April. Christopher calmly commended his son on his diligent study of Scripture, and suggested they take a little walk.

As they passed the barn on the way to one of the tractor paths, David and his dad saw Samson and Dancer cavorting playfully together in the bright spring sunshine, across the fresh green grass of a pasture field. As the two of them watched, the young equines came to a halt, nuzzled one another fondly, and suddenly turned so that Samson was behind the red jenny—and mounting her. David looked at his dad, who was laughing out loud about the living parable before them, relative to the subject of their walk—instead of birds and bees it was mule and donkey! Our philosopher composed himself and, with one hand on his son's shoulder, explained the essential anatomy of mammalian sex, with reference to the human case, and how God had made man and woman to marry, one to one, and to live faithfully in marriage. A loose woman (and there were loose men too) was one who was personally unfaithful in marriage, or who tempted married men (or women) to be unfaithful—because sex could be a powerful temptation. David replied that he thought he was attracted to Magdalena a little bit, in that way, but that didn't mean they were *loose*, did it? Putting his arm around his son's shoulders, Christopher explained that feeling such an attraction didn't make anyone *loose*, as long as they didn't do anything that only married people were supposed to do—according to the Almighty Creator. David nodded silently. He did not, at that time, raise the question whether he might one day marry Magdalena, somewhat to his father's relief. That question would have to be faced eventually, but the delay was welcome.

Another preoccupation of David's during that period—not unrelated to his boyish romance with Magdalena—was planning the world premiere of White Stone, which was looking to be a world premiere in more ways than one. In addition to the act itself, the four parents had decided that the safest way to broadcast the first performance was over the AeviComNet, given that the Chairman was expected to launch the *Therion* surveillance system by mid-year; and given that White Stone was to be hurled directly *at him*, it appeared more than prudent to employ the clandestine network. The main theme of the premiere performance was the heroic opposition of Enoch and Elijah to the Man of Sin, the Son of Perdition who was currently consolidating his peoples and nations, and would consist of a single three-minute song in their sweet new style, beginning with the following stanza.

Enoch and Elijah came
To oppose the Antichrist,
To oppose him in God's name,
In the name of Jesus Christ.
They bear witness to the lies
He continues to devise:
They are bringing him to shame!

While David and Magdalena worked on perfecting their song, with instrumental accompaniment, Chris and Maria completed the technical specifications of the protocol by which they could instruct the angels on the size, placement and orientation of the desired RPD. The trial run transpired in the middle of May, the plan being to generate, on the side of the barn facing the farmhouse, a virtual screen twenty feet square on which would appear a series of short video clips and static images, including text, and which would also emit sound. On that pleasantly warm spring evening, Chris and Maria took their places inside *Synaxis* while John and Rosa, Max and Sophie and the kids sat on the farmhouse porch, at the end facing the barn, and waited almost breathlessly, yet somehow subtly hyperventilated. "The angels are here," Magdalena observed matter-of-factly. As if on cue, the wall of the barn lit up like a video screen, an icon of the Synaxis of Angels appeared vividly for a moment, and Christopher's voice was heard, loud and clear, "Welcome to AeviComNet—

the network that's out of this world!" As several pairs of eyes rolled ironically at the slogan, there followed a series of brief cinematic segments, lovingly edited from the family archives by Sophie and Maria, with commentary from the latter and her brother from their stations inside *Synaxis*—morphically copied from control screens there to the side of the barn, acoustic vibrations and all, with no intervening electromagnetic signal. The broadcast ended as it had begun, with the angelic icon, and the virtual screen disappeared from the side of the barn as the family cheered and applauded. The remote planar display function was all but ready for action.

John and Rosa never ceased to be amazed by the things their kids and their spouses kept getting into, or discovering, or inventing—and now their grandkids, not surprisingly, were following suit. Given the signs of the times and the drift of events, the grandparents were naturally somewhat nervous about David and Magdalena going public in the very face of the Lawless One—but if this was the Lord's will, how could they oppose it? If these two nine-year-olds were destined to confront the Antichrist, at least the ACN would provide cover as to their location, although for how long was unknown. But for now they were safe, Providence had given them a happy childhood, and John and Rosa were glad to have had a hand in that happiness. *Thy will be done*, they prayed in the words of Jesus, *on Earth as it is in Heaven*.

The period from January to June of 2054—or liturgically speaking, Christmas to Pentecost—marked the first half of Father Maxim's second year at Philadelphia Chapel, as he continued to grow spiritually in that ministry. He had come to love that compact, consecrated space adorned with windows of Heaven (as the holy images were sometimes called), where he had by now celebrated the Divine Liturgy well over fifty times. He could almost hear the reverberations of chant as he sat in the chapel on weekdays, frequently preferring to pray and meditate there instead of in his study, unless he particularly needed privacy. Twice a day, morning and afternoon, Maxim would perambulate leisurely about the campus, choosing his route as he fancied, with an evangelical gleam in his eye. His tall figure, robed in a black cassock, tended to make the students notice him, and gauging their reactions by their faces, Maxim would sometimes make eye contact with someone he could speak to about Christ—someone capable of understanding their need for a Savior.

Those same evangelical perambulations, however, were sometimes occasions of temptation, particularly in relation to Maxim's most poignant personal flaw, which, as the reader of these *Romances* may recall, was concupiscent sexual lust. He had been noticing a shift in the makeup of the student body since Killgower's retirement as Dean of the College, and one of the signs of this shift was the way some students, including several extremely attractive young women, were dressing. The hallmark of these handsome hussies was the way they displayed their bodily figures, their most exquisite contours, by attiring themselves in apparel both skin-tight and scanty, and so presenting themselves as objects of sexual attraction, fit for exciting the lust of fallen mankind. According to *Genesis*, Adam had no carnal knowledge of Eve, nor even was aware that she was naked, until after they had eaten the forbidden fruit—after the Fall—which implied there was no lust in Paradise. But this was no longer—and not yet—Paradise. Father Maxim was still a fallen man in a fallen world, and when his eyes fell upon the bodily form of a beautiful woman, then despite his baptism into the Body of Christ and his ordination as a priest of the Church, a flare of desire would arise from the depth of his soul. It had nothing to do with his love for Maria, which was inviolable, nor with any lack of the marital remedy for lust prescribed by St. Paul, and his commitment to conjugal chastity was unshaken. But let a pretty lass of twenty parade before his gaze, clad in such raiment as to reveal the contours and convergences of her feminine shapeliness, and there was lust—no matter how often confessed nor how frequently staved off. It was like St. Paul's *thorn in the flesh*, which the Lord had said He would supply the grace to live with, and Maxim trusted it would be so for himself.

Theologically, he continued to meditate on the letter of Christ to the church in Philadelphia, as recorded in St. John's *Revelation*, in light of a connection with the letter to the church in Pergamum, which had occurred to him during a conversation with Maria on the latter subject. Assuming the *pillar in the temple,* ascribed to each of the faithful Philadelphians, would be made of stone, both letters made reference to stones with names written on them— three names on the *pillar*, and one *new name* on the *white stone* described to the church in Pergamum. Moreover, the stone pillars would also presumably be white, as portrayed in his mother's icon, so that both letters described white stone inscribed with one or more names—and in both cases it was the one *who conquers* that would receive the *white stone* (along with *some of the hidden manna*), or who would be *made a pillar in the temple of God*. The conquest in question was perseverance in the faith, during the time of trial preceding the End: to keep the Word of Jesus, and refuse to deny His name, in the face of whatever the great Tribulation might bring. And now the Lord had called Maxim's own daughter, along with his dear nephew, to go public with their performances under the name White Stone! Earnest conversations on that subject were still underway, but Maxim found in these matters much food for meditation.

Another such matter emerged in the merry month of May, when Maxim was joined in the chapel by the Reverend Doctor Killgower one fine morning, the latter bearing some news to share with his chaplain. The network of evangelical prophets, to whom the Director fondly referred as his Invisible College, had recently reached a consensus regarding a new set of dreams and visions received by several of its fellows. The context of these private visions was the twelfth chapter of *Revelation*, where the figure of a celestial Woman, bearing a male Child who was immediately *caught up to God*, symbolized the Church, and where the said Woman quickly became the quarry of *the Dragon, that ancient Serpent, who is called the Devil, and Satan*. At this dire moment, according to St. John, *the Woman was given the two wings of the great Eagle that she might fly from the Serpent into the wilderness*. The recent consensus of the

Invisible College had reference to the identity of this Eagle, and of its two wings, the former being interpreted as the principle of religious liberty, and the latter as two nations: America and Russia. Further food for meditation, indeed!

Our blond, blue-eyed Thucydides of the Apocalypse, in the meantime, was keeping close tabs on her subject. Maria observed with astonishment the almost clockwork procession of current events in accord with biblical prophecy. As spring was breaking in the woods of Pennsylvania, the Antichrist announced that the consecration (his word) of the new Temple in Jerusalem would be held on the first of July, and that he himself would have an important message to the world on that occasion. The same date would also see the inauguration of *Therion* as Chief of Global Intelligence, and the activation of the worldwide system for monitoring all electromagnetic signals. Enoch and Elijah were expected to mount some sort of spectacular protest at the event, and accordingly our Metaphysicals (all six of them) proposed to augment that protest by projecting the world premiere of White Stone onto the façade of the new Temple. David and Magdalena had pretty well finalized their three-minute tribute to the two ancient prophets, musically replete with their sweet new style—lute, vocals and flute—with lyrics tightly rhymed and trenchant, and movements reminiscent of some courtly dance. The kids made several recordings of the act in early June, studied them carefully, and after a few more rehearsals announced they were ready to record the final take, to be uploaded to the *aeviternum*, from where it could be copied onto the front of the Adversary's Temple.

Maria was far from fearless regarding this proposal,

but the signs were unmistakable that this was what they were meant to do; so the fear, like any other obstacle, was simply to be faced. Another such obstacle, from a spiritual point of view, was pride, of all things—her own personal temperamental flaw. After all, not only had she been instrumental in the development of AeviCom—although the technology had been revealed to her twin brother—but her own sweet daughter was to play so salient a role in the current eschatological drama, of which Maria herself was the historian. Yet, in order for this whole operation to be God-pleasing, pride could have no place in it—this was axiomatic, and she knew it, no matter how many times she had to remind herself. Max had a marvelous way of helping her with this, when she happened to give voice to some prideful sentiment: a certain ironic look in his quiet brown eyes; a certain subtle movement of his beard and mustache. It was one of the things she loved about him.

Maria had been so busy with various matters over the course of several months that the *Journal of Jeremiah Jefferson* had lain untouched. Picking it up again in mid-spring, she found her bookmark still in the copious sheaf of pages devoted to the pivotal year of 2022. In the entries for early October the outcome of the Nuremberg 2.0 tribunals proposed by Russia was still unknown, but plenty of ink had been devoted to the burgeoning campaign of the Russian military to circulate and distribute documentation of crimes against humanity, gathered during their special military operation in the Ukraine. In a major speech, the Russian President asserted "certain Western elites" had conspired to subjugate all sovereign nations to global governance, and that Russia would defend its sovereignty by all available means, urging other nations to do likewise. This latter-day Vladimir also made reference, in an exchange involving the naming of a falcon, to a special military unit named "Storm" which was instrumental to the current operation—at the same time that the unseated American President was making frequent reference to an imminent Storm. As Grampa Jefferson amply documented, "Storm" was also a major symbol deployed by the clandestine Q-operation, in reference to a sweeping visitation of justice upon certain domestic enemies culpable of treason—ultimately by military tribunals. In late September of that year the unseated President began openly acknowledging, at rallies and in social media, the reality of the clandestine operation; and in mid-October a federal special counsel brought to trial a case that mapped out a criminal conspiracy to subvert a sitting President, which implicated a presidential candidate and the national committee of her party. Jeremiah's anticipations were palpable.

II.

The Chairman of the Global Emergency Council had barely slept on the eve of the calends of July, and when the sun rose over Jerusalem he greeted the day with a sort of fiendish joy. Because of the summer heat, the sacrilegious ceremony he had planned for the dedication of the Third

Temple was scheduled for the evening, giving him all day to doublecheck all the preparations, and to concentrate his psycho-mental energies upon the evil plan he was to carry out. The Temple site was meticulously adorned with red and green brocades decking out pillars of polished black marble, forming a somewhat somber backdrop to a white marble podium topped with an ornate golden throne. Elaborate security arrangements had been seen to, as a large crowd was expected, and elite members of the global financial cabal supporting the GEC, who were expected to be present, required assurances of their safety no less than did the Chairman himself. Final tests of the *Therion* technology had proceeded smoothly, and the system was ready to be activated that day as planned, so that no electronic communication on Earth, cabled or wireless, could escape the surveillance of the "Beast." Mentally, the Chairman's concentration was turned toward the infernal spirit who inspired, or rather possessed him, the fallen angel who had seduced mother Eve to disobedience, tempted the Son of God to betray His Father, and now at the End of Time was to have his final fling. All was in readiness as evening arrived in Jerusalem, on the memorable first of July. The assembled crowd, prompted by enthusiastic operative planted in its midst, was chanting loudly, "Hail Chairman Nabal! Long live the Savior!" and similar panegyrical phrases; while the cabal elite stood in small groups to the left and right of the gleaming podium, politely applauding the Chairman as he approached the golden throne. A group of religious leaders representing all major religions also stood facing the podium, nearer the golden throne than the shadowy financiers, and inclined their heads as if in reverence when the tall, imposing figure took his seat. We shall not describe in detail the oration delivered by that figure, so splendidly robed and enthroned, in a voice orotund of tone, announcing the inauguration of his One World religion, which would thenceforth supplant all traditional religious authority. In order to preserve Peace on Earth, religious dissent and disputation would no longer be permitted, whether involving doctrines offensive to the vision of One World, or actions deemed illegal by the Council. This directive, Chairman Nabal added, would be rigorously enforced by the new Chief of Global Intelligence—the most powerful and sophisticated artificial intelligence entity ever developed.

Pausing for effect, the august-looking figure enthroned before the Temple was about to introduce *Therion*, which was to deliver a short address of its own, when events took an unexpected turn. Enoch and Elijah suddenly appeared, standing directly in front of the podium and, raising their arms, began to denounce the Abomination of Desolation represented by the demonic pride of the one who wished to usurp the throne of the Most High. Without even rising to his feet, Nabal gestured to the nearest security detail, and four armed men quickly seized the two ancient witnesses and slew them with knives on the spot, according to previous orders. With a sinister sneer, the would-be divinity ordered that their bodies be exposed on the Temple steps, where the public could view them as examples to be avoided, and perhaps the birds of the air would view them as meat. At just that moment, however, events took yet another turn, for behind and above the figure on the throne appeared a shimmering surface about thirty feet square, like a screen, and on that screen the angelic icon of the ACN. Accompanying the icon was a ten-second audio clip from the *Sanctus* of Bach's *Mass in B Minor*, and then the screen went white and the audio announced, "We are White Stone," clearly pronounced in the voices of two children—who promptly appeared, garbed in white, on the virtual screen. Before the Man of Sin could even react, a lute and a flute were heard in sweet strains of sound that enveloped the Temple Mount—such was the volume of the audio—and then, the flute falling silent, the voices of a boy and a girl combining most beautifully with each other, and with the chords of the lute.

At first the audience was entranced, even Nabal himself appearing momentarily captivated, but as the *meaning* with which the lilting lyrics were loaded began to dawn upon those assembled, exclamations of shock and dismay arose. The Chairman stood, covering his ears with his hands, and loudly demanded that security put a stop to this outrage and arrest everybody involved—which turned out, to his chagrin, to be impossible. There in the forecourt of his new Temple, the big shimmering screen continued for three full minutes to display two charming children, in white tunics girded with golden belts, playing and singing a ballad recounting the bold interventions of Enoch and Elijah in the plans of the Man of Sin. At the ballad's end the boy and girl joined hands and, cradling their instruments, nodded solemnly to the audience, repeated the phrase, "We are White Stone," and faded into a blank screen which briefly displayed the angelic icon before disappearing altogether.

Without a trace. No chemical residue, no electronic signal. Nothing for Nabal's investigators to go on.

The perspective on all this from the Eckhart farm was, of course, completely unique. Chris and Maria again managed the transmission from *Synaxis*, uploading the recorded clip to the ACN for duplication on the virtual screen in Jerusalem, then joining the rest of the family in the farmhouse to watch the global network coverage. Several networks captured nearly half of the performance before orders to switch programming were confirmed, and local channels continued to play the truncated performance for hours before they, too, were gagged. David and Magdalena were delighted at the outcome, especially since the second half of their act repeated the lyrical stanzas sung in the first half, with musical variations, so the part that the networks captured contained the whole ballad. At the same time, everyone was saddened by the murder of Enoch and Elijah—even though it had been clearly prophesied in *Revelation*—as well as appalled at the public exposure of their bodies, which was to be broadcast around the clock by webcam. Keeping the same prophecy in mind, however, the family marked with pious anticipation the following three days and a half, which given the meridianal separation of Jerusalem and New Bethlehem, would conclude just before midnight on the Fourth of July. Having no neighbors near enough to be disturbed by their customary pyrotechnics, the latter were delayed until the prophetically designated time, eighty-four hours after the murder of the venerable ancients.

Half an hour before midnight, the whole family

gathered in the living room of the farmhouse, where the video console was tuned to the webcam in Jerusalem, where the bodies of the venerable witnesses lay undisturbed, according to the Adversary's directive. It was early morning in Jerusalem, and already a small crowd had assembled around the prostrate corpses—which strangely showed no signs of decay—jeering at the fallen prophets and celebrating the cessation of their furious denunciations. As the family assembled in the farmhouse looked on, a cry of alarm ran through the crowd surrounding the bodies, which suddenly began to stir, then sat up and slowly rose to their feet. At once, something like an articulated rumble of thunder was heard, and the two old men rose into the air, disappearing from the webcam and, as reported later, enveloped by a brilliant white cloud in the sky. David and Magdalena were the first ones out the farmhouse door to where the fireworks were staged, and as the others emerged onto the porch they were pointing into the sky and shouting excitedly, "There they go! There they go!" The children insisted they had seen the venerable ancients transiting the constellation Cygnus—which was especially bright because of the motion of the stars toward Earth—and then vanish into the distance toward that celestial Swan. Although no one else could confirm their observation, it was clear in any case that the prophesied resurrection and ascension of the apocalyptic witnesses had indeed transpired, on time, and the annual Fourth of July fireworks at the Eckhart farm assumed an additional significance that year.

The world premiere of White Stone, and of the RPD function of AeviComNet had both been brilliantly successful, so while the children immediately started planning their next episode, Christopher turned his technical attention to the handheld mobile devices. It was not so much a question of further technical development just then, as of figuring out the most efficient deployment and use of the handhelds, and how many of the latter were accordingly to be acquired, which led to considerations of cost. To begin with, Max, Maria, Sophie and himself should each have one, and these could be shared with John, Rosa and the kids as needed. Killgower had requested four of the devices for maintaining communication with his Invisible College, and had sufficient funding to cover those. Sheriff Jones, upon being informed confidentially of the technology by John Eckhart, figured he could scrape enough out of his budget for four more, at least to start with; and Pastor Cornelius, desiring to communicate secretly with the other six churches of the Illumination, thought that the seven congregations could raise enough for one unit apiece. That came to nineteen units in all, minus the two already in hand, so that seventeen additional units were desired. Fortunately, the crystallographic lab where Christopher had sourced the supercrystal components was only a couple of hours away, and the fabricator was right in new Bethlehem. Purchase orders were in place by the middle of August, secured by cash deposits.

About that same time, Chris and Sophie found themselves alone one evening on the veranda, side by side on the porch swing outside their cottage door, swinging gently to simulate a breeze in the still summer heat. Their minds were not at that moment enthralled with thoughts of the agricultural season, which was still at that time looking pretty good, nor with plans for the fall term at the Institute, when the third-year Masters candidates would begin their independent research. As darkness fell, pale moonlight could be seen flooding the vegetable field to their left, and the pasturage to their right; they were holding hands. Christopher was remembering the first time he had seen his Sophia, remembering indeed how he had known she was his, in an instant, in the glance of an eye. Her face was a perfect synthesis of a uniquely Slavic beauty with a mesmerizing mestiza loveliness, and there was something in the form of that synthesis, something like a dart or an arrow, that utterly transfixed him, not only that first time but still, virtually every time he looked—really *looked*—at her. Over the decade of their married life, Christopher had come to believe that something like *purity of heart* was prerequisite for the kind of looking that really *saw* the perfect beauty implicit in the face of his wife. And the interesting thing about that conclusion, he thought to himself as he sat by the side of his beautiful beloved, was that purity of heart was precisely the quality named by the Lord in the beatitudes, as pertaining to those blessed ones who *will see God*. This then was the standard he had set for himself, whenever he gazed into his Sophia's face: to purify his heart by the sight of her, in the fire that his love for her enkindled in his spirit.

Sitting by his side in the moonlight, Sophie was feeling how strangely her love for her husband was immersed in the enveloping love of Christ, which had been ever more evident in her inner life since she and Chris had been attending Divine Liturgy at Philadelphia Chapel several Sunday afternoons a month, in addition to their usual morning attendance at Jerusalem Lutheran. More and more, she was coming to understand the words of St. John in his first letter, *God is love, and those who abide in love abide in God, and God abides in them.* And also *if we love one another, God lives in us, and his love is perfected in us.* On one level, Sophia's love for Christopher was quite natural: she admired his intellect, appreciated his gentleness, adored his rugged good looks, and was attracted to him sexually. But the silent conversation of their hearts, the inward communion that united them, touched upon something supernatural, something declaring the glory of God as much as the heavens do, and declaring the work of his hands as much as the firmament does. For *those that abide in love abide in God*, and *God lives in us* when we love, which meant that her most heartfelt affection for her husband, like his for her, situated their romance in the supernatural love of Christ, in whom the love of God was fully incarnate.

Their silent conversation was at length interrupted by a topic they needed to articulate. Sophie reminded Chris, with a gentle squeeze of his hand, that they needed to figure out how to contact her parents over the ACN, since they did not want *Therion* to be privy to the travel plans. One possibility was to ship them a mobile device via the air transport corridor secured by the American and Russian militaries, but such a small item might be at risk of being lost in transit, or even falling into the wrong hands. Another approach would be to deploy an RPD screen, say four feet square, inside the cottage in Ozerki, provided the angels could configure the network to return input from there to *Synaxis*, as well as displaying input from the command vessel. After querying the angelic crew by keyboard, Christopher would learn that they could indeed configure the virtual screen to receive and return, as well as to display, video and audio content, and would be provided with a character string to specify this function when desired. In addition, he would broach the problem of placement—of actualizing the planar display inside the Losskys' cottage, preferably placing it on a wall—and be informed of the appropriate procedure. Next they would contact Sergei and Manuela electronically to obtain, by certain circumlocutions, the GPS coordinates of the center of an appropriate wall in their cottage, and to establish a time for their next conversation. But that would be several weeks after their moonlight communion on the veranda.

In Russia, meanwhile, the elder Losskys were firming up their plans for returning to America sometime in late winter, as soon as the air corridor was open for passengers. Cargo flights were underway, and Manuela had already shipped her second rendering of the Philadelphia icon by that route, in fulfillment of Maxim's request. She planned to leave the original with Amvrosy at the Lavra, much to the delight of the old Hieromonk, who blessed her when she told him, and offered a prayer for her continuing inspiration. Our painter was presently preoccupied with her final Russian watercolors, her last renderings of now-beloved landscapes around Ozerki—gently rolling expanses of grass dappled with trees and copses, divided by waters flowing or still, and crowned with a wide-open sky. Manuela abstracted a variety of motifs from the scenery she perceived in certain carefully selected perspectives, and painted their coloration rather playfully, striving for a surprising beauty in scenes that might appear, at first glance, to be lacking in sublimity. Her very favorite view was one that was seen from a certain perspective on Ozerki Lake, looking out over a bank of reeds across the broad sheet of water fringed with trees—although Sergei insisted it was no match for Natty Bumppo's Glimmerglass.

One evening toward the end of summer, the two of them were enjoying an equestrian outing which took them past the aforementioned prospect, and they halted their mounts to see what new aspect the familiar view might have in store, as the sun sank toward the horizon across the lake. A broad trail of reflected sunlight stretched out over the water toward them, gradually turning from golden to orange as they watched—when Whitman whinnied ever so softly, and the whistling of swans was heard. The noble birds were approaching them from behind, headed for the lake, and passed no more than thirty feet over their heads, continuing perhaps a hundred yards over the water before landing on the surface of the lake. As the swans, of which there were seven, descended gracefully onto the glimmering orange trail of reflected sunlight, a single instant caught Manuela's eye—a single image traced in her memory like a photograph. She saw the seven swans touch the water at the same time, framing in that instant a roughly circular patch of orange light, and—just like that—she saw a human figure in a shimmering aureole, surrounded by angelic forms. Manuela's intellect tingled with supersensory scintillations as she apprehended what she had seen, as if she were hyperventilating yet breathless: she had seen a Synaxis of Angels on Ozerki Lake! Whitman whinnied again, restoring her quotidian consciousness, and she immediately pulled out her sketch pad to capture a motif while the image was fresh. Sergei had seen only the swans, but he did, he assured his wife, consider them messengers relaying, by the direction of their flight and the trail of light they landed on, an unmistakable directive: Westward to America!

Sergei had given notice at the university that the fall term would be his last, but he was looking forward to that final fling at teaching American Literature, at least in Russia. Among the authors he covered that term was Taylor Caldwell, a Pennsylvania native whose fictional tours de force included portraits of St. Luke, St. Paul, Cicero and other ancients as well as classic delineations of American characters. Focusing on the latter works in keeping with his Whitmanian-archetypal approach, Professor Lossky laid particular emphasis on Caldwell's rendering, in *Captains and the Kings*, of a 19th-century Irish immigrant and his son— Joseph and Rory Armagh, respectively. The elder Armagh arrived in Philadelphia as a penniless orphan responsible for younger siblings, set his mind upon becoming rich by any available means, and honed his will to forge a commercial empire comprising petroleum, newspapers, and houses of prostitution. As such, he portrayed the archetypal Tycoon. Upon reaching the upper echelons of the wealthy, Armagh was admitted to a secret group of powerful operatives, of whom he offered this description:

> My—friends—have no ideologies though
> they will solemnly use those of others if it
> serves them. They are men of many interests,
> politicians, merchant chiefs, mineowners,
> industrialists, bankers, railroaders, oilmen,
> shipbuilders and owners, munitions makers,
> men of inherited wealth, men of illustrious
> family both here and abroad, princes, if you
> will. Landowners. They have several things in
> common: None is devoted to his particular
> country. None cares about the people's welfare
> in any nation. ... They want to be the Elite,
> with absolute authority over the lives and
> deaths and destinies of the world.

Joseph Armagh colluded with this group for the sake of his own wealth and power, hoping they would ultimately enable his son to become President of the United States, and accordingly arranged for them to meet him. At that meeting, Rory formed his own opinion of these illustrious gentlemen:

> They had looked upon the world and made
> that world their own. They were a criminal
> conspiracy, but they did not regard themselves
> as either criminals or conspirators. They were
> businessmen, realists. What gave them power
> was, in their eyes, virtuous and righteous and
> reasonable, for who was more worthy than

themselves to control and manipulate the
world of men.

Now Rory Armagh did not like what he saw in that plush
boardroom. He knew very well that America was not perfect, "but, after all, she was his country," and was not to be
subordinated to an international cabal of criminals.

> To obtain what they had plotted for so long,
> from grandfather to father to son, they must
> first throw the world into chaos, dismantle
> governments, incite violence and fury among
> the mindless masses, cause enfeebling wars
> which would weaken any nation ready to
> contest with them, raise up tyrants who
> would subdue the people, destroy the validity
> of nations' currencies. Then, in the general
> catastrophe they could exert their unbelievable
> power and assume command.

Taking up his father's suggestion that he run for President
independently of the cabal, Rory launched his campaign in
direct opposition to several of the policies they were backing,
and instead promoted measures beneficial to Americans. He
was consequently assassinated at a political rally, portraying
yet another archetypal character, the Patriot-Martyr whose
effort to defend his country, as Sergei pointed out to his
students, was grounded in the discernment of her true
enemies. He invited them to examine the history of their
own century in the optic of *Captains and the Kings*.

One afternoon in late August, Sergei was in their small barn currying Whitman after a short ride, when Manuela called from the cottage that Chris and Sophie were on the i-screen. It was a curious call, of which the main purpose seemed to be selecting, by virtual tour, the best interior wall of the cottage for some unspecified purpose, determining the GPS coordinates of the center of that wall as well as its directional orientation, and agreeing on a time when the two elders would be in the room. Ten days later, at the appointed time, Sergei and Manuela were startled to see on the designated wall a large, square screen of light displaying an angelic icon, which quickly faded to a view of the living room in the Eckhart farmhouse, from whence the whole family waved and voiced their greetings. Christopher quickly explained the technology, assuring the Losskys that the channel was secure from interception by the Beast, and there followed the most lively and joyous conversation the reader can imagine. Anticipations of their planned reunion figured largely in the flow of talk, along with anecdotes of daily life and broader themes, some of them troubling, like the Communist coup in China and the suppression of news about the massive earthquake that had struck Jerusalem just as Enoch and Elijah were disappearing in a cloud. Before ending the conversation, they agreed to make contact again in another ten days, which would be David's and Magdalena's birthday.

The following week, Maria had scheduled a day at the farm to help with harvesting and putting up the late vegetables, packing some into boxes for the CSA clientele and canning or freezing others. Late summer rains had kept the vegetables coming, and though there were increasing difficulties in getting produce to the city due to GEC interference, there was plenty of local demand. Magdalena of course came along, and she and David helped in the garden for a couple of hours before shedding their muddy boots and heading up to their studio to rehearse their act. By mid-afternoon the goals Rosa had set for the processing of garden produce had been met or exceeded, and when she announced that she was ready for a nap, Sophie and Maria decided to take Sable and Honeysuckle for a ride before Maria and Magdalena headed back to Pinecreek. On their way to the barn, the young women encountered Chris on a tractor, hauling a load of fresh hay to the mow, and after saddling and bridling their mounts, and trotting them out of the farmyard along the same path he had come in on, they soon spotted John baling a field.

Both of our heroines had been thinking for some time about riding to the top of Christmas Tree Hill, where their children had last seen the Christ Child, who had there christened them "White Stone." They took the logging path toward the woods, entering through the Barrier Oaks and continuing past woodlots and timber stands toward the evergreen-covered knoll. Maria and Sophie were chatting amiably, pleased with the work they had accomplished that day and enjoying the mild late-summer afternoon, as they approached the towering tree that the children had named the Mother Pine. Abruptly, without being reined, the horses both came to a halt, causing their riders to turn their attention to the golden aureole emanating, apparently, from behind that stately conifer. "Absolutely no way!"

Maria laughed. "How utterly improbable!" Sophia agreed with a smile. "And yet …" Her voice trailed off, as out from behind the great grey trunk stepped the radiant figure of the Child, surrounded by a nimbus of golden light and robed in pale yellow with a golden sash—about the same age as their kids. "Peace be with you," He greeted them as they dismounted and curtsied deeply in reverence. "It is time to tell the children," He continued, "of the term of their lives and the limits of their love." Then pausing for an instant, He added, "I shall teach them what beatitude they may share within those bounds." The Child looked both women directly in the eye as He spoke, then smiled warmly, raised His right hand in blessing, and turning away, walked briskly off among the pines and vanished.

Maria had never seen the Child before, except by the lake on Sadronia, and Sophie had only seen His face, as in a vision, and looking much younger. Thus, the numinous impression of His bodily presence on Earth was new to them, and the import of His message all the more emphatic. Not that they had procrastinated irresponsibly in delaying these discussions—after all, the kids were just turning ten. On the other hand, they hadn't exactly been looking forward to explaining to David and Magdalena that the world would probably end before they turned thirteen, or soon thereafter—let alone broaching the delicate subject of the obvious romantic affection they shared, as they approached pubescence. After consultation with Christopher and Maxim as well as John and Rosa, it was decided to have a family conversation at the upcoming tenth birthday party, when the scheduled ACN session with Sergei and Manuela would enable them to participate too.

The date fell on a Monday that year, and taking into account everyone's schedule along with the time difference from St. Petersburg, it was decided to hold the birthday party and family conversation at noontide on the farm, which would be mid-evening in eastern Russia. We shall pass over the superb farmhouse dinner, the huge cake with two sets of ten candles, and the opening of presents, and advance directly to the moment when the family adjourned to the living for the session. Christopher had arranged with the angels to position a virtual screen on one wall, connected over the *aeviternum* with another screen in the Losskys' cottage, and soon there were happy greetings as the two households again beheld one another onscreen. A quarter of an hour or more had been filled with fairly wide-ranging conversation involving all parties, not least the birthday kids—a quick, general catching up—when Sophia took the floor to inform her parents, and the children, what she and Maria had been directed to do by the Christ Child. David and Magdalena, who were sitting side by side on a sofa, holding hands, looked solemnly at each other and around the family, as Maxim and Maria explained the prophecy of the final fourteen years, its apparent fulfillment, and the probable end of the world in about three years. "But that will be the new Heaven and the new Earth!" Magdalena laughed. "But first we have to fight the Antichrist!" David exclaimed. "That went well," Maria remarked with a grin, the family responding with an affirmative chuckle.

Christopher and Sophia then proceeded to broach the

tender topic referred to by the Child as the limits of their love, causing both children to blush deeply, glance shyly at one another, and then break into the most beatific smiles of which their juvenile countenances were capable. Then rising from the sofa, still holding hands, the romantic cousins looked around affectionately at their parents and grandparents, aunts and uncles. "We know that we can never marry," David began. "And we know from the Bible," Magdalena continued, "that some things are only for husbands and wives." "So I can never *know* her as Adam knew Eve," David resumed. "But he knows me so well in other ways, like I know him, and we love each other," concluded Magdalena. After a few seconds of somewhat stunned silence, the six adults in the room converged upon the pre-pubescent lovers, enveloping them in a family hug, while Sergei and Manuela conveyed their blessings from the virtual screen. The gathering concluded with a brief presentation by the children on their developing plans for the second appearance of White Stone, which was to celebrate the resurrection and ascension of Enoch and Elijah after their brutal public murder by the Man of Sin.

Summer passed into autumn, which immediately moved along toward winter with an alacrity that seemed endemic to the times, at least in the experience of our leading characters. This seeming acceleration of time was among the matters mentioned as Maxim and Maria sat on their patio south of Pinecreek, on a Saturday afternoon in late October, enjoying the crisp autumn air and the sunlight on the trees. Their lawn was surrounded by a forest of conifers, gleaming verdantly in the bright sunshine, while several maples of the sunset variety adorned the clearing like orbs of fire, flaming with every shade of yellow, orange and red. Another matter was more than mentioned in that conversation, namely Maria's primary project, *The History of the Apocalyptic War*, which she very much wanted to discuss with her husband the priest. Maria was narrating the titular war in terms of the spiritual enmity of Christ and the Antichrist, as realized in the actions—including the verbal actions—of their respective followers. The principal mode of warfare Maria was tracking was *informational*—otherwise known as *fifth-generation warfare*—the battle for dominance of narratives and metanarratives in the population, beginning c. 2017 and ending c. 2057, thus covering the last four decades of history. The triumph of Enoch and Elijah, for example, not to mention the non-artificial temblor that accompanied it, were very bad optics for the Son of Perdition, and the children's plan for a White Stone encore on that meme would be a damaging attack, insofar as it was widely viewed.

It seemed to Maria that the recent comeback of the Communists in China, viewed in the lens of prophecy, was the entry onto the stage of the great red Dragon in *Revelation*, which threatened the Woman symbolizing the Church. The steadfast protection of religious liberty in America and Russia, in the face of the Chairman's declaration that his One World religion was obligatory, corresponded to the two wings of the great Eagle that came to the Woman's rescue in St. John's vision, as Killgower's collegial prophets had seen. Maxim agreed entirely with these interpretations, adding that it likely would not be long before

Russia felt the Dragon's breath from the east, and America from the west, given China's new alliance with the GEC; and observing how providential was the Russian-American air corridor, for as long as it lasted. Meanwhile, Maria continued, the situation in the States was growing more dangerous as regions that had become enclaves of socialist sympathizers began to form alliances with the GEC. Given the devolved condition of the Federal government and the increasing logistical difficulties in supplying regional military commands, little could the President could do to prevent these globalist beachheads in the American homeland, where the sympathies of the population did not lie with the constitutional Republic. Under these circumstances, the 2054 elections had been suspended, and the President had appealed to the people of the patriotic states and counties to hold fast their God-given liberties, and to keep the spirit of Union alive as best they could.

This memorable conversation meandered through several other matters, under a deep blue sky crowning the gleaming evergreens and the flaming maples that framed the couple's view from the patio behind their brick rancher. Maxim mentioned Chris's prediction of a dismal harvest, because after a promising spring and summer the weather had turned rainy and wet, and looked to continue that way well into November—the beautiful afternoon they were enjoying being an anomaly that fall. Maria replied that at least the vegetable produce had been abundant. The patch was still yielding some greens, beets and turnips, but they'd probably have to cut back on the chickens and beeves if the corn and beans fell way short. In any case, it was looking like the urban relief project was pretty much done for, since GEC operatives in Pittsburgh's inner city were interfering with distribution of the farm produce—even confiscating one truckload after overwhelming the Posse escort at the city limits. Maxim said that, according to Chris, the rural counties including Clarion and Jefferson were in good shape, security-wise, having constitutional Sheriffs and active Posses with operational protocols for arresting armed migrants and extending humanitarian aid to those who were peaceful.

After a moment's thoughtful silence, Maria changed the subject to her father's current study of the seismic data on the Jerusalem temblor—the quake that had coincided with the supernatural ascent of Enoch and Elijah. Having plugged the data into their $\mathcal{G}$-field model, John was finding similarities in the tectonic profiles of the Jerusalem quake and of the earlier Global one (excluding the artificial Temple Mount temblor), confirming that it too was an act of God. This conclusion reminded Maxim of what he had recently learned from Cornelius about the covenant formed by Jerusalem Lutheran with the other six churches of the Illumination—those that had been visited by apparitions of the New Jerusalem. The seven congregations had vowed to resist the Adversary's false religion, to the death if necessary. He was about to continue when he was interrupted by the muted sound of a melodious horn. It was Magdalena on the aeviphone, asking could she please sleep over at the farm that night. Permission was readily granted, and the girl quickly ended the call. Maria looked intently at her husband, and blushed. She would definitely be giving Max some conjugal balm for his personal thorn in the flesh, later on.

YEAR TWELVE

(2055 A.D.)

I.

If our narrative has silently bypassed the last two months of the previous year, suffice it to say that nothing essential to our chronicle transpired in that period; and that besides, if our Metaphysicals had looked back, on the Twelfth Day of Christmas, over the previous two months, their overwhelming impression would certainly have been, "Where have they gone?" But they were already facing full-ahead into the New Year, further into the darkening phase of the final prophetic countdown, ready to assume their predestined places, and play their assigned parts, in the divinely-directed drama of the remaining years.

Christopher was trying to spend more deliberate time with David, in addition to the time they spent working side by side—deliberate in the sense of intentionally devoting his full attention to the boy when they talked about things. David still had lots of questions that his father was happy to expound upon, and though the boy could read almost any book, he still liked Christopher to read to him sometimes—he was pretty good at doing the different voices in *The Chronicles of Narnia*, for example. But David also had things to *say*, sometimes a lot of things, and about some things he had quite a bit to say, his father noted as he listened intently, such as Samson the mule, the arts of poetry and music, and his cousin Magdalena. On the latter subject, Christopher was amazed at how easily the children had understood their situation, the limits of their love, and their liberty, within those limits, to be lovers.

For his part, he loved both children immensely, and devoted no little time to thinking about concealing them from the Antichrist, who already hated them intensely for upstaging his Temple enthronement with the premiere of White Stone. When he saw what they were planning for an encore, he would be desperate to identify and locate them, so additional security measures were being established with the angelic crew. In the case of the world premiere, the children's faces had been vaguely visible to the live audience and the network viewers, but the radiance of their faces had virtually veiled their features, and although the networks had been able to broadcast live, no recorded footage was obtained. Going forward, the plan was to increase the brightness of their faces in the display so that their features were completely invisible, and then to enable the networks and viewers to record and circulate future performances. In addition, Christopher and the angels were working that winter on another advance in the ACN technology, whereby angelic intelligence would override the key servers feeding the network broadcasts and copy audiovisual information into the electronic data feeds—essentially hacking the networks. The plan was to try this out with the next performance, which was also to take place at a prominent event in Jerusalem, so that when the networks cut their coverage the ACN would take over and finish the world-wide broadcast.

Another matter on Christopher's mind that winter was a sort of philosophical sizing up of Chairman Nabal's new Chief of Global Intelligence, an invisible super-genius with a suave and charming voice, and a starring role in the globalist media. Prominent news anchors and talk show hosts vied for an interview with the fabled *Therion*, reveling in his marvelous wit and sense of humor—especially irony—and addressing him deferentially, as a great and powerful personage. Not only were they calling him a person, he had been mentioned for Person of the Year. But was *Therion* really a person, considered metaphysically? Formally, a *person* was defined as a *rational* or *intellectual substance*—a subsisting being endowed with intellect—that is, a created being with created intellect, deriving metaphysically from the Being and the Intellect of the Creator. Created intellect, proceeding by creation from uncreated Intellect, was empowered to fashion artifacts for the use of the person possessing it, and for others. Among these artifacts were complex systems of integrated electronic microcircuitry capable of performing calculations and processing information according to coded instructions. As these systems grew more complex, and their programming codes more abstract, a threshold was crossed when they could simulate intelligence, impersonating created human intellect. Yet no artificially intelligent entity, in Christopher's analysis, could be metaphysically equal to created human intelligence, from the artifice of which the artificial derived its very existence. The media and their masses might hail *Therion's* "superhuman intelligence," but the Beast was actually *sub*human, being a product of human intellect, which was in turn a creation of God—according to the thinking of our philosopher.

His beautiful wife was deeply engaged that winter in the Master's program at the Institute, as Christopher's involvement there gave way to a series of lectures at the College, on topics in the philosophy of science, leaving the management of the aforesaid program entirely in the capable hands of Sophia. There were now six first-year candidates, nine second-year and twelve in their third and final year—the first two classes working their way through the comprehensive and specialized course work, and the third pursuing independent research to be presented as theses in the spring. Sophia was especially interested in the findings of the team that were looking into the apparent extra acceleration of the principal stars of Cygnus as they fell, along with the rest of the heavens, toward Earth. Careful analysis of new data was indeed confirming that Deneb, Sadr and their stellar companions were emitting significantly more-blueshifted starlight than any other stars in the celestial sphere. And not only that, but the blueshifts of the five stars varied among themselves, such that the more distant the star from Earth the greater its blueshift, as though the farther stars were trying to catch up with the closer ones! It would make a solid, if enigmatic, Master's thesis. The interdisciplinary linguistic-genetics team, building on the early work of Jeanson, was compiling and integrating all available data on the geographic distribution of human Y-chromosome haplogroups—populations sharing a common male ancestor. In parallel, current information on the languages spoken by those populations was being correlated with the haplogroup geography, and strong indications were emerging that the geographic separation of the male lineages had been driven by the division of language at Babel.

The geological group was comparing John Eckhart's $\mathcal{G}$-field model of the Global Flood—archived right there at the Institute—with his analysis of the Global Quake, which he was happy to provide. The reader may recall that the latter analysis, assisted by Maria Lossky-Eckhart, discovered a tectonic profile with sufficient specified complexity to imply intelligent design, a "divine signal," and that Sophia had also collaborated in establishing a metaphysical correlation between that profile and the celestial mechanics of the Blueshift. The current group's proposal was to reexamine the Flood model in light of the Quake-Blueshift analysis, and see whether the "divine signal" was also in evidence there—which was looking to be the case. Sometimes, though, Sophia wondered what fate awaited this brilliant work—indeed the Glorious Synthesis itself—as the edicts of the Chairman began to single out specific religious organizations deemed to be in rebellion against his ordinances. Then too, how many years remained of time itself?

And yet however punctual (or otherwise) the prophetic calendar proved, Sophia was continuing to feel herself ever more enraptured in the love of Christ. Enraptured, not in the sense of carried away, let alone in the sense of being snatched bodily out of the Tribulation, but enraptured in the sense of being grasped and held, with the utmost gentleness and even courtesy, but firmly, by an overwhelming sense of being loved. By *the love that moves the sun and other stars*, as Dante sang; the love of an eternal *Logos*, the Son of God, through whom all things were created yet who, for the salvation of fallen humanity, came down from heaven, became one of us, and suffered death for us. It was *that* love that grasped and held Sophia, enraptured her, when she looked at her son David, whose very existence was owing to the command of the Christ Child. How strange, and yet how utterly beautiful, that the Lord had chosen to appear to the Metaphysicals, on Sadronia and thereafter, in that form; and that every time he had appeared since the birth of the children, He had looked to be about their age. When Sophia looked at David she felt, above and beyond the natural affection of a mother for her son and totally enveloping that maternal love, a supernatural affection for this ruggedly brilliant boy. The love of Christ aglow in her heart added its own emotional radiance to the feelings that flowed through her soul at the sight of him—or sometimes just the thought. It felt like she was participating in the love of Christ for David—loving him with the love of Christ Himself.

Sergei and Manuela spent January and February making arrangements for the move to Pennsylvania, wrapping up loose ends in Russia, and trying to imagine what their new life in Americas would look like. One of Manuela's loose ends was perfecting the painting she considered her best of that period, *Synaxis of Angels on Ozerki Lake*. She conducted a series of cartoon studies in coloration of the scenic motif before painting her final rendering of the sky, the trees and the sunlight on the lake, leaving an ovoid space near the center for the writing, in tempera, of the angelic icon: seven haloed angels gathered around the Christ Child. Her intention was to take it along back to the States. Manuela also had to arrange for the sale of her dairy goats, which proved easy enough—except that she had grown attached to them! She cheered herself with the thought that she could start over at the Eckhart farm. Sergei, of course, was also faced with separation from his good grey horse, and the parting was not without its poignancy. He had lost Tolstoy to the raiders, and now he was leaving Whitman behind. Still, he couldn't help thinking about what he would name his next, and final steed. Pushkin?

Meanwhile, although he was no longer teaching in St. Petersburg, Sergei continued to meet informally with students and former colleagues two or three times a week, when he would invariably propose the same topic for discussion. Born and educated in Russia, Sergei had lived in America for more than thirty years, and what he wanted to talk about with the Russian professors and their native and international students was the relationship between the two countries. He shared the prophetic word he had heard through Maxim, relating the two nations to the two wings of the great Eagle in *Revelation*, which generated much lively discussion. Someone mentioned that many Chinese Christians were escaping into Russian Mongolia as the new Communist regime aligned itself with the GEC, and another added that, similarly, Christians were fleeing Canada for those States and regions to their south which remained loyal to the American Republic. Several of the Russian interlocutors commented on the longstanding turbulence of relations between the two countries, which had preceded the final state of friendship at which they had at last arrived. Sergei's response was that he thought globalist propaganda had a heavy hand in the prolonged animosity of many Americans toward Russia, well into the twenties. There was general agreement that the current alignment between the two nations was nothing less than providential, prophecy or no prophecy.

At the end of February the air corridor was opened for passengers, and having settled their lease on the cottage, Sergei and Manuela packed their trunks, boarded a plane on the Ides of March, two days after Ash Wednesday, and were on their way to a military airstrip on the Appalachian Plateau, in northern Clarion County. The flight seemed long but was happily uneventful. Upon landing they were met by all six Metaphysicals, with much merriment and mutual gladness, and carted off with their baggage, in a pickup truck and a car, to the Eckhart farm. There, John and Rosa were genuinely pleased to welcome the arrivals as friends, into the hospitality of their farmhouse, where they could comfortably reside in the guest rooms. The farmhouse was plenty large for four adults, besides which Sergei and Manuela would be staying with Max and Maria several days a week, further reducing the risk of anyone feeling crowded. Rosa was happy to have another woman share her roomy kitchen, as Sophie usually cooked in her own kitchen except for farm-to-table and food preservation projects, and besides, she was looking forward to the milk, yogurt and cheese from Manuela's dairy. The farm could easily feed and graze a few goats, and the farmers had earmarked a corner of the cattle barn for a pen and milking stall.

John and Sergei—the farmer-geologist and the cowboy-professor—were genuinely fond of one another. Each considered the other an interesting character, and both looked forward to some long conversations. Sergei's desire for a horse of his own would also be honored with a new stall in the stable, where four horses, a mule and a burro were already snugly installed. The first thing Sergei wanted to know from John, as soon as the excitement of their arrival settled down to discourse, was his assessment of their security situation, given the decentralized state of the American Republic. First of all, the farmer related, the Posse patrols had been mostly quiet all winter, with only a handful of arrests and fewer than a dozen migrant families to be housed and fed. It appeared that the GEC had inner-city Pittsburgh pretty well supplied with essentials, and military intelligence available to the Sheriff indicated that GEC operatives were now actively discouraging people from leaving the city. So Clarion and the surrounding counties—including Jefferson, where Max and Maria lived—were in an excellent defensive posture with no immediate threat they were aware of, pending Chairman Nabal's next move.

One of the latter's more bombastic moves, however, could hardly have escaped the awareness of anyone on Earth, so powerfully was it publicized. On the Feast of Pentecost, which fell that year on the sixth of June, the Son of Perdition was to be coronated on his throne before the Temple, by the Bishop of Rome and the Orthodox Patriarch of

Jerusalem, as the King of Kings and Lord of Lords—Christ come again. Nabal had faked a series of public miracles, including his own resurrection from death. As Pentecost approached he continued the campaign to present himself as possessing divine powers which, along with the life-saving work he had led since the Global Quake, ought to qualify his appearance as the Second Coming of Christ. The premise of the blasphemous coronation was this: As the Holy Spirit, on Pentecost, inaugurated the Apostles to establish the Christian Church, so on this New Pentecost a new Messiah would be anointed by the same Holy Spirit to establish the One World Religion. The Man of Sin had doubled down on security arrangements for the event, including an array of sophisticated jamming equipment to seal off the area from any incoming signal, ground-based or orbital. It had been nearly a year since White Stone crashed his Temple dedication, and while they had not reappeared since, he had been unable to locate the impudent brats, and he emphatically did not wish to witness a repeat performance. He was to be bitterly disappointed.

Naturally, that day was precisely the one chosen by David and Magdalena, with advice and consent of their parents, for the performance they had come to call "Enoch & Elijah 2.0." White Stone would again perform for exactly three minutes. They planned to sing and play a ballad of three stanzas through twice, with Magdalena adding an element of dance this time. The ballad, of course, was set in the sweet new style with lyrics in David's hallowed heptasyllabic line, as for example in the second stanza:

When these two old men were killed
As the Man of Sin had willed,
On the fourth day they were raised!
Hallelujah! God be praised!
They ascended up on high
Disappearing in the sky
Just as Jesus' Father willed!

Sergei and Manuela had arrived in time to watch the
final rehearsal, performed for the family in the farmhouse
living room, and were as stunned as everyone else at the
polished and courtly manner assumed by the ten-year-
olds as White Stone. Not that these traits were entirely
new to their act, having been present in the premiere—
as well as prominently displayed in their developing play
for years—but here was a difference of more than mere
emphasis, a difference of degree, a higher standard. After
their closing bows, David and Magdalena seemed almost
embarrassed at the exclamations of acclaim that greeted
their accomplishment. After gladly participating in hugs
all around, they promptly headed for their studio in the
cottage to record the show.

We need not dwell upon the sordid scene that Chairman Nabal had set for his coronation and anointing as
Messiah—a scene that suggested something more spooky
than spiritual—nor upon the look of horror and rage
that twisted his face when the dreaded screen of light
again crashed his event. The performance was, of course,
perfect, the bearing of the performers enchanting, the
music enthralling, and the content of the lyrics absolutely

devastating to the narrative promoted by Nabal. The angelic override of the networks functioned flawlessly, so the full three-minute clip was played worldwide in place of the planned coverage, as well as captured electronically for replay and circulation. Unfortunately for many who played, replayed and shared such recordings of White Stone, *Therion* was able to identify them, and lists were forwarded to GEC Security Forces for "corrective action" wherever the persons of interest resided in countries or regions under GEC control. Taking grim note of this outcome, Christopher decided a change of tactics was in order for the next sortie of White Stone into the narrative battlespace of the information war they were waging against the Antichrist. This was not the first wave of arrests owing to the perspicacity of the Chief of Global Intelligence: the first had followed the premiere performance, when *Therion* had swept up many who publicly approved of it, and the second wave consisted of those who protested the arrests of the first.

These developments only intensified Christopher's concern with keeping the children, and the rest of them, under the proverbial radar of the global surveillance apparatus. It seemed essential to conceal the kids' identity even locally, including from folks at church, not out of any fear of betrayal but because, given the swift celebrity of White Stone the word would eventually spread, and the Beast was watching. In fact, it was the folks at church who were most likely to recognize the clandestine performers of White Stone, having heard them sing and play in Evangeline's ensemble. At first, David and Magdalena had hoped to have Roland

and Violet add some horn and violin to the audio in future episodes, but they quickly understood that for the sake of their secrecy, and the safety of all involved, this would simply not be possible. Maxim and Christopher conferred more than once on the matter over the course of that spring. While they felt confident that their area was currently safe from GEC operations in general, they agreed that Nabal would stop at nothing to get hold of their children. And they shuddered to think what he would do, if he ever did.

As spring ran its course, Sergei and Manuela settled in readily to their new home in the Eckhart farmhouse, where John and Rosa made them feel warmly welcome, with frequent stayovers at the rancher at Pinecreek and weekly attendance at Maxim's Divine Liturgy in Philadelphia Chapel. Manuela found she had much to learn from Rosa in the field of agricultural home economics, and was glad to contribute her dairy-goat produce to the research kitchen managed by her friend, while Rosa was in awe of Manuela's artistic talent, especially after seeing her Philadelphia icon at Maxim's chapel. John and Sergei found ample opportunity to share thoughts on the global state of affairs within which the devolved American Republic then existed, particularly in light of what Sergei called "the evident eschatological indicators." They found themselves in consensus regarding the guardian roles of Russia and America, in the face of the final onslaught by the forces of darkness against the children of the Light. The two old men agreed that if the Church were going to survive until the return of Christ, as He promised, it was necessary that citadels of religious liberty—freedom of religion—be defended from GEC domination. They also shared a sense of irony, that these citadels whose security must be assured were yet, perforce, so utterly temporary, given the actual imminence of the End.

Maria, for her part, was delighted with her father-in-law's interest in her historical studies, from the emerging record of which she read him several parts of the work in progress, and allowed him to peruse the MS. Sergei asked how she had chosen her moniker as author of *The History*, given that Thucydides was known as the first historian to dispense with divine actors in the narration of history, whereas she was explicitly framing her *War* as a theater of divine action. Maria explained that what she prized in Thucydides' *History* was the concise, objective realism of the narrative style, which for Thucydides, being a skeptic of pagan Greek theology, meant a purely secular chronicle. Whereas for her, as a believing Christian, objective realism meant interpreting current events in the lens of apocalyptic prophecy, which so clearly appeared to be coming true right before her eyes. For example, the participation of the Bishop of Rome in the anointing of the Antichrist placed the former in the role of the False Prophet who, according to *Revelation*, would lend support to the atrocious blasphemies of the latter. Unless, on the other hand, one assigned that role to *Therion*—in which case the papal action would amount to placing the Roman church in the role of the Whore of Babylon.

Sergei was fascinated by the project undertaken by his daughter-in-law, acknowledging that her narrative style was indeed comparable to that of Thucydides, bringing objective realism to bear upon a historical reality suffused with supernatural action, to which the historian of the Pelopennesian War had no cognitive access. For example, the manner in which Maria told the story of the series of apparent miracles, which the Man of Sin had contrived to simulate for the sake of strengthening his messianic claims, never allowed the reader to forget the foreknowledge of God, reflected in the words of St. John, that permitted these fraudulent deceptions. When fire fell from the sky at his command, incinerating a structure built for the demonstration, *The History* described the scene objectively as transmitted by the networks, analyzed the possible technical means by which the phenomenon could have been faked, and related the energies underlying those technologies to the physics and chemistry of the creation. Sergei also appreciated Maria's perspective on the parallels she pointed out between the early years of her forty-year period, and the latter years through which they were currently living. Sometimes these parallels were drawn in the form of contrasts, as in the case of the devolution of Federal executive functions in the early twenties, and again in the early fifties. The earlier operation had been temporary, and the normal functions of the constitutional Republic were restored after the fraudulent elections were rectified, but this time it would apparently be permanent.

Maria's workdays at the farm, that spring, were enriched by the presence of her mother-in-law in the farmhouse kitchen, by watching Magdalena renew her fond relationship with Manuela, and by seeing David become better acquainted with his other grandma. The kitchen work that season would focus on stocking the larder—with two extra mouths to feed—and on the expanding CSA clientele, as more local families were signing on. The greater New Bethlehem community was no longer shipping produce to the urban relief zone due to overt GEC interference, and after a couple of poor agricultural seasons the locals were beginning to look to their own provisions. By the end of May, Manuela had her dairy up and running, and soon a supply of cheese was available for consumption and sale in addition to the early produce which, despite a fairly dry spring, they were able to bring in by irrigation. Rosa's farm-to-table group hadn't done a supper in New Bethlehem for several years, owing to their involvement in urban relief, but this year they planned to hold two events, one in July and one in August, both at the Moravian Star. Maria was thankful for the chance to participate in these celebrated suppers, of which she had heard so much while she lived in Texas.

But above all, Maria was thankful for Maxim, with his dark curly beard framing a solemn, yet somehow cheerful face and quiet brown eyes—her pillar of strength in those troubling times, and the love of her life. Her passionate husband! It always amazed her, when he assumed his priestly vestments and the full dignity of his office to celebrate Divine Liturgy, that here was the very man who so loved the sight of her nakedness, and to whom, in her nakedness, she so ardently gave herself. It amazed her not so much on account of any apparent incongruity, but precisely because of the question of *congruity* raised by the juxtaposition of the heavenly Paradise symbolized in the Divine Liturgy, and the fleeting, incarnate earthly paradise of a man and a woman, beloved of one another, locked in the ecstasy of carnal union. Maria couldn't help wondering whether some higher form of that carnal union would belong to the experience of Paradise. Jesus said there is no marriage in heaven, she reasoned, but he said nothing about interpersonal relations between the saints in light, and nothing about the anatomy of the resurrection body either. She put the question to her brother, who had given serious thought to the metaphysics of the celestial body. In Christopher's theory the *substantial form* of a human being in the new creation was identical with that of the same individual in the original creation. In the latter, this substantial form united with chemical, corporeal matter to form a physical, mortal body; in the new creation it united with uncreated Light to form an immortal, spiritual body, which might reasonably be imagined to include the same anatomical features as its mortal precursor. The metaphysician would not speculate, however, whether sexual organs of uncreated Light would play any role in the bliss of Paradise. Maria also put the question to her husband, who replied after a moment's meditation that, while it was probably pointless to offer predictions on the specifics of paradisal bliss, there was no doubt whatsoever about the delights of the conjugal use of the organs in question, in the *physical* body. As he said this, Maria noted a subdued sparkle in Max's quiet brown eyes.

The reader will recall that, even as his pert and pretty, blue-eyed wife had an indelible streak of pride in her temperament, so Father Maxim's characteristic passion was lust—the unintended, instinctual rush of desire at the sight of a desirable woman. The fallen psyche, seizing upon such sightings, memorized them as images to be formed into fantasies by natural libido, doubtless with the assistance of demons intending to deploy them as temptations. It sometimes seemed ironic to Maxim, that his unshakable vocation to the priesthood should coexist with an engrained impulse to break the commandment against adultery—and to break it even mentally was to break it. His considered opinion, however, was that spiritual warfare formed the heart of the life in Christ, perhaps the chief prerequisite of the priestly vocation, and that if lust was the battlefield on which the Lord had stationed him, or the direction of attack upon the citadel he defended, then he would join battle there.

Moreover, as noted earlier in our narrative, the campus of Luther-Aquinas offered a formidable front for the conduct of that battle, in the form of a type of female student that had not formerly frequented the Christian college. The young women in question were often shapely and attractive, but what typified them was their choice of attire revealing the full extent of their shapeliness and a great deal of their skin—attire designed to emphasize their attractions. The seductive dress of these women was accompanied by a distinct attitude and demeanor suggestive of flirtation, and students of this type were often followed, or surrounded, by males of the species. One of the freshmen seemed to take a particular liking to Maxim, and whenever the two passed on campus she was sure to ask him something or other, often adding what a "cutie" she thought he was.

Max thought she enjoyed making him blush, but he always answered her question succinctly and invited her to visit the chapel, which so far she had not done.

Regarding Philadelphia Chapel, the space above the doors entering that former planetarium was now adorned with Manuela's *The Church in Philadelphia at the End of Time*, the original of which hung in the Lavra east of St. Petersburg where she had studied. Maxim always contemplated the icon for a moment before entering the chapel—the faithful on Earth, surrounded by the Dragon, and their corresponding pillars in the heavenly Temple enshrined in the golden City—placing himself mentally in that archetypal tableau. The reader will recall that our priest was fond of retiring to the chapel from time to time during the day, for prayer and for pondering whatever was currently uppermost among his concerns—such as the troubling letter he received from Padre Pablo, his Texas friend to whom he had handed over the pastorate of St. Michael and All Angels in San Angelo. The beautiful mission church where Maxim had premiered in his priestly office had been turned entirely into a communal residence for undocumented migrants and completely desecrated, although the congregation had been able to save most of the icons, including Manuela's *St. Michael and the Dragon*. Her *Endtime Nativity* painting, however, had been looted from Pablo's study and used for a shooting target, with the Christ Child as the bull's-eye. Talk about signs of the times! Maxim was deeply saddened by the plight of his former parish, now meeting as a house church, and of his friend Pablo, who were truly feeling the crush of the Dragon, while he and his family had escaped to the relative security of rural Pennsylvania. Yet such, it seemed, had been the will of God.

At the prompting of David and Magdalena, the elder Losskys began attending Jerusalem Lutheran with the family on Sunday mornings, before driving to Philadelphia Chapel for Divine Liturgy in the afternoons. Fresh from the great cathedrals of St. Petersburg, Sergei and Manuela found Maxim's Rite of St. Tikhon, not to mention the Divine Service celebrated by Pastor Cornelius, to be in austere contrast with their recent experience of worship. What dawned on them rather quickly, however, was the continuity transcending that contrast, in the salvific action of a liturgical order larded with prayer and sacred song, and combining the celebration of the Word of God with the Sacrament of His bodily presence. They had attended Jerusalem Lutheran a couple of times before, but only with regular participation in worship there did they come to know that truly, here too was the One Holy Apostolic Church. Manuela always paused before entering the nave to contemplate the paintings of the first two apparitions of the New Jerusalem, seen during worship, which hung above the entrance doors. After the service she liked to linger in the parish hall, musing upon a number of other paintings of the foursquare golden City that hung there, including one from each of the other six churches of the Illumination, so called after the original apparition at Jerusalem Lutheran. Then, on Sunday afternoons, they would repair to Maxim's beautiful little chapel, after which they would usually stay over in Pinecreek overnight. It made a wonderful Sunday routine.

Cornelius and Evangeline Chen, after six years of happy marriage, had grown more or less resigned to remaining childless despite their most ardent efforts to achieve parenthood. In view of the darkening signs of the times, they told each other, perhaps it was providential that they had no young children of their own to care for, as it freed them to minister to the children of the congregation, as well as to occasional migrants. Over the years, the pair had grown particularly fond of David Eckhart, and with the arrival of his cousin Magdalena upon the scene had immediately been taken with her as well. Evy, as the reader knows, had taught both children to play their instruments and built her ensemble around them. Of course, she had surmised, and covertly confirmed with the Eckharts, that these two dear children were White Stone, and in personal danger from the Antichrist. She and Cornelius were devoted to protecting their secret identities, and consequently several decisions were made regarding future performances of the ensemble: There would be no vocals, no pieces in the sweet new style would be played; performances would be limited to the church building; and no recordings or broadcasts would be allowed. Secrecy, it seemed, had to become the watchword. By the end of spring, Cornelius managed to distribute handheld ACN devices, acquired from Christopher Eckhart, to the sister churches of the Illumination, whose pastors could now conduct clandestine communications.

II.

As the year moved into summer, Christopher found himself finishing up some technical details of the AeviCom mobile network, consisting of twenty devices in all, distributed among the Eckhart family, Killgower's Invisible College, the Clarion Sheriff's Department, and the churches of the Illumination. Each device was assigned a unique number and logged electronically at the communication control center inside *Synaxis*, and each holder of a device was instructed on how to contact others in the network. There was no particular expectation that, for example, the county Sheriff would need to contact an evangelical prophet or an Illumination pastor (except perhaps the one who resided in his county), or vice versa, but the topology of the network made such contacts possible. Once the network was activated, the Eckhart-Lossky family soon became aware that Killgower's Invisibles were engaged in discussing a point of biblical prophecy, namely the flood of water said to be spewed from the Dragon's mouth *after the woman, to sweep her away*, once she had been rescued by the Eagle. The prophets were exercised over the question of the identity of this demonic flood, in the flux of current affairs, and had not yet arrived at an evangelical consensus on the matter, but in the meantime the Illumination pastors were soon following their discussion with interest. It seemed the angels had launched a small-scale social media platform— in a roundabout sort of way.

Of course, Christopher's work on the aeviphone net-work was confined to evenings and rainy days, given the seasonal demands of the farm: the barley and wheat harvests, the hay and silage, manuring and weeding the vegetable patch. The spring had already been difficult, weatherwise, exhibiting a particular permutation of the ele-mental patterns of weather adverse to farming, which our philosopher had steadily observed over more than twenty years. What the farmer needed was a relatively favorable arrangement of the combinations of temperature and precipitation, parceled out over the seven or eight months of the agricultural season, and as of midsummer the season at hand was already looking less than prosperous. Sufficient examples of favorable and unfavorable patterns of weather have been described in our narration of previous years, that the reader may here be left to imagine the particulars of the season at hand.

On the theoretical side, most of Christopher's thinking that summer was done while driving tractor, and the main matter he found himself pondering was a question his sister Maria had asked him regarding the celestial body. Maria's question had been specific as to the presence or absence of sexual organs in the resurrection body, and her brother's first thought had been, "Leave it to a farm girl," but then the metaphysics of the matter had persistently aroused his interest. At first, he had assumed that the substantial form united with chemical matter in the physical body, and the substantial form united with uncreated Light in the celestial body, were one and the same. After all, the human substantial form was essentially the intellectual soul, and the doctrine of the general Resurrection was that souls who have departed from their physical bodies will receive new, celestial bodies, like that of Christ after He rose from the dead. So if the substantial form is the same, he reasoned, then the features of the body of light should resemble those of the body of flesh—including presumably the sexual organs—though in Paradise they would not be "genitals" because they would not be reproductive. Whether or how such organs might participate in the bliss of Paradise, however, was matter for speculation or even fantasy, in neither of which our philosopher was inclined to indulge.

Nevertheless, the subject of the anatomy of the celestial body continued to fascinate Christopher, and as he considered his initial assumption that the substantial form of the physical was unchanged in the celestial, it occurred to him that there could, after all, be an alteration of the substantial form itself. Since the identity of a person was anchored in the *idea* or *logos* of that person in the divine Intellect, a change in the substantial form for the sake of adapting the new body to a novel habitat was, after all, entirely plausible. In that case, for example, since the sexual organs would not be needed for reproduction, their ontological specification might be deleted from the original substantial form, as likewise the organs of digestion and excretion. Regarding the latter, even though Scripture spoke of eating and drinking among the modes of paradisal bliss, it seemed unlikely that metabolic processes and the associated organs would be required in a body composed of eternal Light. But Christopher was far from closing the book on this subject, and further considerations were likely to ensue.

His beloved wife Sophia continued to revel in the presence of her parents after nearly five years of separation. She loved talking with Sergei in Russian, which somehow she and Maxim never seemed to do, and she especially liked hearing her father describe, in his mother tongue, salient scenes and experiences from his and Manuela's sojourn in the vicinity of St. Petersburg. With her mother, she would often speak Spanish when they were alone, for Manuela had taught her that tongue just as Sergei had instilled her love of Russian, perhaps unwittingly inspiring their daughter to take up linguistics along with astronomy. Also, they were so good with David, who loved to show his cowboy grampa how adeptly he could handle Samson, and how well he could shoot his sling from muleback, and to question his gramma the painter on certain fine points of her art, such as the meaning of style. The boy also liked to watch Manuela milk her goats, and to help her feed and water them. He was already helping to feed and water the cattle, but milking was new to the Eckhart farm, and David was intent on learning to do it himself. Despite the darkening times, all these things brought joy to Sophia, as she pondered them in her heart.

Because of her ongoing engagement with the Glorious Synthesis, as she guided three classes of candidates through the Master's program, Sophia was finding ramifications of the love of Christ in that illustrious *summa* of biblical creation sciences. Objectively considered, the Synthesis represented a comprehensive codification of the principal sciences of nature, conceived according to the biblical creation paradigm and grounded, each in its own way, in a metaphysical formalism relating the cognitive content of each science to Divine Knowledge—the Creator's own cognition of His creation. Now according to her husband, that Knowledge began with the Father knowing the Son, in whom all things were made, the *Logos* containing all the *logoi* of things, and that primordial knowing was fraught from the first with love! Her brother Maxim, besides confirming Christopher's view of the matter, added that the Western church had traditionally personified the mutual love of the Father and the Son as the Person of the Holy Spirit, whereas the Eastern church had generally avoided that identification, considering the Spirit as proceeding directly from the Father, in parallel with the Son. But the point that focused Sophia's mind was the transcendental identity of knowledge and love in the act of knowing by which all things were made. Upon that identity the Glorious Synthesis was metaphysically founded. It gladdened her heart to think that the love of the Father for the Son, returned by the Son to the Father, had included the *logoi* of all creatures from all eternity; and that when that Love, which was also Knowledge, spilled over into time and formed creation by the intellectual brooding of the Holy Spirit, the whole creation was consequently infused with that very Love. And was it not fitting to celebrate the divine Love, which was also Knowledge, engrained in creation, primarily in the name of the Person who "came down from heaven" and lived in a physical body born of woman to save His fallen creatures—and to call it the Love of Christ?

But despite Sophia's expanding sense of the love of Christ, in her inner life and in the world around her, there was no escaping the residue of regret she felt for the temporal truncation of earthly life that was apparently approaching. No matter how often she parried that feeling, fended it off by prayer or faced it down by faith in the promise of Paradise, it would return like a hen to the roost at unexpected moments, often when she was most happily engaged in one of her favorite pursuits. She might be watching David and Magdalena perfect their courtly play, or working in the kitchen with her mother, or holding her husband in her arms—the moment she happened to reflect on her present happiness, the eschatological regret would return. Sophia knew very well to what roost in her soul that rueful hen kept returning: it was her temperamental tinge of envy that furnished the foundation for her regret, in this case her envy of those who had lived full earthly lives, and seen their children grow up, because they had not been born less than forty years before the End of Time. But she also knew very well, though she evermore had to remind herself, that many of the faithful *had* lived full earthly lives in less than forty years, and that she herself had already lived a fantastically full and marvelous life. But such were the ways of the psyche: certain moods, however often parried or fended, would yet arise unbidden, offering further occasions for spiritual warfare.

David and Magdalena were working more hours in the vegetable patch that summer than in previous years. As their eleventh birthday approached, both were strong and fit, careful workers, and their contribution to bearing the farm's work load was becoming significant. They also found time to exercise Dancer and Samson, while sharpening their own equestrian skills, occasionally showing off a bit for their cowboy grampa. But when it came to their imaginations, one principal theme preoccupied them at that time: the next appearance of White Stone. One afternoon in late August, having accomplished their chores in the morning, our precocious players holed up in their studio for a session of prayer and brainstorming on that very theme. After praying for inspiration, they tri4d out some new melodic variations in their signature style, pausing periodically to exchange a few words or phrases by way of suggestion.

During one such pause, as the voices of David and Magdalena alternated in melodic dialogue, a third voice was suddenly heard in the room: "Peace be with you." When they looked, a stalwart and handsome boy of about their age stood just inside the closed door, his right hand raised in blessing. They recognized the Lord at once, although he was clad this time in a simple tunic and was not surrounded by light as before, but stood before them without so much as a visible halo. Something was different about his face, too, for though he transparently looked upon them with kindness and affection, there was a spark in His eyes of something more fiery, more martial in mood, warlike even. "I have earnestly desired to play this game with you," He said, "and my Father has granted us His favor. You will be given what you need to know. And lo! I am with you till the End." When He had finished speaking these words, the Child approached David and Magdalena, momentarily took their hands in His, and disappeared as abruptly as He had arrived.

It all happened so quickly that it took our young musicians a few deep breaths to start processing this latest appearance of Jesus in juvenile form. First of all, they had physically felt His hands, and this was the first time He had ever touched them. His simple dress suggested work clothes, like He might have worn in the carpenter shop, and the fact that He had put off His investiture of light seemed to remove a sort of barrier between them—meaning He was dressed to work with them? Then there was that fiery sparkle in His eyes—like a warrior awaiting battle, said David, and Magdalena added that her mom said they were waging an information war with the Antichrist. By the time they had gotten thus far it began to dawn on them what He had meant by, "You will be given all you need to know." For they found, when they thought of it, that now they knew more or less exactly what White Stone would do next: a virtual world tour entitled "Glory Be to Jesus Christ." Apparently, the Child had communicated the idea directly to their minds, and as they talked it over, more and more details came into focus. It would be a virtual tour in the sense that, instead of relying on a single, large-scale display at a prominent event and broadcasting from location, they would directly override local networks and stations, replacing their programming with White Stone, in different regions over a period of time. The performance would also be more than three times longer than previous shows, running a full nine minutes of song with two instrumental interludes, and thoroughly choreographed in the most courtly style. The piece, of course, had yet to be composed, and would then need extensive rehearsal, so the *wunderkinder* had their work cut out for them.

At their birthday dinner several weeks later, Sergei asked David if he had any thoughts about turning eleven, to which our boy genius readily replied that the number eleven reminded him of Dante's line of so many syllables, in which he had composed his *Commedia*. Then glancing with a smile at Magdalena, he added, speaking of Dante, that the poet had been only nine when he first loved Beatrice. The girl responded with the most demure little blush, and the conversation moved on to other topics, including the newly-conceived world tour of White Stone—about which, however, the principals had little to say except that they were hard at work on it. Another discussion was prompted by two of David's birthday presents: a bone-handled hunting knife and a high-powered slingshot. After several years of honing his skill with a beginner's sling, the boy had approached his dad about learning to hunt squirrels, to which Christopher was entirely amenable on one condition: David had to skin and gut his own kills, wash off the blood, and hand them off to the kitchen. Chris and John had both done their share of hunting over the years—mostly small game since they had little need for venison with their own supply of grassfed beef—but in recent years their interest in that rustic sport had waned. When David expressed his own interest, however, his father gladly took the time to show him the process by which a fat squirrel, slain with his trusty sling, was rendered a kitchen-ready carcass to be food for the family. The season began in early October, and David was set to go hunting.

This new facet of our boy hero's character did not escape the journal kept by his fair lady, a combination chronicle and album of attributes, with illustrations and tender asides. In fact, Magdalena insisted on going with David at least once, even if it was a mostly solitary sport, in order to enrich her romantic narrative with real experience. Her lover could hardly say no, and the result was a bit of a pageant, with simple but elegant costumes—and mounted, of course, like the lords and ladies of old—all of which must have been most astonishing to the squirrels! But they did maintain silence as they walked Samson and Dancer slowly through the woods—except once, when Magdalena giggled. David did actually bag two squirrels on one of the innermost Guardian Oaks, which was a major den tree. Back at the farmhouse, his devoted journalist lingered to observe the bloody rite known as cleaning the game, in order to round out her portrait of the mighty hunter.

Manuela was thankful for how easily she had been able to blend into the life of the farmhouse, where she and Sergei were beginning to feel truly at home. The Ozerki Lake painting with her vision of the angels hung in their bedroom, and one of her watercolors of the Texas Hill Country adorned another wall in their quarters. The artist was saddened by the fate of her *Endtime Nativity*, yet she knew the loss was small in the context of the desecration and destruction that had occurred. Maxim had a copy of the book with that painting on the cover, so at least it still existed in that form. While awaiting inspiration for another icon, Manuela was sizing up a set of landscapes to be abstracted from the Eckhart farm, which accordingly, in addition to the crops it was already producing, was now poised to produce a harvest of paintings. Meanwhile, the stalls built by the Eckhart men in a corner of the cattle barn suited her perfectly; her little flock of goats was thriving, and the contribution of their produce to the economy of the farm made her feel even more at home. The kids liked the goats too, especially David.

Sergei was similarly pleased with the empty stall that Chris and John had added to the horse barn, to accommodate the new steed he was still seeking. In the meantime, he was free to ride any of the other horses—even old Alba was still good for a gallant jaunt—but the old afficionado of cowboys had his heart set on one last horse of his own. Aside from that point of interest, however, Sergei had something else to think about as autumn approached: Max and Sophie had secured an invitation for him to deliver a series of lectures at Luther-Aquinas in the fall term. He decided to devote those lectures to comparing classic works of American and Russian Literature, allowing himself a certain intuitive whimsy in their selection. In the first lecture, for example, he paired Charles Brockden Brown's *Wieland*, published in 1798, with Feodor Dostoyevsky's *Crime and Punishment*, which appeared in 1866. Each of those novels offered a portrait of a brutal murderer—the Russian Raskolnikov killing two old women for motives as much philosophical as financial, and the American Wieland slaying his own wife and children for pseudo-theological reasons.

Writing in the earliest years of the American Republic, Brockden Brown's intent was to portray in his protagonist a dangerous tendency in Protestant religious traditions then active in American Christianity, which were in conflict with the emerging Enlightenment ideology. Yet here was

how Wieland's sister, journaling the history preceding his
heinous crime, described his religious background:

> Our education had been modeled by no
> religious standard. We were left to the
> guidance of our own understanding, and the
> casual impressions which society might make
> upon us. ... He was much conversant with
> the history of religious opinions, and took
> pains to ascertain their validity. He deemed
> it indispensable to examine the ground of his
> belief, to settle the relation between motives
> and actions, the criterion of merit, and the
> kinds and properties of evidence.

It seemed to Professor Lossky that these were curious credentials for a character supposed to typify Christianity in
the early Republic, Protestant or no. Setting out with "no
religious standard," Wieland had proceeded not according
to faith seeking understanding, like a Christian, but by
understanding seeking to construct its own faith, like a
secular Enlightenment man. His sister continued:

> Moral necessity, and Calvinistic inspiration,
> were the props on which my brother thought
> proper to repose. ... All his actions and
> practical sentiments are linked with long and
> abstruse deductions from the system of divine
> government and the laws of our intellectual
> constitution.

Within the novel's eerie atmosphere of occult, quasi-supernatural occurrences, heightened by the trickery of a sinister ventriloquist, the character thus constituted became convinced by his long and abstruse deductions that it was God's will he should murder his family. In Sergei's view, Brockden Brown portrayed in the character of Wieland not a Christian at all, but a thoroughgoing critical modernist typifying a dangerous tendency in the tradition of Enlightenment rationalism: the logical justification of murder.

Two generations after the publication of *Wieland*, Dostoyevsky's Raskolnikov added a further refinement to that dangerous tendency, or rather development, of the Enlightenment ideal: the autonomous individual radically criticizing all received tradition. Toward the End of *Crime and Punishment*, the murderer's sister questions one of his acquaintances regarding the motivation, "the causes," of her brother's diabolical axe murders. "A theory of a sort," her interlocutor replied, "that a single misdeed is permissible if the principal aim is right, a solitary wrongdoing and hundreds of good deeds!" He went on to explain that Raskolnikov, living in poverty, had been in dire need of a substantial sum of money to launch his career—in the course of which he intended to accomplish much good—and had believed the old pawnbroker woman to be in possession of such a sum. It all seemed quite logical. But then he brought to bear the refinement already mentioned, in the dangerous tendency of Enlightenment rationalism:

A special little theory came in too—a theory

of a sort—dividing mankind, you see, into
material and superior persons, that is persons
to whom the law does not apply owing to
their superiority, who make laws for the rest of
mankind, the material, that is. … Napoleon
attracted him tremendously, that is, what
affected him was that a great many men of
genius have not hesitated at wrongdoing, but
have overstepped the law without thinking
about it.

If Wieland had been driven to murder by logical deductions from a muddled theology, then Raskolnikov assumed
an entitlement to murder by identifying with a class of
"superior persons … to whom the law does not apply."
Sergei saw these two characters as landmarks on the
route taken by the modern mind from the eighteenth-
century enthronement of reason, through the ideology of
superior individuals and elites fostered by the romantic
century, toward the brutal Socialist systems, national and
international, of the twentieth. He intended to make sure
his students got the point.

Sergei also lost no time signing up for the Posse, and
not solely for the cowboy-western connotation the word
conjured up in his mind, although he was hoping to ride
at least some patrols on horseback, once he secured his
new steed. This meant he would ride along up to Clarion with John and Chris one Saturday a month, where as
many as a thousand Posse members, including women,
would assemble for training supervised by the Sheriff and

his Deputies. Sergei was especially interested to learn more about the development of the constitutional county system, which seemed to play so essential a role in the devolved state of the Federal Executive currently maintaining the American Republic. The Constitutional Sheriffs movement had begun to gain traction back in the twenties, as more and more citizens became aware that the County Sheriff offered a final line of defense against overreach by Federal or State agencies. Duly deputized by the Sheriff, the Posse was a well-regulated militia as called for in the Constitution, organized at the county level to bear arms in defense of Liberty. Constitutional counties, in which the whole county government formally adopted the constitutional standard, had also begun to appear in the early twenties, but it was not until the thirties that these principled polities, embedded in the Federation of States, had multiplied rapidly, mostly in response to globalist infiltration into State governments. The result was essentially a network of free counties loyal to constitutional principles, Federal and State, yet standing in opposition to any government agency that would violate them.

Sergei's gleanings on this topic from the Posse training provided helpful background for discussions with his daughter-in-law, the historian of what she called the Apocalyptic War, for her focus was so much upon current events that some of the antecedent details were not yet filled in for him. Indeed, Maria was up to her ears, as she liked to say, in *The History*, although she chipped in at the farm two days a week all summer, and helped with both of the farm-to-table suppers at the Moravian Star, working side by side with her mother, her mother-in-law, and her best friend. Maria's coverage of the War remained her major intellectual undertaking, and she had settled on three modes of collecting information: the global networks for the GEC version of events, a military intelligence backchannel available through Posse contacts, and a clandestine data-capture function of the ACN still under development by Christopher and the angels.

The GEC networks were reliable enough when it came to things the population was supposed to know, such as the establishment and location of Governance Regions loyal to the Council, along with the laws, rules and regulations to be observed by those residing there. When it came to reporting on the enforcement of these codes and the enactment of penalties upon violators, the accuracy of the report depended upon the particular case, and the desired effect upon the population. The Chairman was still attempting to maintain the benevolent persona proper to his messianic pretension, so in general the more brutal details of the suppression of dissent tended to be glossed over in media reporting. At the same time, sufficient coverage was afforded to the frequency of arrests to ensure a certain degree of intimidation. Assessing the aforesaid details required going behind the media façade by clandestine channels, whether military or angelic, and it was thus our historian learned of the use of torture by Global Security forces attempting to compel believers to renounce their faith. These measures were being applied not only to confessing Christians but also to Muslims, Jews, Hindus, Buddhists—anyone faithful to a traditional religion in defiance of the False Messiah and his One World religion.

In other circumstances, when a desired point could be made by detailed and repetitive coverage of some event or phenomenon, the globalist media expertly assured that the subject would be deeply imprinted in the public mind. For example, as unfolding events made it ever more clear that the global Chairman was indeed the dreaded Antichrist, and therefore that the great Tribulation was indeed underway, certain groups of Christians who had placed their faith in a "pre-trib rapture" began to despair, abandoned the faith entirely, and even committed suicide! This unfortunate phenomenon was seized upon by the networks as an opportunity for the ridicule of Christianity, and for weeks on end the masses were never allowed to forget about "Rapturecide," especially as an example of "dangerous tendencies inherent in ancient cults."

In early autumn, the global news launched a fresh metanarrative: a deadly new virus had emerged from the African jungle, highly contagious and expected to produce high mortality. Described by GEC doctors as a "lycovirus," the pathology it produced was given the designation "Lyvid-55," a moniker that would be dunned with ominous redundancy into the consciousness of the terrorized masses. Maria immediately suspected that a psychological operation was afoot, especially when she learned that a team of technicians sponsored by the Council had been conducting classified research on this novel type of virus in the region where Lyvid-55 had emerged. Not only did historical precedent exist for use of biological agents in psychological actions upon populations; the resemblance of the current operation to the one in the early twenties was nothing short of uncanny. The exposure of the Covid-19 operation in 2023, following the publication of secret social media communications of key operatives along with evidence obtained by Russia in the Ukraine, tribunals had eventually been convened in which globalist operatives, mostly American, had received justice for crimes against humanity as defined at Nuremburg after World War II. Since that operation had involved the invention of both a novel virus and a new type of vaccine that proved equally deadly, Maria was not surprised to hear that vaccination was on the current agenda as well. In the context of the Apocalyptic War, Lyvid-55 could be counted among the *golden bowls full of the wrath of God* given to a cadre of angels to *go and pour out on the Earth*. The forces of the Adversary had no power save what was granted by God, *for a little while*.

While his beautiful, blue-eyed blond wrestled with her apocalyptic *History*, Father Maxim found himself unexpectedly taken with a strain of theological thought completely new to him—a strain not uniquely Orthodox and yet not *un*orthodox to Christian tradition, and certainly worthy of pious consideration. When he had learned from Padre Pablo of the destruction of his mother's painting, Maxim pulled out his copy of *Arts of Love in the Endtime*, on the cover of which the ill-fated painting was reproduced, to share with his mother. In so doing, he opened the romance and began rereading the Author's Preface. This time he was struck by a reference that had previously escaped his notice, to the

Anglican theologian and novelist Charles Williams. The latter's *Outlines of Romantic Theology* had proven useful to the romancer in developing the relationship of his two traditional-Christian characters and, by contrast, displaying the dysfunctionality of the efforts of the other two principal characters to live out their mutual attraction. Intrigued by Williams' title, Maxim acquired a copy through the College bookstore and was soon reading it in parallel with the romance, enriching his experience of the latter while providing fodder for his personal reflections.

Williams began by defining *romantic love* as "sexual love between a man and a woman, freely given, freely accepted, and appearing to its partakers as one of the most important experiences in life—a love which demands the attention of the intellect and the spirit for its understanding and its service." He went on to observe: "It has been part of the work of Christianity in the world to make men aware of the spiritual significance of certain natural experiences. This has been attempted with sacrifice, it has been attempted with death; it has been attempted very little with romantic love." Williams boldly proposed to remedy this theological deficiency: "The principles of Romantic Theology can be reduced to a single formula, which is, the identification of love with Jesus Christ, and of marriage with His life. ... Romantic Theology, like the rest, is therefore first of all a Christology. ... So each marriage was lived in His life, though—in terms of time—it waits its due time in the order of the universe to become manifest. ... It is His manifestation of Himself in marriage that is the subject of Romantic Theology."

The whole notion struck Maxim as extraordinary. He of all people, given the hot streak of sexual desire in his fallen temperament, ought to be devoting intellectual attention to the spiritual significance of his sexual love for Maria. But the idea of marriage as a life of Christ, and of the love between husband and wife as Christ Himself, was completely new to him—not to mention the concept of each marriage preexisting, as if aeviternally, in the life of Christ until its time for material manifestation! Then there was Williams' romantic exegesis of the most gruesome event in the Savior's life, the crucifixion: "The lover knows himself also to be the cross on which the Beloved is to be stretched, and so she also of her lover." Father Maxim had to smile at that one, since the first thing that came to his mind at the thought of his Beloved stretched out on him, was assuredly *not* crucifixion, but the unspeakable erotic joy of union with her. Yet the Englishman's point was undeniable: in taking the form of marriage, romantic love entailed a daily proximity in which the worst features of each lover must, by turns, come into play, making each of them part of the other's cross to bear. He and his Maria were no exception.

The season of Advent, in the Year of Our Lord 2055, was marked by cries of woe from Christians worldwide who lived in countries and regions under GEC control, as all public and private assemblies larger than five people were banned in the wake of Lyvid-55, and even house churches became impossible to sustain. At the same time, arrests of religious leaders loyal to their traditions and not to the counterfeit Messiah were increasing in frequency and violence, though globalist media still downplayed the latter.

The little flock at Jerusalem Lutheran praised God for their relative safety, and prayed for the protection and deliverance of those who were fully exposed to the onslaught of the Man of Sin and the Beast. Cornelius and Evangeline carried on their ministry with the steadfast good cheer commended by Christ, to those who faced tribulation—sustained perhaps as much by their love for each other as by their unshakable faith. The Eckhart-Lossky family celebrated Christmas Day at the farmhouse and the following day, a Sunday, worshiped together at Jerusalem Lutheran in the morning and at Philadelphia Chapel in the afternoon, with Father Maxim celebrating the Rite of St. Gregory for the occasion. A week later, in the dark depth of winter, the year came to an end.

YEAR THIRTEEN

(2056 A.D.)

I.

The winter of 2056 was marked by an abundance of clear, cold weather in western Pennsylvania, resulting in numerous days of deep blue skies followed by nights of unbelievably brilliant stars. There was more to this incredible sidereal luminosity, however, than the frigid clarity of the atmosphere, as our astronomer had been documenting for some time. The still-accelerating fall of the astronomical orbs toward Earth had progressed to a stage at which their diminishing distance was now plainly visible to the naked eye. Moreover, the increasing blueshift of their starlight was also becoming visible in varying shades of azure or indigo tint, from pale to surprisingly saturated, depending upon the incoming velocity of each star. And the bluest stars in the clear night sky were the five major stars of Cygnus! This information was obviously damaging to the narrative of the Antichrist, whose claim to divinity was called into question by a cosmic phenomenon which he could not control, and of which the scientific explanation was terrifying. The globalist media were still dismissing the Universal Blueshift as a mass delusion generated by conspiracy theorists, and there were reports that the Council was experimenting with ways to mask the night sky, reducing the visibility of the phenomenon. Given that one of the master's dissertations to be published in the spring was a deep dive into that very topic, Sophia couldn't help thinking about its possible impact.

In any event, she was glad that at least twelve able scientists would be receiving the Master of Science in the Glorious Synthesis, which it had been her honor to design and administer, with some initial help from her husband. A cadre of capable souls would go forth from the Institute, equipped to defend the biblical worldview against those committed to the modern scientistic paradigm of reality, in which everything was merely matter in motion. And this in a world more and more under the control of a brutal regime resolutely committed to scientism, suitably spiced with a sprinkling of occult mythology. The second-year class was smaller but equally capable, and by spring would be ready to choose their research topics, while the first-year group, a mere half-dozen, faced another full year of comprehensive coursework. There were no new applicants for the following term. It did not escape Sophia that her beloved program appeared to be dwindling away, but then, considering the times ...

She and Chris had several interesting conversations that winter, regarding the romantic relationship between David and Magdalena, in light of what Maxim had shared with his friend about his discovery of Romantic Theology, as envisioned by an Anglican savant. They found it note-worthy that, although the latter spoke of theological romance primarily in terms of the marriage relation, his archetypal instance was Dante and Beatrice, who not only never married, but whose romance consisted at most of a series of the most demure and infrequent encounters. It seemed to them that David and Magdalena, whose encounters were neither infrequent nor especially demure, could validly be viewed in the optic of Romantic Theology, despite the impossibility of marriage in their case. They would be twelve that year, and they certainly had their crosses to bear with respect to the bond of affection that united them. Besides, the identification of their love with Christ required no feat of imagination, given the integral role of the Christ Child in their lives, and His manifest approval of their romance. Most recently, He had spoken of playing a game with them, which presumably had to do, at least in part, with the tactical moves of White Stone in the war with the Antichrist, but maybe their romance itself was part of the game to which He had alluded.

Christopher, no less than Maxim, found the perspective of Romantic Theology utterly fascinating, and was soon bringing it to bear upon his earlier thinking about the spiritual or celestial body. After all, part of those considerations had to do with the presence or absence, in the spiritual body, of those organs which, in the physical body, were used in making love. Christ had taught that there was no marriage in Paradise, but he never denied that some indelible intimacy might remain between two souls who, in their physical bodies, had been romantic lovers, when those two souls arose in their bodies of Light. This did not mean, so far as our philosopher could see, that analogues of the physical organs of love would necessarily be involved in the romantic intimacies of Paradise. In fact it seemed fitting to him, in a way, that the organs of love in the body of Light would occupy the region of the heart—the seat of individual intellect—as well as the spiritual organs of speech, hearing, and vision, so that the act of making love would consist of the most intimate knowledge of the beloved's mind, visage, and voice. Given that the sexual organs per se would be superfluous with regard to reproduction, just as the organs of digestion and elimination would be with regard to heavenly feasting, it seemed almost probable to Christopher that all of these organs would be absent from the body whose habitat was Paradise.

As for the metaphysics underlying this possible ana-tomical difference between the physical and spiritual bodies, he was of several minds. There was much to be said for his initial theory involving substantial forms, which was of Aristotelian-Thomist provenance, but Luther's Augustinian notion of modes of *esse*—*naturae*, *gratiae*, and *gloriae*—offered perhaps a more elegant model. The prin-ciple of *esse* was the act of being by which a possible creature came to actually exist—the possibility of the creature being indicated by an uncreated *idea* (St. Maximus called it a *logos*) in the Intellect of God. The Creator's *idea* of a creature defined *what*, and for intelligent creatures *whom*, that creature would be; and the divine act of *esse* gave it real being. In the modal theory adapted from Luther, an act of *esse naturae* brought into being a creature in its natural state, subject to ontological corruption since the Fall, and was applicable to all created beings. The other two modes were applicable only to human beings: an act of *esse gratiae* transposed the natural person into a state of grace, corresponding to the life of faith; and the final act of *esse gloriae* would bring into being the resurrected person of a saint in Light, resident in the New Creation. In this optic, any change in the anatomy of the spiritual body could simply be brought about by the action of *esse gloriae* upon the uncreated idea of the corresponding person. Well, it was all speculation, true; but speculation of that kind, in Christopher's view, was one way of loving God with his mind.

A less speculative occupation of our philosopher's mind, during the first half of that winter, was documenting a standard operating procedure for the network override function of the ACN. The strategy for White Stone's virtual tour called for three major dates, deriving from the Feast of the Transfiguration, on which multiple metropolitan areas and rural territories would be targeted for a ten-minute performance of *Glory Be to Jesus Christ*. The first of these dates, drawn from the Western liturgical calendar, fell upon February 13, presenting a deadline for the protocol to be worked out with the angelic crew of *Synaxis*—the trusty band of bodiless intelligences who would actually carry out the operation. Christopher rather enjoyed spending time in his captain's seat inside the vessel, communicating with the crew by keyboard as they established the geographic coordinates of the target areas and indexed key network servers feeding content to those areas. Once the kids had recorded their final take, the video was uploaded to the ACN and configured for copying onto a large screen inside the former starship, where the image could be adjusted for reasons of security. After the proper filtering had been applied, the viewer could see the two performers with marvelous clarity from their shoulders to their feet—every motion, step and posture, every courtly bow and curtsey. But the appearance of each of their heads was like an orb of light, with eyes the color of fire, and each was crowned with a golden band which looked like a halo. The band on the female figure bore a large white rosebud, while the halo on the male was adorned with a round white stone, on which some kind of marking could be seen.

The Man of Sin, having declared himself the Messiah, had begun hour-long weekly broadcasts featuring himself in that role, which were aired every Sunday morning on all GEC-licensed networks, and it was this broadcast, on Transfiguration Sunday as celebrated by the western churches, that White Stone was scheduled to override. The elaborate song which formed the content of the performance was, as usual, cast in their signature style, with heptalinear stanzas in heptasyllabic verse, sung and played to seven-tone melodic lines. In nine stanzas, this biblical ballad touched upon key points in the history of salvation, with emphasis upon the role of the Savior, beginning with His involvement in Creation and ending with His Judgment and its aftermath. The opening stanza, for example, ran thus:

> Glory be to Jesus Christ!
> Praise to the eternal Word
> Who from darkness called the light,
> As the holy angels heard.
> Through Him everything was made;
> He the world's foundation laid,
> And without him nothing stirred.

The deployment of this stunningly beautiful video in the designated battlespace required its coordinated repetition in each of the targeted time zones, which presented no problem at all for the angelic operators, and the technical part of the mission was executed just as brilliantly as its artistic messaging. The subsequent assessment of impact continued into early spring, as Maria queried her sources and reported to the family, and the emerging picture exceeded all expectations. The ACN operation had been specified to permit home recording of *Glory Be* in a manner undetectable by the overridden networks (and thus by *Therion*), and thousands of DVDs had been burned to be circulated secretly in the GEC's Governance Regions. White Stone, already on people's radar from the two earlier appearances, was now indisputably world famous, and with two more Transfiguration dates to come, both in the month of August. The anonymous celebrities themselves were torn between an amused hilarity over the game that Christ, in His juvenile form, was playing with them, and a troubled concern for the safety of those who had recorded and shared *Glory Be*. David and Magdalena found some comfort in the thought that, surely, it was because of Jesus that those intrepid souls risked the wrath of a tyrant to traffic the forbidden White Stone, and not because of the personal charms and abilities of their humble selves. And if these personal qualities were used by the Lord to bring those souls to Him, or to strengthen their faith in Him, then that was to His glory too. Besides, they knew very well that they were not exactly out of danger themselves, despite all precautions, since Chairman Nabal had announced a large reward for the capture of the perpetrators of White Stone, making it clear that he wanted them taken alive. But their abiding belief remained, quite simply, that the Lord and His angels would protect them.

Manuela was working steadily on her Pennsylvania watercolors that winter, selecting from her sketchbooks the best of the motifs she had collected around the farm and its environs—including a view of the Guardian Oaks from the path approaching the woods. One afternoon in mid-March, as she sat by the north window in her small studio adding another layer of color to that particular painting, she paused for a moment to rest her eyes, gazing briefly out of the window into the blue northern sky. Relaxing the focus of her vision, Manuela stared vacantly into the empty air, then closed her eyes for a few seconds—when a radiant smile suddenly shone on her face. For in those few seconds, she had seen the holy image to be written as her next—and possibly final—icon, about which she had been praying for more than a year. Put simply, what our iconographer had seen in that prolonged blink of her eyes was a vision of the New Jerusalem, in much greater detail than shown in any of the paintings produced by the churches of the Illumination. Most remarkably, the visionary space in which Manuela saw the celestial City was such that all four sides of the foursquare wall of radiant jasper were visible simultaneously, as were the enormous triple gates in the middle of each side—twelve gates in all. Also clearly visible were the massive gemstones forming the foundation of the golden City, variously opaque, translucent or transparent, and ranging in color from red to russet, orange, amber, yellow, green, blue and purple, with several showing bands of white, black or grey.

The structure of the great triple gates was most ingenious: at first glance, it appeared that one gigantic pearl encompassed all three of the adjacent gates, but immediately the artist's inner eye discerned the intricate beveling by which three pearls, one framing each gate, had been fashioned into the elaborate, tripartite portal apprehended originally. Even more amazing to Manuela, though, were the photographic glimpses, burned into her visual memory, through one set of gates and into the New Jerusalem. Again, the embedment of multiple perspectives in the visionary space gave her two different views of the luminous interior: one downward, from above the gates, through which she saw a broad golden boulevard divided in the middle by a river, bright as crystal, running parallel to the gated wall, with a bridge across the river for each gate and a hedge of fruit-bearing trees on each of its banks. The other view was upward, from below the level of the gates, showing only the crests of the vaulting bridges against the distant background of what appeared to be the base of a great mountain, with a crystal-clear waterfall cascading toward the golden plain below. Manuela apperceived all of this in those few seconds, and the details were cemented in her memory. Now an artistic challenge lay before her: how to translate the multiple perspectives of the visionary space on a two-dimensional surface. We shall see, in due time, how she managed.

Her husband, in the meantime, was happy to have found himself a horse—a handsome roan stallion, gone a bit grey in the muzzle at eighteen years of age. A farmer friend of John's had told them of the horse, and at first the idea of taking on a stallion gave them pause, since Alba and Thunder were both gelded and it was unclear how Samson, not to mention the mares and the jenny, would take to having a stallion around. But the geriatric status of the steed was a major mitigating factor, and after inspecting the animal in person John and Sergei agreed he was a mellow old fellow, and in excellent physical shape for his age. Besides, there was something about the way the old roan looked at him, with a very specific sort of nicker that smacked somehow of irony, that told Sergei this was indeed his horse, and by the end of winter the stable at the Eckhart farm was filled to capacity. The questions of equine sociability, about which some concern had been harbored, were quickly laid to rest in the most amiable manner, as the roan stallion quickly befriended Samson and the geldings, and showed an almost gentlemanly reserve toward the females.

The horse's name had been Rusty, but Sergei rechristened him Pushkin, after long and careful consideration of possibilities, according to his habit of naming his horses for literary figures. When those considerations arrived at Alexander Pushkin, the professor remembered what Dostoyevsky had observed about that poet—that he was in effect the wellspring of Russian Literature, especially in the sense of producing its first gallery of "artistic types." Pushkin had presented powerful literary archetypes of "Russian moral beauty sprung directly out of the Russian soul," but also of "our negative type, the disturbed and unsatisfied man, who can believe neither in his own country nor in its powers." Dostoyevsky had also noted Pushkin's "capacity for universal sympathy, and for the most complete reincarnation in the genius of other nations," going on to observe that this capacity is "a completely Russian faculty. Pushkin only shares it with the whole Russian people." So here was a poet who practically typified the subject Sergei had pursued academically, and who had died before the age of forty, and here was a horse who had reached a ripe old age, and whom Sergei intended to ride until the End of Time: somehow it seemed fitting. Furthermore, the old roan stallion had most certainly shown signs of a "capacity for universal sympathy" in his relations with his stablemates—and for a clincher, "Hi ho Pushkin, away!" had a very satisfying ring.

Perhaps partly in honor of his new mount, but largely on account of the foregoing literary considerations, Professor Lossky's last lecture of the spring term proposed to compare Pushkin's novel, *The Captain's Daughter*, with *The Narrative of Arthur Gordon Pym* by Edgar Allan Poe. These two first-person narratives had been published within two years of each other, Pushkin's in 1836 and Poe's in 1838, although *The Captain's Daughter* was *set* some sixty years earlier, while *Arthur Gordon Pym* was roughly contemporary. Pushkin portrayed Peter Andreitch Grineff, the first-person narrator of his own adventures, as the only surviving child of a retired military officer and a doting mother. Peter was assigned to the tutelage of his father's gamekeeper, Savelitch, a God-fearing man from whom he learned to read and write Russian, among other things, by the time he was twelve. From then until he was sixteen, Grineff confessed, he "lived the life of a spoiled child," a status which came to an abrupt end when his father enrolled him for military service at a remote outpost, far from the desired amenities of St. Petersburg. With faithful Savelitch by his side, Grineff journeyed to the "dreary and distant country" to which he had been assigned, encountering on the way a sudden massive blizzard from which he was rescued by a Cossack peasant, who later turned out to be the leader of a peasant uprising which threatened the fort to which Grineff was headed. Moreover, it was the Captain of that very fort whose daughter provided the title of Pushkin's tale, and Maria Ivanovna Kouzmitch (Masha) was a heroine to whom Dostoyevsky's "type of positive and indubitable beauty in the person of a Russian woman" aptly applied, although that description originally referred to another of Pushkin's heroines. In the same optic of literary types, the faithful servant Savelitch typified traditional Orthodox Russia, being a serf of the most unshakable loyalty to his master, and the most humble submission to God. The character type of Grineff was more complex, displaying development from spoiled child to brave soldier in the course of a series of adventures that involved him in hardship, suffering, and romantic love.

Arthur Gordon Pym, by contrast, displayed no development whatsoever as he endured the series of harrowing storms and shipwrecks described in his first-person narrative, for counting himself among the "race of the melancholy among men," he confessed at the outset of his misadventures that his "visions were of shipwreck and famine; of death or captivity among barbarian hordes; of a lifetime dragged out in sorrow and tears, upon some gray and desolate rock, in an ocean unapproachable and unknown." Pym's melancholy visions came true in abundance, and were carefully narrated with exact scientific objectivity—everything from the most distressing situations involving extreme terror and intense, agonizing despair, to the most novel and fascinating natural phenomena, the speciation and habitations of birds, the proper disposition of stowage and riggings for various kinds of weather at sea, and precise latitude and longitude coordinates along the way—all detailed in the most objective, almost clinical style. Unlike Grineff, Pym showed no development of character in the course of the adventures he narrated: his melancholy temperament encountered the very miseries it sought, and recorded with cold objectivity both technical details germane to the voyage and experiences of genuine horror, often side by side. Sergei knew very well that the juxtaposition of these two works was somewhat whimsical, for after all, aside from narrative form and time of publication, what connections existed between the two tales? What had the nobly maturing young Russian in common with the melancholy American phenomenologist of horror? Or what significance lay in their contrast? Did it imply an analogous contrast between their two nations of origin, for example? The professor was pleased to put these questions to his class in the form of an essay assignment, and promised to post his own response after further ruminations.

Sergei's son, Father Maxim, received shocking news on the Ides of March: a letter arrived from San Angelo informing him that his friend and colleague Padre Pablo had been brutally murdered in his study by anonymous assailants. He had continued to convene the congregation of St. Michael's in several different homes, after their expulsion from the old stone mission, which had been confiscated by GEC authorities for housing. A large swath of the Southwest had fallen to the globalist regime, and Pablo had nowhere to turn for protection after receiving several threats from a "friend of Lucifer" in the weeks preceding his murder. Packaged with the letter was the icon of *St. Michael and the Dragon*, which Manuela had written more than a decade earlier when Maxim became priest at St. Michael's: Pablo had left instructions that, if anything happened to him, the holy image was to be sent to Maxim. The first thing that struck the latter, upon receiving the fateful package, was not the personal grief that swiftly followed, but the thought that his dear friend was now numbered among the martyrs *coming out of the great Tribulation*, envisioned by St. John in the *Apocalypse*. There was also the grief over his old congregation—sheep without a shepherd now, scattered by the wolves—from whom such good fruits of the spirit had been forthcoming, and who had boldly stood, at least as a remnant, with their now-martyred priest. Solemnly, Maxim mounted the St. Michael icon on the iconostasis in Philadelphia Chapel, next to the large icon of St. John.

Another shocking experience confronted Father Maxim only a few weeks later, on a rainy afternoon in April, while he was working in his study on a short theological piece for the Institute newsletter. We have noted before, as the reader may recall, that a particular female student had appeared on campus who was prone to exacerbate our worthy priest's "thorn in the flesh," being both physically attractive and shamelessly flirtatious. On the afternoon in question, there came a knock on the door of Maxim's study, to which he responded with an invitation to enter, and in walked this young woman, carrying a broad-brimmed pink hat and wearing a knee-length raincoat of the same color. Having invited her several times to visit the chapel, Maxim assumed she had come for a quick tour, during which he could speak with her more about the faith, and he rose with a smile to greet her. As the student approached his desk, returning his smile, she casually tossed her hat on a chair and then suddenly, in a single swift motion, she unzipped her raincoat and slipped it off of her shoulders and onto the floor. She wore nothing underneath. If much of the clothing regularly worn by the temptress left little to the imagination, regarding the exact topography of her figure, there was now no need for imagination whatsoever.

For a split second the priest was transfixed by the sight of the woman's nakedness—her pretty face, her perfect breasts and thighs, her delta of fur—but already the smile on his face was turning to the sternest of frowns. "How dare you!" he thundered, heedlessly heading around the desk with the thought of retrieving the raincoat to cover her naked form, when she suddenly ran to meet him, throwing her arms around his neck. At that moment, the door of the study swung open and two other female students entered, both pointing video recorders at the embarrassing scene. Placing his hands under the woman's arms and forcibly pushing her away, Maxim snatched up the pink raincoat and tossed it to her, then turned and pointed at the videographers: "May God have mercy on you all for this shameful deception!" Picking up the phone on his desk, the chaplain asked the Reverend Doctor Killgower, who happened to be in his office at the time, to please come to his study immediately. So swift and decisive had been Maxim's reaction that when Killgower arrived on the scene, all three of the perpetrators were in tears, readily agreeing to erase the video files and to sign a statement exonerating the priest from any accusation in the matter. After the students had departed, the Reverend Doctor could not help teasing his chaplain about the missionary methodology he was developing to evangelize the new pagans now appearing at Luther-Aquinas, having glimpsed the videos before they were deleted. As for Maria, although she did not see the videos, she heard all about the incident from her faithful husband, and while she could no more help teasing him than could Killgower, in terms of how terribly tempted the poor dear must have been, she promised to help him deal with any libidinal repercussions of his stressful afternoon—and faithfully kept her promise.

Maria was also faithfully working away on *The History of the Apocalyptic War*, with her bust of Thucydides perched on her desk, overseeing the careful attention with which she studied each day's information capture—excepting farm days and Sundays. Shortly before Easter, Killgower's Invisibles had announced their evangelical consensus on the interpretation of the *water like a river* poured from the *mouth* of the great Dragon *after the Woman, to sweep her away*. Having previously agreed that the Dragon, described by St. John as being red, signified Communist China, the circle of prophets now concluded that the river poured from its *mouth* was a stream of propaganda, essentially verbal though amplified by visual imagery and musical refrains. In our historian's narrative framework, it signified a flow of memetic information into the cognitive battlespace of the Apocalyptic War, where the struggle—strategic and tactical—was for the hearts and minds of the target audiences, to turn them toward the truth of Christ, and away from the claims of the Antichrist—or vice versa. Since China had again become Red, her psychological operations command had been quietly broadcasting certain programs and advertisements into the Mongolian regions of eastern Russia, subtly seeding the narrative that Russia's occupation of those lands was illegitimate, and that the destiny of the Mongolian people was unity with China. Maria could readily see that such a move would threaten the Chinese Christians who had fled to eastern Russia from the Communists, and thus that the red Dragon's *river* of propaganda would threaten the Woman—the Church in the form of Chinese and other Christians in the Mongolian lands. Not to mention the threat to Russia itself.

Another major development our historian was tracking that spring concerned the military supply shortfalls that were beginning to occur, due to poor domestic harvests and low industrial productivity, coupled with the effective curtailment of foreign trade by the GEC. Sheriff Jones in Clarion County was having discussions with the regional military command about how the county might support their operations, even possibly billet several squads locally where they could work directly with the Posse. Rosa's farm-to-table network was drawn into these discussions by way of John's connection with the Sheriff, and the group was working up an estimate of what provisions they could supply—always depending of course upon meteorological factors. The importance of keeping the county garrisoned with U.S. Military personnel was elevated by recent reports that the Son of Perdition, operating though his Emergency Council, was preparing to take a more aggressive stance toward the regions that continued to resist his control. It was still uncertain what form this new aggression might take, but the intelligence suggested that, along with incursions into eastern Russia, special operations teams were being formed in certain GEC enclaves on American soil, including possibly Pittsburgh. Those teams could include robotic personnel—a new generation of military automatons directed by AI with satellite links to *Therion*—equipped with acute sensors and multiple weapon systems. In light of these developments, it made sense to secure whatever military and paramilitary defensive resources could be plausibly sustained, and as a matter of fact, Maria wished the Sheriff of Jefferson County, where both the Institute and her home were located, was showing as much concern as Sheriff Jones.

The saga of Lyvid-55, in the meantime, was unfolding apace, as numbers of infections increased rapidly in all regions under GEC governance, and death rates, primarily among those over seventy, also soared over the winter. In the areas protected by the wings of the great Eagle, where free communication remained, it quickly became known that several treatment regimens prescribing inexpensive neutriceutical and pharmaceutical agents were highly effective in reducing the severity of the disease, and even in preventing it. This information, however, like the therapeutics themselves, was largely unavailable in GEC territories, being banned by the Council as dangerous to public health, and anyone suspected of being informed of it was likely receive a cautionary visit from Security Services. At the same time, a tremendous advertising campaign was underway on the global networks, advocating a series of injections which, it was claimed, would best protect the general population from the ravages of Lyvid-55. The Council was hoping that the propaganda push, together with social pressure, would suffice to conform the population to the desired regimen, but the subliminal implication was that any popular contumacy on the matter would be firmly confronted. What Maria found most remarkable, as the pandemic saga unfolded, was how closely it resembled the Covid-19 operation in the early twenties—remarkable in that the globalist cabal would use the same playbook twice, barely a generation apart. She figured their audacity was a testament to the mass trauma inflicted by the Global Quake, followed by the GEC's well-funded rise to the occasion, including their rapid consolidation of power and strict censorship of mass media. In any event, this remained a major front in the Apocalyptic War, of which our Maria was the historian.

John Eckhart was praying hard that spring, for a season of weather more amiable to the needs of his crops and herds than Providence had provided for the past two years. They had already reduced the number of beeves and brought the chicken flock back down to its previous size, before the urban relief scaleup, and now there was a need for provisioning troops. He and Rosa devoted considerable discussion to the matter, and drew up a plan that, God willing, should yield a significant contribution to the rations of the billeted personnel. They hadn't much to offer in the way of housing since the Losskys had moved in, unless a squad wanted to bivouac in a pasture—but they needed the grass acreage to feed the beeves, too. The other farms on Rosa's network were also planning to contribute produce, and several of the farmhouses had space for a couple of soldiers, which was typical of the responses countywide. Sheriff Jones announced in early June that implementation of billeting would begin by midsummer, so that Clarion County would be hosting a full platoon of Special Forces operators before the year's end. The Posse was getting reinforcements, to say the least.

Cornelius and Evangeline Chen, still deeply in love and still childless, remained profoundly devoted to the little flock of the faithful at Jerusalem Lutheran, and to a group of aspiring musicians there, both choral and instrumental. But now they were having a prolonged and difficult controversy, which began in midwinter and continued well into spring, pertaining to a plan that Cornelius and the other Illumination pastors had been discussing over the aeviphone network. These seven pastors—four of whom were still Lutheran while the remainder had led their congregations into the Orthodox Church in America—finally arrived at a consensus that the Holy Spirit was calling them to hold a convocation at which they would celebrate the Eucharist seven times over three days, each of them presiding in turn. Between liturgical celebrations they would pray for the preservation of the Church, for all Christian believers, and for all human beings who suffered under the tyranny of the Antichrist. By the command and example of the Lord, they would also pray for the enemies of the Church, beginning with the Man of Sin himself, that they might turn from their wicked ways and repent of their evil deeds. Evangeline was utterly dismayed at the idea, especially since her husband insisted he must go alone, for even though the rendezvous they had chosen was in Federal territory, Cornelius would have to traverse several areas of uncertain security. The reason they needed to assemble in person, Cornelius explained, was that Holy Communion played so central a role in the convocation, since it simply was not possible for the celebrant and communicants in that Rite to be spatially dispersed and not assembled, no matter how clearly they might hear and see one another remotely. But who would preach and preside at Jerusalem, his wife demanded, for surely he would be away at least one Sunday? Cornelius had cajoled his friend Father Maxim, who often attended Sunday morning Divine Service, to stand in for him in his absence, and Maxim, having reminded the OCA bishop of western Pennsylvania of the spiritual charismata of the congregation, received permission to do so. Jerusalem Lutheran was to experience the Rite of St. Tikhon for the first time in its history, provided the choirmistress would be so gracious as to prepare the choir, which the gentle pastor was hoping his accomplished wife would undertake.

Eventually, Evangeline relented, perhaps inspired by the choric challenge just mentioned, and plans were cemented for the departure of Cornelius in mid-July.

II.

The beginning of that summer was an eventful one for our Sophia, for not only did the first class of her master's program receive the degree, and not only were their research findings brilliantly defended and subsequently published; they actually provoked a bit of a firestorm in the globalist media. Given that a dogmatic scientism, claiming ontological status for a fundamentally mechanistic worldview, formed a major component of the ideology of the Antichrist, the Glorious Synthesis in general, and the recent findings in particular, amounted to an information attack on that ideology. Accordingly, the media attempted to prevent the circulation of these items of science news, and seemed to be succeeding rather well, when Sophie and her ingenious husband happened upon the idea of using the ACN for a "newsblast." Since they had perfected the network override function through the *Glory Be to Jesus* tour, it was simple enough to put together a slideshow presentation, upload it to the ACN, and "blast" it onto millions of screens worldwide. In terms of the information war, the Glorious Synthesis newsblast scored a major hit on the ideological bulwark supporting the Man of Sin's tyrannical governance, and the offense was impossible to ignore. The networks could no longer suppress the new science shoring up the Babel paradigm of the emergence of human languages, rigorously demonstrating the high probability of divine action in the Global Quake, and highlighting the rapid approach of the principal stars of Cygnus. Chairman Nabal was practically apoplectic with rage. After a brief consultation with the Beast, he announced over all media that the collection of pseudo-scientific fantasies known as the Glorious Synthesis consisted of dangerous misinformation, and that possession or circulation of any part thereof would thenceforth be considered criminal activity.

If these developments weren't eventful enough, in the middle of July her brother Max became embroiled in a media scandal that implicated the Institute where he was chaplain and she directed the master's program. It turned out that one of the video devices used to record the staged mock-sexual encounter in Maxim's study had, only a split second before the file was deleted, been transmitted to a list of other devices. In this way it came to *Therion*'s attention by way of its connection with the Institute that housed the archives of the Glorious Synthesis. It made perfect tactical sense to connect this scandalous imagery, suitably edited, of course—the priest in his cassock, embraced by the naked woman—with the hated scientific synthesis anathematized by Nabal. Eventually, stronger measures would have to be taken, despite the complications posed by the Institute's location in American Federal territory, for the Beast was quite confident that any trifling complications could be overcome. In the meantime, a media campaign was underway to vilify the Institute of Biblical Creation Science, home of the "Notorious Synthesis," along with the Christian college on whose campus it was located. The Reverend Doctor Killgower was preoccupied most of that summer with damage control, defending both the scientific integrity of the Institute he directed and the moral integrity of its chaplain, through whatever medial outlets he could find. But even though the scientific data spoke for itself, and Maxim's innocence had been thoroughly documented, Killgower found he was unable to make the case to any significant audience due to *Therion*'s control of the networks and social media. Morever, it was impossible to do another ACN newsblast on the matter without linking Maxim and the Institute with the mysterious, untraceable technology deployed in the White Stone broadcasts. The first newsblast had already been risky, and they weren't going to hazard a repeat. On that front, therefore, they were stymied.

On the White Stone front, however, the month of August saw a double offensive which brought *Glory Be to Jesus* to millions of screens around the globe, the first performance falling on the sixth of the month and the second on the nineteenth. The two dates marked the Feast of the Transfiguration in the Orthodox calendar—one being the Gregorian date and the other the Julian—which afforded the opportunity for a sort of one-two punch to the messianic façade of the Son of Perdition. Again the broadcasts rotated through the time zones as necessary, to interrupt the Chairman in the midst of some solemn program of self-promotion, maximizing the contrast between his pretended role and the reality of the One to whose role he pretended. In token of this double performance, we here inscribe two stanzas of the balladic song.

> To Jesus be the glory,
> As once upon a mountain
> He shattered categories
> By shining like a fountain
> O brilliant light before three
> Disciples dazzled, showing
> His nature to their knowing.

* * * * * * *

> Glory be to Him who died!
> Christ for us was crucified,
> Dead, and risen from the grave,
> From our sins our souls to save!
> Then ascended higher and higher
> Into heaven, where He bides
> Till He comes again with fire.

Should White Stone strike yet again, we shall be sure to mark the occasion with another stanza of the Christological ballad at the heart of their virtual tour.

Late in the evening on the day of the second performance, Chairman Nabal sat alone in his private den, where none but *Therion* was permitted to penetrate, watching replays of David and Magdalena performing their impermissible piece. He was weary that night, and his grim face was haggard as he watched with hatred this boy and girl who so recklessly flaunted his authority—to which he intended that all should bow down—and who did so with such enchanting style as to be deadly to his pubic dignity. This White Stone had become a major problem for him—first the two Enoch and Elijah shows and now the "Glory Be" tour—and the Beast was keeping him well informed of the disastrous impact they were producing. He had been working systematically for several years to eradicate the remnants of traditional Christianity, along with other religious traditions, in the regions accessible to his authority, and that with increasing success, despite the usual fanatics who insisted on martyrdom. But the cultural influence of White Stone was beginning to create an increase in the number of these criminal extremists, who were actually willing to die rather than renounce their pitiful crucified Christ. Yet still Nabal had no clue whatsoever as to *how* these video attacks had been perpetrated, by what inconceivable technology they had been carried off, which lent further fuel to the fury that possessed him at the thought of those two children. Furious hatred, however, was not the only passion aroused in the Man of Sin at the thought, and especially at the sight, of those two anonymous children. Among the most demonic manifestations of evil in human history had been the desire of certain adults to have access to children for sexual purposes, and our chief villain was very fond of that perversion, as were most of his closest associates. Nabal knew well that one of the latter had a penchant for boys, while he himself preferred pubescent girls; he definitely wanted them taken alive.

Never suspecting she was the object of a sexual fantasy in the dark soul of the Son of Perdition himself, Magdalena's major project that summer, above and beyond the various chores she was now doing, was interviewing her mother about the amazing voyage into outer space undertaken by her parents and David's in the starship *Synaxis*—as narrated in Book I of these *Romances*. Our wonder girl was working on her own narrative of that voyage, of which she had heard bits and pieces over the years, and her gramma Manuela had promised to help her with illustrations. Maria loved the time spent with her daughter in these interviews, delighted especially with the intelligent questions by which Magdalena guided her recollections, eliciting details long submerged in the flood of other concerns and commitments. Magdalena laughed gaily at hearing of the overwhelming scent of roses that greeted the voyagers the second they stepped outside the spacecraft on the planet Sadronia, and of the high-leaping white unicorns with horns of gold which carried them to the shore of the great Lake. Her face grew solemn as she questioned Maria about the appearance of Enoch and Elijah at the lakeside, beside the stone table, and about the swans that came trumpeting toward them, and the giant Swan with the Christ Child riding on its back. Her bright blue eyes widened with wonder at how the Child had served them Communion from a gold ciborium, then rinsed the ciborium in the Lake, and the water turned all shimmering and golden! The images mesmerized her: the trick was figuring out how to write it all down. "Wait! The gold ciborium was filled with the gold-shimmering water and put back inside *Synaxis*?" she exclaimed at one point. Being told that it was so, she asked whether it was still there. Indeed it was, her mother assured her. Magdalena grew thoughtful for a moment, before going on to question Maria in detail about what happened after the Child rinsed the golden vial in the Lake and refilled it: how quickly had the golden shimmering spread across the entire Lake, and how far away the great golden City had been as it rose from the luminous water; and while they were riding the unicorns back to the starship, how many legions of angelic warriors had they seen training in battle formations, mounted on their celestial steeds? The girl took copious notes during these interviews, and devoted much thought to how she would arrange her narrative of the awesome journey her parents had made, along with Uncle Chris and Aunt Sophie, before she and David were born.

Her literary grandfather, besides pitching in around the farm and getting Pushkin acquainted with his new terrain, was thinking about his first lecture for the fall term, in which he had promised further reflections comparing Edgar Allan Poe and Alexander Sergeevitch Pushkin. Specifically, having compared the former's Arthur Gordon Pym with Peter Andreitch Grineff, he had then posed the question whether the contrast between these two characters implied a corresponding contrast between America and Russia. He had solicited the opinions of his students on this, and had received a number of interesting comments which he considered in forming his own view. The question had been framed naively to provoke discussion: could those two literary characters possibly typify the national characters of their countries of origin, such that America and Russia could be contrasted by analogy with Pym and Grineff? Pym was melancholy of temperament, as was the author who imagined him, but not all Americans were melancholic. Pym was a character of "negative type" in Dostoyevsky's sense, as was Melville's Captain Ahab, whose mad quest for the great white whale bore strong resemblance to the wild ecstasy of horror sought by the seafaring Pym. Melville's masterpiece and Poe's narrative also showed another family resemblance: their close attention to minute details in the observation of natural phenomena and technical equipment, and this trait, Sergei believed, was authentically American. Pym, along with Ahab, doubtless typified a certain strain in the American psyche, but given the negativity of that type, comparing Pym with a positive type like Grineff was hardly "apples to apples."

Perhaps a fairer comparison with Pym, Sergei considered, would be Pushkin's Eugene Onegin, the titular hero of what Dostoyevsky called "that immortal and unequaled poem," in which "the real Russian life is embodied with a creative power and perfection not seen before Pushkin." Dostoyevsky identified Onegin as a "negative type" representing "the very inmost essence of (Russian) high society that stands above the people." He called this type the "Russian wanderer," always "disturbed and unsatisfied," as in the case of Onegin, a wealthy and rather dandified fellow whose rash and arrogant behavior caused him to kill a close friend in a duel, meanwhile spurning the love of the girl Tatyana (Tanya), described by Dostoyevsky as a "type of positive and indubitable beauty in the person of a Russian woman." Onegin's perverse obstinacy in a course that brought him only misery could aptly be compared with Pym's headlong rush from disaster to disaster, although the former transpired largely within the circles of St. Petersburg society and the latter on the high seas. It was interesting, Sergei thought, that Dostoyevsky expected Onegin's type to have "enormous significance in (Russia's) destiny to be," for it was precisely among the westernized upper class in St. Petersburg that the fateful revolution of March 1917 found crucial support. It made him wonder what role the American "negative type," represented by Pym and Ahab, had played in the history of the past two centuries. Here lay food for further thought.

As it turned out, the lecture which Professor Lossky had studiously prepared was not delivered at the intended time and place, for the very weekend before the fall term was to open, two truck bombs were detonated on the College campus, both targeting the building that housed the Institute. The explosive charges in the trucks had been shaped to focus the shock waves in one direction, and the vehicles were parked with precision to take out the whole front of the building, which in fact the double blast succeeded in accomplishing. Though no other buildings on campus were damaged, the College administration prudently postponed the opening of the academic year to a later time, to be announced. Many courses would be available online as soon as the faculty network was in place, Luther-Aquinas having long shunned the virtual mode of instruction in favor of face to face pedagogy, and it was over the new network that Sergei's lecture was eventually aired, from his little study in the Eckhart farmhouse.

But the attack on the Institute was devastating in more ways than one: not only did it completely derail Sophie's academic program after graduating only one class—and breach one wall of Philadelphia Chapel, strewing the sacred space with rubble—it resulted in the death of the Reverend Doctor Killgower. The Director had been working late in his office, writing a report to the board of the Institute and to its supporting donors on the delicate, if not precarious situation created by the global Chairman's vendetta against the Glorious Synthesis. As the hour grew late, he had decided to recline for a moment on a sofa he kept there for precisely this purpose, being now in his mid-seventies and prone to occasional napping, usually for half an hour or less. Closing his eyes, he fell into a deep and prolonged sleep, in which he did not notice the two trucks quietly parking in front of the building, nor the car in which the two drivers escaped. He had been reported missing by his housekeeper the following morning, and by that evening his remains had been identified in the rubble.

The Jefferson County Sheriff quickly ascertained that the perpetrators of this devastating attack had had come down Interstate 80 from the east, exiting less than five miles from the College to approach the campus on local roads. By the time the bombs were exploded remotely, just before 1:00 in the morning, the getaway car was most likely back on route 80 headed east, probably toward the GEC enclave in New York. Within seventy-two hours, Sheriff Jones of Clarion had convened a council of his peers from the surrounding counties—Armstrong, Butler, Venango, Forest and Jefferson, where the attack had occurred—as well as a lieutenant colonel from the regional military command and the commanding officer of the special operations platoon now billeted in Clarion. Representatives from the Posse of each county were also present, including John and Chris Eckhart and Sergei Lossky, and the consensus of the council was that the conflict with globalist tyranny had now entered the "grey zone" of irregular warfare. The attack was not carried out as a regular military operation, possibly having utilized private contractors, and was well coordinated with network news disclaiming GEC involvement, and spinning the event as an unfortunate but understandable reaction to a dangerous extremist cult. It was clear that the globalist enemy was taking the war to a new level, which called for a shift in defensive strategy, including increased surveillance of roads intersecting I-80, and strengthening the Posse in several counties—including Jefferson—whose sheriffs had not recruited as vigorously as had Sheriff Jones. Further intelligence was also shared at the council regarding the development of military robots by GEC forces: production was currently being scaled up from a well-tested prototype of a humanoid warbot, eight feet tall, capable of rapid movement on any terrain, equipped with acute 360-degree visual and auditory sensors, and armed with a variety of lethal weaponry, including high-caliber automatic riflery and rocket grenades. Military intelligence was still trying to hack the design specifications of this deadly monstrosity, specifically its self-defense capabilities, with a view to discovering any fatal defects, any chinks in the armor of this "Giant Operator Lethal-1AΘ," as it was technically designated. The "1A" of the suffix was reported to signify the model number, and the "Θ" to represent the wireless uplink to *Therion*, being the first letter of his name in the Greek. Christopher Eckhart, as he listened to the briefing, thought to himself that this might be just the job for *angelic* intelligence, making a mental note to follow up on the idea.

As a result of the intercounty security council called by Sheriff Jones, Posse patrols were coordinated between the six counties, four of which were intersected by the Interstate, in order to cover the key points of vulnerability more comprehensively. These patrols were also coordinated with reconnaissance activities of the billeted troops, who sometimes accompanied them in two-man teams, and communication links were established, some employing the aeviphone network, so that resources could be rallied to a point of conflict as needed. Concentration on the major thruway, however, had to be balanced by continued attention to the border areas, and several of the Posse, including our cowboy professor, volunteered to cover some of the less accessible stretches on horseback. These missions were accomplished by hauling the noble Pushkin in a trailer behind the Eckharts' truck, dropping off Sergei and his mount to conduct a sweep over a given area, and picking them up at a designated spot. Meanwhile, John and Chris covered a specified route on nearby roads. Constant contact was maintained by aeviphone, and the horseman was only to report, not engage with, any unusual movement of people or equipment, withdrawing to the pickup point to wait for backup. If attacked, he had his Colt 45 in his holster and his Winchester rifle on a sling. From the middle of September, just as the kids were celebrating their twelfth birthdays, and on through the months of autumn our trio conducted such patrols on a weekly basis, and for quite some time these remained uneventful.

While her dear husband was happily riding his horse as part of the Posse, our painter and iconographer was praying her way through the problems of composition posed by her polydimensional vision of the new icon. The reader will recall that Manuela had envisioned the New Jerusalem—the same cubiform, golden City seen by St. John on the island of Patmos, by our original Metaphysicals on the planet Sadronia, and by the seven churches of the Illumination during worship—and that she had seen all four sides of the foursquare wall of jasper at once, while enjoying both upward and downward perspectives, through the pearly gates, upon the interior of Paradise. In two dimensions, Manuela began with a board four feet high (viewed vertically) by two feet wide, divided into three panels: a two-foot square in the center, with a one by two rectangle above and below it. In the central panel, one vertical edge or corner of the foursquare crystalline wall, flanked by the two sides it joined, was inscribed as viewed straight ahead from a moderate distance, so that essentially half of the great glassy circumvallation was visible. In the lower panel, one of the threefold gates was rendered in closeup, looking downward through their openings, and here Manuela devised a view of the City's interior foreground, where a broad street of burnished gold ran left to right, with a crystal-clear stream separating the aureate boulevard into two wide lanes, lined on both banks of the river with trees of multicolored foliage. Just inside each of the three gates, an elegant bridge arced across the crystalline stream, joining the two lanes of the divided highway, and through the central gate, beside the far end of the bridge a tributary could be seen pouring into the river, apparently originating further within the shining City. In the upper panel, looking upward through the gates and glimpsing only the tops of the arching bridges, a great verdant mountain was visible in the distant interior, and descending from its unseen heights a diamond cataract aligned with the central gate—apparently the origin of the tributary seen in the other panel. As Manuela prayed and labored over the icon it amused her to think that, if the End of Time were really at hand, she would hopefully soon be able to verify the iconography of Paradise in person.

John and Rosa Eckhart were finding that sharing the farmhouse with the Losskys had made them more conscious of their need for time alone together, which in turn proved to enhance the quality of that time. They found themselves, in reverie, recollecting the forty-odd years of their life together, recalling their meeting at Penn State, their first dates (Rosa would blush at some of these), and their move to the farm after John made his small fortune in the gas fields. The birth of their unbelievable children, and the experience of bringing them up, featured much in these recollections, but all the way along, every challenge, every difficulty had drawn them closer together. John remembered well the sassy Afro-Italian girl he had courted and won, and he marveled at the mature beauty she had attained at sixty-eight, beauty not only of face and figure but beauty of soul, beauty that came with the gifts of the Spirit: the joy, kindness, patience, gentleness she exuded. Rosa remembered John too, the muscular, bearded farm boy from Perry County, the brilliant geologist, the passion-ate lover who had completely captured her heart within three days of their first meeting, so ardent had been his pursuit and so winning his case.

Christopher had shared with John, once upon an uneventful Posse patrol, what Maxim had related on the subject of Romantic Theology, and the old farmer found it worthy of reflection regarding his marriage with Rosa. Their early attractions and their underlying compatibility notwithstanding, the amorous feelings they had felt when they first fell for one another were far too intense to be sustainable, and their love, in order to live, had to mature. The analogy with the life of faith, which was the concern of theology, was not far to seek: just as romantic love had to grow in order to remain compatible with marriage, so faith had to grow in the knowledge and love of Christ to survive the vicissitudes of life. The other analogy, the one proposed by the English fellow, John found to be quite applicable as well, because considering love as being Christ, and marriage as being His life, offered any number of interesting parallels, opening up a new dimension in his reading of the Gospels. The healing miracles, for example: how often had their conjugal love healed emotional wounds inflicted in the heat of some supremely trying moment? Likewise the forgiveness of sins which generally accompanied Christ's healing: was it not the mutual forgiveness issuing from their love that actually healed those emotional wounds? John had never studied much theology, but it seemed to him that this point of view permitted an exaltation of human romantic love, in, with and under the form of Christ, without making an idol of it. A perspective well worth pondering.

The agricultural season had been a modest one: cool, wet weather had dominated the summer months, and then September brought early frosts, bringing crop yields well below expectation. The larder was stocked for the winter, and the CSA clientele had been served—though in reduced quantities due to provisions supplied to the billeted military—but the farm account books were not entirely devoid of crimson figures. This was a new experience for John and Rosa, whose hard work had generally been rewarded with prosperity over the years, but they owned the farm free and clear thanks to John's initial investment—or rather they held it in trust for the Lord until He came for it. Thankfully, the natural gas well in the back pasture continued to produce abundantly, and John was able to sell or trade cylinders for a little extra cash, besides powering the tractor and heating the house.

Maria Lossky-Eckhart was increasingly appalled at the progress, in the course of that spring and summer, of the Apocalyptic War of which she was the historian. The Sino-Mongolian invasion of eastern Russia, carefully prepared by a propaganda campaign from the *mouth of the Dragon*, had been accompanied by a prophetic sign: the Euphrates River ran completely dry, which was said, in *Revelation*, to *prepare the way for the kings from the east*. Then followed the massive propaganda assault on the Glorious Synthesis and the Institute, coupled with the misleading pictures of Max, which paved the way for the bombing of the Institute and the martyrdom of Thomas Killgower. Maria's sources informed her that the same Chinese PsyOp group responsible for the eastern Russian operation had also been involved in the media attack on the Institute—again, the stream from the *mouth of the Dragon*. The Lyvid-55 operation, meanwhile, proceeded with an almost comical predictability—though dark indeed the comedy—because of the way it so closely resembled the "plandemic" of the early twenties. It was almost as though the latter had been a rehearsal for the present one, and several elements of the plot had been altered to fine-tune the outcome. For example, the mandatory series of injections administered in the GEC regions produced a surge of mortalities, beginning soon after the first two rounds of mass injections and increasing with each round of boosters—just as in 2021. At that time, however, the agenda in play had been depopulation, and mortalities were high in the young and middle-aged as well as in the elderly, whereas now, with the population thinned by the Quake (on top of the Covid-19 shots), the goal was a robust working class, and accordingly, mortalities were almost entirely confined to the elderly. The earlier operation had been exposed to the public over the course of 2023, and the present replay had been delayed for over thirty years by the Restoration, which got underway in earnest with the return of the providential President in 2024—as documented in the *Journal of Jeremiah Jefferson*.

But now the Apocalyptic War, of which our Maria was the historian, had struck close to home. The bombing of the Institute, the death of her dear mentor, the closure of the College—all indicative of the threat to her family by the deadly reach of the Dragon—fundamentally altered her attitude concerning security. Beneath the western wing of the great Eagle she had grown somewhat complacent about the danger they all faced, as the forces of evil geared up for their final assault on the saints. Max would be unemployed after the end of the year, since the board of the Institute had declined to attempt reconstruction under current conditions, though they kindly continued his salary, along with that of the other staff, to the year's end. Since that was exactly when the lease on their rancher was up for renewal, Maria had been praying for a solution when the answer emerged providentially from an otherwise unfortunate turn of events. Pastor Cornelius had successfully navigated to the pastoral convocation in July, returning without incident, while Father Maxim served the congregation at Jerusalem Lutheran on the Sunday of his absence. So profound had been the experience of the seven pastors, which included a brief glimpse of the cubiform apparition along with other things they struggled to articulate, that it seemed to them the Holy Spirit called them to convene once more, on the Eve of All Saints, also hallowed for the posting of Luther's *Theses*. Reassured by previous success, Evangeline was more readily reconciled to the plan this time, and Father Maxim was asked to administer the Service as before. This time, however, Cornelius did not return, and as the pastors had agreed not to take their aeviphones to the convocation lest the enemy should capture one, there was no word of him.

This heart-breaking turn of events, by which Evangeline was utterly devastated, nevertheless provided a solution for Maria's (and Maxim's) problem. For the congregation immediately called the unemployed priest to replace their lost pastor, at least until such time as he should return. Evangeline welcomed the company of Maxim, Maria and Magdalena in the otherwise lonely parsonage, where they began by staying over a few days at a time, until the next turn of the apocalyptic screw caused them to expedite their move to Clarion County. During the week of Thanksgiving, a series of hostile encounters occurred in which both Posse and military patrols engaged with paramilitary intruders in Jefferson County. This was no longer a matter of groups of undocumented migrants, with or without armed accompaniment, as in the early phase of GEC tactics. This was a paramilitary operation probing security perimeters, and it looked as if the enemy considered Jefferson to be vulnerable. Consequently, by the third Sunday in Advent, Father Maxim's little family was settling into the Lutheran parsonage in New Bethlehem.

Amid this relentless cascade of occurrences, Maxim was especially grateful for the rigorous practice of the Jesus Prayer that had formed the heart of his spiritual life from his seminary years onward. He had loved sitting in Philadelphia Chapel, with the great icon of Christ Pantokrator overhead, passing the black woolen knots of the *tschotki* though his fingers as he repeated the confession of faith and the cry for mercy combined in the ancient formula: *Lord Jesus Christ, Son of God, have mercy on us sinners.* Thankfully, the icons were not damaged by the blast, and with the exception of the Pantokrator, which was written directly on the plaster of the dome, our priest was able to remove them, clean them up, and remount them in the parish hall at Jerusalem, where he had so suddenly and unexpectedly become pastor. He arranged the icons to form a "beautiful corner" in the rectangular hall so that, facing it, the *Philadelphia* icon stood centered athwart the corner, flanked on opposite walls by *St. John* and the *Key of David*, with the *Theotokos and Child* mounted above the former, and *St. Michael and the Dragon* above the *St. David with Key*. The corner was divided from the rest of the hall by a movable wooden screen, and it was there, in that hallowed space, that Father Maxim now preferred to pray the *tschotki*—not to contemplate the holy images while in prayer, but for the sense of the sacred they imparted to the space. Then there was a certain awkwardness he felt about using the study of his missing friend Cornelius. In any event, he was glad to be able to accomplish what Cornelius had long considered, by conducting the congregation into the episcopal fold of the Orthodox Church in America, as three of the Illumination pastors had already done. With approval from the diocesan bishop, the congregation was renamed New Jerusalem Evangelical Orthodox Church, and retained the right to use the Old Red liturgy on desig-nated occasions—though the Western Rite of St. Tikhon would be their liturgical norm—and to sing their familiar hymns. Maxim remarked to his wife the historian that apocalyptic times made strange ecclesial bedfellows, and yet, as he thought about it, how far apart had traditional Lutherans—leaving aside the various revisionists—ever really been from the fullness of Orthodoxy?

Maxim also mentioned to Maria, as Advent drew to a close, the startling thought that this Christmas might actually be the very last Christmas of all, *if* the evangelical prophecy they had taken as a working hypothesis were indeed proving true, as certainly appeared to be the case—unless the End fell in the final week of the following year. That same thought occurred to him again after Vespers on Christmas Day, as he sat in the *beautiful corner*, lit only by icon lamps in the darkened parish hall, Maria and Magdalena having headed back to the parsonage with Evangeline. Could this really be the last Christmas? Reverently running his gaze over the holy images, left and right, Maxim focused intently on the central *Philadelphia* icon for a moment, then closed his eyes, breathing slowly and deeply in rhythm with the silent prayer that spontaneously arose in his mind: *Lord Jesus Christ, Son of God, have mercy on us sinners.* Our priest was fingering the hundredth knot of the *tschotki* when he was interrupted by an adolescent male voice, directly in front of him. The Child had never appeared to him before, but when Maxim opened his eyes, he had no doubt upon whom he was looking, or from whom he was hearing. The Son of God Incarnate, in his boyhood form, was clad in battle dress, with greaves, breastplate and plumed helmet of bright gold, over a woolen robe of deep crimson matching the plume of the helmet. "I have had mercy on you, and I shall have mercy on you," He was saying. "The Day and the Hour draw near when our endgame will be played. Be mindful of the celestial water I sent with you from the Lake. You will have need of it. You also will have need of these three verses, breathed by my Holy Spirit through my forefather after the flesh." Gesturing to the icon of David, the Holy Child chanted in an ancient mode probably used in the Jerusalem Temple worship:

Thou shalt hide them in the secrecy of thy presence
*   from the disturbance of men.*
Thou art my refuge from the affliction which
*   surroundeth me; O my Rejoicing, deliver me*
*   from them which have encircled me.*
The angel of the Lord will encamp round about those
*   that fear Him, and will deliver them.*

Then, with a grave smile, and a gesture of blessing that somehow resembled a military salute, He resumed invisibility.

YEAR FOURTEEN

(2057 A.D.)

I.

Despite the numerous factors of gloom that were active that winter—the winter at which our chronicle has at last arrived—our Sophia was finding comfort in feeling completely fulfilled by her life at the farm, with no remaining obligations to any outside institution. Even when her attention had been more divided, she had always been happy here with Chris, David, John and Rosa, and now her dear parents were right there as well, and Maria was closer in New Bethlehem than she had been in Pinecreek. This feeling of fulfillment was one of her consolations amidst the aforesaid factors, which included the gloomiest winter anyone could remember, wet and cold with very little sunshine; even on sunny days the light was filtered by a translucent haze. There was substantial evidence that the GEC had been deploying light-reflecting nanoparticles in the stratosphere, with the intention of attenuating the increasing brightness of the stars, several of which were approaching daylight visibility. In the process they had dimmed the light of the sun, which led to lower temperatures and increased cloud cover, boding ill for the coming agricultural season and facilitating psychological depression among the unprepared. Nevertheless the stars continued to fall, apparently faster and faster, as the current astronomical data showed not only continued acceleration in the approach of the sidereal bodies toward Earth, but a second-order increase *of the acceleration*! Sophia was initially surprised, given the massive precipitation of inertial matter toward Earth, that no tectonic effects were being observed, but a closer look at the physics (and metaphysics) of the cosmological-geological coupling indicated that the spherical symmetry of the incoming mass was conducive to gravitational stability in the center of convergence.

Daily life at the farm afforded an analogous stability to the soul of our learned astronomer, as its diurnal routine revolved symmetrically around her heart—in the sense of her spiritual center—evenly balancing her central concerns and commitments upon the fulcrum of her consciousness of Christ. Sophia's conscious awareness of the presence of Christ in her heart formed the ground of her daily experience—sometimes the background, sometimes the foreground—from which all the familiar movements and activities seemed to emerge. At morning prayer, when everyone assembled in the farmhouse living room for psalmody, Scripture and prayers, her participation in the simple rite brought Christ into the foreground, as did the regular table blessings, as well as whatever spontaneous moments the Spirit graced her with. Otherwise—as for example when she was feeding animals, or working in the kitchen, or doing laundry—her immediate awareness of Christ might recede into the background, yet it remained the *ground* of all she did in the course of those dark and dreary days, and of the comfort she found in her life at the farm.

Another facet of Sophia's farm life, as she often reflected

that winter, was the manifest presence of the bodiless intelligences on and about the premises. The subtle but unmistakable supersensory ambience associated with the angelic habitat had been familiar to Sophia and the other Metaphysicals ever since they first activated the angelic field around *Synaxis* for the voyage into outer space. Sophia always sensed this ambience—which they had agreed to designate as *aeviternal*—in the vicinity of the silo that housed the starship, but in other places as well (in the farmyard, the grass fields, the woods) she had been suddenly *zinged* with it, only to have it subside just as suddenly. Her husband the metaphysician had explained the ontology of those purely spiritual beings, intellectual essences brought into existence by divine *esse*: intellectual substances, therefore *persons*, albeit bodiless persons. Sophia loved those invisible associates assigned them by the Lord, who had helped and served them in so many ways over the years, even as she loved their Lord, King of the Angels, the Lord of Hosts in whose burning love her own love was enkindled, and by whose light she was living through those days of darkness.

Christopher's first priority in the new year was once again to team up with those invisible associates in a search for technical specifications detailing the operating system of the GOL-1AΘ warbot, of which the first lot of field units was already in production. The word was that these deadly automatons would be infiltrated into regions designated as being in rebellion against the GEC, where they would conduct search-and-destroy missions, either in free-fire mode or with specific targets. Thus the urgency with which our philosophical farmer approached the angels, seeking to establish a dialogue by which he could guide their search for crucial files, within the archives of digital information comprised in the global cybersphere. The target specifications of the bot were of course deeply encrypted in layers of code, but the pure intellectual power of the bodiless operators proved more than capable of cracking every security barrier erected by the Beast. By Groundhog Day the essential documentation was in hand, and was quickly relayed to the Sheriff and the military command for tactical analysis, which thankfully revealed at least one "Achilles heel" in the design of the murderous behemoth. In the structure of its head, critical nodes of microcircuitry were clustered around and immediately behind a spherical sensor array embedded in the upper facial armor, appearing from the outside like an eye in the middle of its forehead. If a bullet consisting of a supermagnetic alloy could be fired straight into that sensor, it should effectively *fry* the command-and-control system, rendering the robot incapable of movement or other activity. The military quickly commenced the procurement process for supermagnetic ammunition, but it would be some time before significant quantities would be available, so small-scale local efforts were encouraged. Christopher found that the specialty lab which had supplied him with batches of supercrystals was able to provide the alloy in the form of spheres, which could be sized to fit shotguns or muzzleloaders. By April Fools' the regional defense coalition had 100 rounds to distribute. This ammunition was precious; every shot had to count.

When Christopher looked at the whole diabolical design

of this GOL-1AΘ, or "Goliath," as it came to be commonly known, he found himself confronted yet again with the characteristic vice to which his irascible temperament ever urged him. Wrath and fury were the words for this indulgence, a raging anger at the evil, twisted intelligence that would design, test and build such a brutal monstrosity, and then unleash it upon innocent people who were merely upholding their liberty, and their faith, against a usurping tyranny. He sought release in the imprecatory psalms, and found certain passages adhering to his memory:

> Arise, O Lord! Deliver me, O my God! For You strike
>   Your enemies on the cheek;
> You break the teeth of the wicked.
> Make them bear their guilt, O God; let them fall by
>   their own counsels;
> Because of their many transgressions cast them out,
> for they have rebelled against You.
> May his days be few; may another seize his goods!
> May his children be fatherless, and his wife a widow!
> He loved to curse; let curses come upon him!

Parsing his burning rage into the dialect of Scripture helped him sublimate, to some extent, the visceral urge to violence that accompanied extreme ire, but he knew full well that the Gospel demanded something more, something he still struggled with: not merely to forgive one's enemies, but to love them!

Providentially, the press of current activities left Christopher little time for brooding on the wrath-inducing evil of the Adversary, for no sooner had he and the angels hacked the design of "Goliath," than yet another project presented itself to him and his bodiless collaborators. When Maxim described to him the appearance of the Child at the church on Christmas Day, repeating the words he had spoken and chanted, the psalmic verses of protection also imprinted themselves in Christopher's memory, reinforced by the intriguing tones of the Temple chant, as if overlaying the verses of imprecation. He found comfort in those declarations of defense and deliverance, and began to repeat them to himself spontaneously as he went about his work on the farm. During the last days of winter, as he was spreading manure on one of the fields, he was actually chanting the verses aloud when a sudden idea occurred to him at the phrase, *the angel of the Lord will encamp round about*: Couldn't the angels deploy defensive perimeters around specified locations? After a couple of keyboarding sessions inside *Synaxis*, this now-familiar method of dialogue with the invisible crew produced a protocol by which a cubic boundary of specified volume could be deployed symmetrically around a designated location, and activated to effectively repel any incursion exhibiting hostile intention or destructive potential. The beauty of this Angelic Defense Perimeter (ADP) was that the operative intelligences were able to detect hostility and destructiveness intellectually, by direct knowledge, and then to activate instantaneously an appropriate physical force or energy field to repel or destroy the aggressor. As in previous deployments of new functions or applications of aeviternal technology, an activation rite would be necessary. Due to the death of Thomas Killgower, whose dreams had previously provided key elements of these rites, Christopher would presumably have to work it out with the crew. He hoped the ADP would be ready to launch by about May Day.

David and Magdalena had decided, after prayerful discussion, that the fourth and final showing of *Glory Be to Jesus* should be aired on March 25, The Feast of the Annunciation, which fell that year on a Sunday. The Feast commemorated the conception of Jesus in the womb of the Virgin, at the moment the Archangel announced it—falling thus nine months before Christmas—and our illegal superstars found it a fitting date for their performance. They also decided to work up a completely new arrangement of the balladic song, instrumentals and all, as well as a new dance routine in which the romantic involvement of the players was tastefully apparent. Their elegant white tunics, belted with cloth-of-gold, revealed that the figures of the two, now in their thirteenth years, were distinctly adolescent, although their physiognomies were veiled in light. Their voices also evinced the maturation of their persons, David sounding distinctly deeper in tone, though mostly free of the cracking so common to adolescent male voices, while Magdalena's clear, girlish timbre, so long an almost birdlike soprano, was definitely tending toward alto. After much rehearsal, the final take of *Glory Be to Jesus 2.0* was a thing of beauty, airing flawlessly on Annunciation Sunday, right in the middle of Nabal's weekly broadcast, as it rotated through the longitudinal time zones. Here is another representative stanza:

Behold! The stars are falling!
He soon returns with power!
O, harken to his calling
Before that fiery hour
When elements dissolving
Bring Judgment to all beings,
Heaven or Hell decreeing.

Not being the kind to rest on their laurels (nor shrink from the price on their heads), the pair was already planning one more show, which they fully expected to be their last, and of which we shall hear more in due time.

Magdalena's collaboration with her grandmother was proceeding apace, illustrating her narrative on the fabled adventure into outer space which culminated on the planet Sadronia in the heart of the Swan, where a necessary condition of her own existence had been decided upon. It was this latter motif that formed the central thread of the tale as she told it, for though Magdalena did not pretend to know what all the Lord had intended, and accomplished, by leading her parents, aunt and uncle on that incredible journey, one thing she knew: He had accomplished their decision to marry and have children—herself and her beloved David—and for that she thanked Him with all her heart. A sense of the shape of her little romance can be gleaned from a survey of the illustrations, in which Manuela handled the compositional motifs and figurations, and Magdalena added details and color. The first plate was an interior view of *Synaxis*, looking down from the apex of the cabin on the four Metaphysicals, with the Participator, blue and polyhedral, in the center. This was the setting in which all of the action, except for the landing on Sadronia, would occur, and the romantic pairing of the two couples was already evident in the direction of their respective gazes. The second plate was from the perspective of the Participator, looking up at four large screens in the hemipolyhedral ceiling, each displaying the angel of one of the four outer stars of the Swan: this completed the view of the cabin, including the essential display screens, and represented the stopovers at the corresponding stars.

Plate three cut straight to the Rose Garden on Sadronia, with the four voyagers dancing on the green before the azure starship, and four white unicorns with horns of gold approaching: here the two couples are explicitly paired, continuing the motif of romance. Plate number four depicted the Metaphysicals, still paired, standing on the lakeshore facing a low stone table and flanked by Enoch and Elijah, as the Christ Child approaches with the golden ciborium. Ranks of swans can be seen in the background, surrounding the giant swan on which the Child had ridden: the pairing of the lovers was here shown to be sanctified by Christ, implying His instruction to marry. The fifth plate showed the Child kneeling by the Lake and rinsing the golden ciborium, while the lake water, in contrast to the previous illustration, shimmered like gold, and in the distance, a great foursquare City rose from the shimmering surface—associating the romance of the lovers with the New Creation. Plate six displayed the heroic foursome astride their leaping unicorns, returning to *Synaxis* by way of a wide green expanse where several battalions of angelic warriors were wheeling their celestial steeds in battle formations; introducing the theme of the Apocalyptic War. And the final plate portrayed the double wedding of the two couples in the old chapel at Luther-Aquinas, a theme whose relation to Magdalena's central motif requires no comment. As she put the finishing touches on the narrative thus illustrated, our ingenious girl was already plotting a sequel narrating the comic romance of two cousins.

Magdalena's partner in that romance, especially as the return of spring began to soften the harshness of that dismal winter, was noticing more and more a new edge in his feelings for her, in the sense of a sharpness that pertained less to love per se, than to desire. In short, it was the advent of a new and powerful type of attraction to Magdalena, an attraction he knew could never be fulfilled the natural way, and yet a definite urge that would not yield to reason, and an urge that sometimes brought his male organ to attention in embarrassing circumstances. Not only that, but one April night he awoke from a dream in which he and Magdalena had been naked in his bed, and had done the thing they weren't supposed to do, and he had ejaculated on his bedsheet. He talked it over with his dad, and they agreed that probably the Devil had been involved in targeting the natural urge of David's adolescent body on Magdalena in particular, aiming to corrupt the sanctity of their love—and yet, in any case, that this was another factor the boy would need to face, and learn to control. It was almost a week before he confided in Magdalena, who greeted the news with the most charming sense of humor—not mockingly but with spontaneous gaiety—wondering aloud, with a mischievous grin, why David got to have all the fun! At that, the two of them dissolved in laughter, then held one another in their arms for a timeless moment, and finally dropped their hands to each other's waists, with their foreheads touching. "We can do this, David," she whispered gently. "Let's see what Jesus has in mind for us in Paradise." "Amen, my beloved," was her gallant lover's reply.

That gallant lover's other exploits during the period at hand had much to do with strength training and with development keen marksmanship skills. As he approached the birthday that would make him a teenager, the same hormones that produced his sexual temptation also facilitated the formation of muscle, and David was determined to develop his share. Besides handling hay bales, feed bags and water buckets in the course of his routine chores, our boy hero had a regimen of calisthenics and special exercises to which he rigorously adhered, and accordingly, in the vernacular of his mother, he was eating like a mule. One of the exercises was to pull back his high-powered hunting sling as far as he could, then relax and repeat the motion a set number of times, and finally hold it extended as long as he could—to the point that his dad had to get a couple more sets of elastomer cords to maintain dependable shooting power. Desiring to strengthen his arms in order to deliver the maximum power of which the sling was capable, and wishing to be ambidextrous in its use, David trained both of his arms by this exercise, while developing a deadly aim either way.

The consequent augmentation of his prowess was well demonstrated one spring evening, as he and Samson were just returning from a little ride around the farm. As they approached the farmstead, Manuela's goats could be heard bleating in their paddock, as if alarmed about something, and riding over to investigate, David saw a mountain lion crouched about forty feet from the fence, obviously stalking the herd. Samson voiced a warning hee-haw as David rode him between the wildcat and the paddock, but surprisingly, instead of retreating toward the woods as expected, the beast stood its ground, snarling and turning toward the boy and the mule. This proved to be a fatal mistake, for on these little rides around the farm, David always carried his sling and ammo at the ready, taking an occasional shot at targets where a clear hit-or-miss could be readily determined. Within seconds the sling was drawn and released, and a forty-five caliber slug entered the cat's left eye socket, incapacitating its brain and dropping it to the ground like a rock. David was lauded for days for this feat, not least by his beloved girl. His dad and grampa showed him how to butcher the animal (just like a squirrel only bigger), saving the hide to be tanned, and his grammas cooked him a savory stew of the meat, and his favorite goat milk caramel pudding.

David's other grampa, our cowboy professor, had several things at the forefront of his brooding mind at that time. Among the most prominent was his newfound vocation in the Posse, in which he considered himself to be aligned with the cowboy values he had imbibed as a Russian boy, from the tales of Louis L'Amour and others. Western Pennsylvania was like a frontier again, as it had been three centuries earlier; only this time the paramilitary threat was not from displaced Indian tribes but from a global tyranny seeking to extirpate the surviving strongholds of liberty. When the American frontier had moved farther west, heroic cowboys were confronted with yet another kind of threat: unscrupulous individuals driven only by greed and lust for power, as captured in the reflections of one of L'Amour's heroes: "His life had been lived among men who played ruthlessly for the highest stakes. It was no shock to him that men would stoop to killing, or a dozen killings, if they could gain a desired end." The struggle for a civilized order under the rule of law, where neither tribal animosity nor individual rapacity were permitted to disturb the peace of a society of free people, did not originate in America, Sergei reflected, and yet for America it was like a founding myth. Furthermore, no sooner had the constitutional Republic filled out the continental roster of the States than it encountered another adversary to the civilized rule of law, in the very government that was supposed to uphold it. This was where the Posse, deputized by duly elected county Sheriffs, took its place in the epic struggle, interposing as a constitutional militia against lawless actions by State or Federal agents upon the people of their counties. Now things had come full circle, as the Posse defended the remnants of the Republic against enemies more dangerous than the Indians and outlaws of old.

Related to this theme in Sergei's thinking was his on-going consideration of the role of the "negative type" in American Literature—the individual driven by obsession—in the actual historic destiny of the nation. The melancholy Pym and the vengeful Ahab, among the exemplars of this type, were perhaps less apposite to this question than Caldwell's Joseph Armagh, the starveling Irish immigrant boy who became a business tycoon of fabulous wealth and power by the most ruthless obsession with becoming so. Armagh's fatal flaw had been to love America too much to collude with an international cabal of bankers, merchants and manufacturers to the detriment of American workers, having underestimated their power to undo him— but other Americans had proved happy to sell out their country. Long and bloody wars had been fought to the drumbeat of propaganda paid for by parties who stood most to profit from such prolonged seasons of destruction and death, and the American military, long employed to impose "banana republics" in Central and South America, by the middle of the twentieth century was serving mostly the interests of these masters of deceit. In short, Professor Lossky concluded that indeed, the spiritual heirs of Pym, Ahab and Armagh had left their mark in the history of the nation.

Another thing Sergei had been thinking about was a subject both Maxim and John had mentioned to him, and which, the reader will observe, had been making the rounds of our characters—the subject of Romantic Theology. He had carefully questioned both of them about the amorous doctrine, interested in how each of them understood it, and had finally read the book himself. One point that especially struck Sergei, in the author's comparison of the life of Christ with the life of romantic love, was the interpretation of the Ascension, when Christ rose bodily into the sky and disappeared into heaven. "Love that was visibly present, a light and a wonder, withdraws Himself into the secret and heavenly places; and in His stead there descends on the lovers the indwelling grace of the Spirit, nourishing and sustaining them." Sergei remembered well the light and the wonder that had bedazzled him when he met the lovely Latina painter, just graduating from Angelo State as he arrived from Russia to assume his teaching post. He recalled with what passion he had courted her, his delight when she accepted his proposal, and the joy they had shared settling into the little ranchero in the Texas Hill Country— their beloved Lucky M. Forty years later, looking back over their life together, Sergei could not deny a certain cooling had occurred, ever so gradually, from what could only be described as a very hot beginning to a sort of cozy warmth. The mature romantic climate of their relationship, while not so exciting as its torrid origins, lent itself well to the sort of serenity they both desired in the seventh decade of their lives—a serenity akin to grace, as he now saw—to nourish and to sustain them in their marriage.

As noted, that serenity was equally welcome to the "better half" of Sergei's marriage, for Manuela had grown up in the quiet of the Hill Country, and her soul was inclined to aesthetic contemplation—the more so as she grew older. The Eckhart farm and its environs provided fertile ground for a fresh crop of watercolors, in which she sought to capture the spirit of the land underlying the elegant vistas of overlapping slopes, lining the little valleys carved by runnels feeding the Leatherwood Creek and Jack Run. Here was a treasury of landscapes distinct from those of her Hill Country, or the flats around Ozerki. Manuela sought to capture them in line and color, and the framed results soon graced the walls of farmhouse and cottage, which took on the semblance of a gallery. Then there was her work with Magdalena, which was doubly gratifying, in that it was fun to bring the mastery of her art to bear in composing a series of book plates—something she had never done before— and because the dear girl was such a delight to work with, besides being her beloved granddaughter. Manuela could not avoid a certain bemusement in contemplating the theme of Magdalena's narrative—not so much the origin of the two children in the Child's instruction to their parents, per se, as the subtle tone of a romantic destiny spilling over from the four parents to their offspring. It never ceased to amaze her how Magdalena and David had developed, by the tender age of nearly thirteen, into a pair of celibate, courtly lovers worthy of celebration in verse or prose, on that score alone, not to mention the incredible game they were playing with the Child, and their worldwide fame! Maybe the girl would tell their story herself—unless she literally ran out of time.

Manuela was also happy to see her icon of the New Jerusalem mounted above the doors into the nave at the Evangelical Orthodox Church now named for the same celestial City, flanked by the principal paintings of the series of apparitions of the same, by which the congregation had been visited during the pastorate of Cornelius Chen. Now, in the rush and swirl of events, it was Maxim who was pastor, and she loved to visit the *beautiful corner* he had arranged in the parish hall, but her heart just ached for poor dear Evangeline, who seemed to be utterly inconsolable. So inconsolable, indeed, that when the first wave of warm weather finally arrived in late April, she went missing, leaving behind a note of touching thankfulness for everyone's kindness during her happy years in New Bethlehem, and adding simply that she had gone to find Cornelius. The foremost practical consequence of Evangeline's departure was that someone needed to assume leadership of the choir. Without undue delay, Rosa Eckhart was more or less drafted to fill in, given that she combined seniority of choric service, a good strong singing voice, and a popular personality. David and Magdalena were saddened by the departure of their beloved music teacher. The parsonage, now solely occupied by Maxim's little family, seemed subtly different in her absence. But life went on.

It was the eighth of May before all arrangements were in place to activate the Angelic Defense Perimeter (ADP), and Maxim duly pointed out that the date, on the Western sanctoral calendar, was assigned to an Apparition of St. Michael that had portended a historic victory for Christian forces. The elements of the activation rite had been assembled from several sources, including the psalm verses chanted to Maxim by the Child, a sort of daydream of Sophia's, and a dream of John Eckhart's which clarified the overall order of the rite, as Killgower's dreams had formerly been wont to do. The six Metaphysicals gathered inside *Synaxis*, with Maxim in his cassock and the rest in their albs, and solemnly recited the simple rubrics of the rite, several with instrumental accompaniment by White Stone. The latter continued to pipe and strum harmoniously as Maxim, advancing to the Participator, opened a small hatch. Reaching inside, he retrieved the gold ciborium from its interior. Reverently removing its lid, he carefully poured a few drops of shimmering fluid on the apex of the blue polyhedron, then stepped back and replaced the lid, watching with the others the transformation of the azure orb, from the top downward, into a sphere of dimly shimmering gold. At that point the rite concluded with the Doxology, and the deed was done. According to specifications developed by Christopher and the angels, a cubic barrier was thenceforth in place around the farmyard and houses with roughly ten acres of surrounding land, that would repel any hostile intrusion or dangerous pro-jectile. But the system had another feature as well: with an aeviphone mounted directly atop the Participator, any other mobile unit in the network could simply call that phone, and receive a local perimeter of cubic dimensions up to twenty-five yards, centered on the receiving phone. This technology was literally unbelievable; furthermore, it was somewhat difficult to test, since hostile intent or dangerous potential would be all but impossible to fake, as it would require hoodwinking the bodiless intelligences! After much thought and discussion on the matter, John proposed that they take rifles just outside the perimeter nearest the house and fire at one of the windows—a proposal that elicited much jollity, but no consensus on which window might be tested.

In any event, the activation of the ADP was timely. The Adversary appeared to be gearing up for a final assault on the regions and regimes that had thus far successfully resisted his hegemony, and his personal vendetta against White Stone was no secret to the world. Now, by the grace of God and the genius of the angels, they had a safe haven at the farm as well as mobile protection via the aeviphone network, and this option was quickly shared with the Invisible College, the Illumination pastors, and the Sheriff. Maxim was now in regular contact with the group of pastors, none of whom had heard from Cornelius since his disappearance, though all reported their growing concern about their security as traditional, confessing Christians since their regions were coming under the threat of GEC penetration. The pastors were uniformly delighted with the newfound ability to deploy local defensive perimeters, especially since a twenty-five yard cubic barrier could protect an entire congregation at worship. Indeed, it was one of these congregations that provided the first practical proof of the ADP's effectiveness. One Sunday morning in mid-June, a pair of well-armed assailants attempted to enter the church in question but were astonished, upon reaching the invisible barrier, to find all of their weapons reduced to a molten state, with resulting burns on their bodies and complete loss of vision. The crippled antagonists were being treated for their injuries by several nurses in the congregation when police arrived, the latter wanting to know, upon observing the melted weapons and corresponding injuries, what sort of defensive system had been deployed—to which the pastor would only reply that the church was under angelic protection.

Maxim was also in constant touch with Killgower's college of prophets, to whom he had become a sort of honorary dean after the Reverend Doctor's martyrdom, and was always careful to share any new commentary from that circle with his wife, the historian. It was they who had first drawn attention to the significance of the altered appearance of the sun and moon, in light of the prophecy of Christ Himself in *Matthew* 24: *the sun will be darkened, and the moon will not give its light.* These were indeed the effects produced by the Council's effort to screen from visibility two other signs prophesied in the same passage, that *the stars will fall from heaven*, and *then will appear the sign of the Son of Man in heaven*, the latter being fulfilled by the increasing predominance of the principal stars of Cygnus, the Northern Cross, in the night sky. Maria was grateful for this collegial backup in matters of prophecy, for she had plenty of grist for the mill of her *History* just keeping up with the accelerating pace of developments in the Apocalyptic War of which she was the historian. She also appreciated their counsel, along with that of Maxim's Orthodox sources, on a question arising from a passage in *Revelation* 20, where St. John described the period to come after the *thousand years* symbolizing the dominion of the Church: namely, the epoch of the Antichrist. The latter would *deceive the nations* and *gather them for battle*, so that they *marched up over the broad Earth and surrounded the camp of the saints and the beloved City.* Historically, many Christians had believed this beloved City was the earthly Jerusalem, where Christ was crucified, but now, in the End, Maria could authoritatively report that *that* city was the capital of Antichrist, and was entirely unsafe for any saints of the sort intended, and exemplified, by St. John. No, the *beloved City* was the one St. Paul, in *Hebrews* 12, called the *city of the living God, the heavenly Jerusalem*, and the *assembly of the first-born who are enrolled in heaven*; and that City, that *camp of the saints*, existed wherever the faithful were gathered in worship and prayer.

Secret citadels of that assembly were scattered about the globe, besides the public ones protected by the two wings of the great Eagle, in America and in Russia, and each of those camps of the Kingdom of God was host to the real presence of the Lord. All of them now, as the final battle approached, were threatened by the combined forces of those who were deceived, intimidated, or bought off by the Man of Sin—this was the fulfillment of the Johannine prophecy. In the case of Russia, that ancient bastion of Orthodoxy was again in the dire position so familiar in her history, of being attacked from the east and the west at once, with the powerful Sino-Mongolian alliance gaining ground on the former front while French and German forces mobilized along the latter. The American situation was more complicated, since the GEC had established a number of urban enclaves in metropolitan areas, early in the post-Quake relief operations, and these had subsequently become entrenched. Declining Federal revenues had forced the military into a defensive posture including the billeting and provisioning of troops by civilians, as in Clarion County. Prophetic signs were accumulating thick and fast in this final year of the hypothetical Fortnight. How much more of her *History*, Maria wondered, remained to be written?

Maria also continued to study, at intervals, her Grampa Jefferson's *Journal*. She was frequently amazed by how astutely he had analyzed current events in the optic of information warfare and psychological operations. In March of 2023, for instance, a leftist District Attorney had announced an indictment of the providential President, who was then actively campaigning for the 2024 election, on charges widely deemed frivolous by legal and political commentators. Many of the candidate's supporters were predictably livid with indignation, but Jeremiah, a supporter himself, was more nuanced in his assessment: Was this indeed a deliberate action of the Left, driven by extreme desperation to prevent the President's reelection—or, given the absolutely terrible optics of the move *for the Left*, had the President's people themselves somehow tricked the DA into doing it? Maria had learned a lot from her black grandfather.

II.

The arrival of summer did not herald the hoped-for hot weather to boost the growth of the newly planted corn and beans, let alone to help with the harvest of the barley, oats and wheat—mostly due to the engineered dimming of the sunlight. Even John Eckhart had to admit he had never seen such a dismal prospect for an agricultural season, neither in his forty-two years on this farm nor as a boy growing up in Perry County, and even worse, this was the prevailing situation worldwide. A global famine was looming, and the GEC was reportedly scaling up certain manufacturing operations geared to the production of synthetic foodstuffs—production from exactly what raw materials, was not entirely clear. Whether or not the family would be able to put up enough food for another winter, let alone fulfill the CSA orders while helping feed the troops, was questionable—although some comfort lay in the thought that, perhaps, there would not *be* another winter on this old, woefully fallen Earth.

With all of the foregoing in mind, Christopher found that his *philosophia* remained his chief consolation next to the Lord—excepting perhaps his Sophia incarnate, whom he so fully loved, body and soul. Having long been preoccupied with technical matters relating to the angels, he now found his mind returning to his namesake the Meister, specifically to an axial theme in his thought, namely the direct procession of created intellect from uncreated Intellect. That procession, the Meister taught, established a relation of union, an immediate link of the human intellect with the divine Intellect, the metaphysical *Logos* who became incarnate as Jesus Christ, and that relation of origin afforded a unique possibility to the created intellect of a human person. The Meister referred to a *transposition* or inversion that could be effected—*by divine grace alone*—through which the human intellect could realize its principial identity with the *Logos*, the infinite Intellect of God. This transposition was also described by the Meister as the *birth* of the *Logos* in the human intellect, and the very possibility of such a divine action had fascinated our philosopher since he first understood what it meant. As Psalm 119 put it, *Intellectum da mihi et vivam; Give me intellection and*

I shall live—or Psalm 61, *Set me upon the rock that is higher than I.* Somehow his understanding of this metaphysical paradox anchored his mind in the midst of those murky circumstances.

Another theme much on Christopher's mind that summer, perhaps not surprisingly, was the Last Judgment, which as Scripture abundantly testified, would form a significant part of the eschatological pageantry at the End of Time. Not that he was unduly concerned about his own verdict in that tribunal, or for the eternal destinies of those he loved, for one and all had thrown themselves upon the mercy of Christ, and believed unshakably in His promise to save them. No, it was the metaphysics of the matter that fascinated him, considering that the Judgment was traditionally attributed to Christ, and that Christ Himself had said it was not He who would judge, but rather His *words* (*logoi*). In this light, it seemed to Christopher that the Judgment would amount metaphysically to the direct confrontation of the resurrected person with the uncreated *logos* (in Christ) which was God's original idea of that person. Those who had undergone the washing of regeneration in Holy Baptism, and who had died in the faith, would find their records expunged of all the transgressions for which they had asked forgiveness, and their names inscribed in the *book of life*. The destinies of the rest lay in the mystery of mercy and justice, deep in the mind of God. That was all that he, as a Christian philosopher, was able to say.

Sophia's mood was mostly retrospective during those summer months, as troubles around the farm kept pace with the melancholy state of the world—crop failure, including grass and hay, calves getting sick, chickens dying, and in the middle of July a windstorm that leveled every tree on Christmas Tree Hill, except for the Mother Pine. More and more Sophia found herself in a welcoming posture toward the End that was evidently approaching, and it was this attitude toward the future that set her to reflecting on her past, all of it, from her earliest memories. The Lucky M had been a marvelous place to grow up, beginning with her father setting her in a saddle on old Tolstoy when she was two and a half, which was the very earliest thing she could remember. Then she could recall Manuela letting her spread the icing on her and Max's third birthday cake, and how she blew out all three candles before Max was ready. The two of them had loved to race their horses in the bottomlands, and once had been soundly scolded for stampeding the sheep. A couple of boys had pursued her in high school, but nothing resembling romance had ensued, at least on her part, although she'd enjoyed going out with them occasionally. When Max had decided on Luther-Aquinas for college, she had been leaning toward staying closer to home at Angelo State, but after praying about it for a couple of weeks she was swayed, by what providential prompting she knew not, to share her brother's collegiate adventure in Pennsylvania.

And what an adventure in Pennsylvania! College had just been the start of it, or rather her meeting up with Christopher there, for it was to him, after a three-year detour through graduate school and a virtually timeless round trip to outer space, that she had delightedly plighted her troth and utterly given herself. Her marriage with Chris had been wonderful beyond belief, not totally devoid of fractious occasions, but overwhelming all such exceptions with a steady sense of joy in the whole exquisite enterprise of their life together. Then there was David, who had appeared rather promptly after their nuptials had been properly solemnized, and whose demeanor had consistently pleased them, while his accomplishments exceeded all expectations. To have been wife to such a husband, and mother to such a son, Sophia counted the richest blessings in her life, next to the grace of God in the love of Christ.

Her intellectual life, of course, was also on her list of blessings: how she had been given the aptitude and opportunity to pursue both astronomy and linguistics, and to make significant contributions to both sciences. Not only had she been among the principal architects of the Glorious Synthesis, she had been privileged to direct a master's program focused on that *summa* of biblical creation sciences. Here, however, was where Sophia's romantic retrospective turned ironic. She had graduated her first class of twelve with the M.S. in the Glorious Synthesis, then the Institute was destroyed and its Director killed before the second class could finish, and the whole splendid subject was now considered a criminal enterprise in the category of thought crimes. This ironic turn, however, had been a recent development, and pointed directly to the approach of the End, reminding our Sophia that the return of the Lord Jesus was close at hand, that she was already abiding in His love and His love in her, and that she knew she was safe in the love of Christ.

David and Magdalena, in the meantime, had been working hard on what they expected to be the final episode of White Stone, with a brand-new balladic song and a musical score that highlighted novel variations of melody, harmony and rhythm in the seven-tone system they called their sweet new style. Magdalena's choreographic gift never failed to find fresh sequences of graceful movement that accentuated the meanings emerging in the song and the mellow intonations of the lute, punctuated by her piping. They had perfected a courtliness of style that was mesmerizingly unique, complemented by a sound so sweet that it tugged at the heart of the hearer The magisterial result was the show they entitled, *Final Call for Paradise*, which opened and closed on the following stanza.

> Final call for Paradise!
> Christ the Lord is coming soon!
> Waken! Open wide your eyes:
> Dark the sun and red the moon!
> Turn to Jesus, we advise
> By the portent of our tune:
> Final call for Paradise!

Keeping to precedent, the swan song of White Stone was timed for maximum impact upon the Son of Perdition's propaganda operations. Perhaps from concern about the increasingly evident signs of the times, Nabal had commissioned a musical farce with elaborate pageantry, mocking the idea of the Second Coming of Christ—"the defunct Carpenter," as the Chairman preferred to call Him. The world premiere was scheduled for a special holiday in early August, and all populations under GEC governance were required to tune in to this lavish production, laced with obscenities, of ritual ridicule aimed at an unshakable article of faith for traditional Christians. No sooner had the extravaganza gotten underway, however, than the hundreds of millions of viewers, both willing and unwilling, were startled with delight or with horror to see the call sign of the angelic override, followed by the appearance of the two familiar figures robed in white.

Among those who reacted to the event with horror, of course, was Nabal himself, whom was watching in his private den, alone save for *Therion* and Satan—the former by a sensor array surveilling the room, and the other, to whom Nabal had long since surrendered his soul, by psycho-mental means. Once again the Chairman's erupting rage was commingled with another passion, constelled in a sexual fantasy involving the female figure in this dangerous duo that called themselves White Stone: how he lusted to get his hands on her! Losing his temper, he shouted new orders to *Therion*: all GOL-1AΘ warbots operating in North America were to set as their highest priority the live capture of that boy and girl—especially the girl!

That very girl, having put the finishing touches on her Sadronia story, was daydreaming now about how she would tell the tale of her romance with David—an impossible love of two cousins, made possible by the shortness of their lives. Magdalena could see how awkward it would have been had she and David lived into their twenties and beyond. What could they have done, chosen celibacy? But it was looking like thirteen was about as old as they were going to get, and then they could be lovers forever in Paradise, in whatever way Lord Jesus would arrange. Ever since David had told her about his naughty dream, and they had come to an understanding, the young couple had been hugging and kissing more than ever, although with renewed awareness of the boundaries set by the Lord. Her girlish heart was utterly enchanted with that gallant boy, who was himself so enamored of her. Yet how on Earth would she tell their tale, assuming there were even time enough?

The hero of Magdalena's love story, meanwhile, continued fitting himself for the role, not failing to present his damsel with occasional poems of love, usually accompanied by a bouquet or garland of hand-picked wildflowers, while training his muscular frame in the knightliest fashion. Having proven his prowess in the affair of the mountain lion, David prevailed upon his father to let him have one of the precious supermagnetic slugs, which he kept in a special pocket in his ammo pouch, in the event he ever came face to face with one of the killer bots. Chris had retained four of the slugs, three of which had been loaded for shotguns carried by John, Sergei and himself, so David was able to requisition the extra one. It was not expected that anyone would get more than one shot at a Goliath, anyway.

David also liked talking to his Aunt Maria about game theory, which he knew she was employing in her historical analysis of the Apocalyptic War. The Christ Child had spoken to Magdalena and him about playing a game, and Aunt Maria had hypothesized, half-jokingly, that divine Intelligence was using game theory to set up His archetypal Adversary for his final downfall. First of all, she

317

had explained to her nephew, the final War was clearly a zero-sum game of competition for human souls, every one of which, reembodied in the Resurrection, would end up either in the City of Light or in the Outer Darkness. At the End of Time, the sum of all souls would be fixed, with every soul ending up in the Light a victory for the Lord and a loss for the Devil, and every soul ending up in the darkness vice versa: every gain was also a loss, so the sum was zero, and the interests of the players were diametrically opposed. Aunt Maria had also spoken of the distinction of finite games from infinite games, where the goal of a finite game was for one of the players to win, ending the game, while the goal of an infinite game was to keep on playing. In this optic, the Devil would presumably prefer an infinite game, while the infinite Intelligence had revealed His intention to conclude the game with an ultimate victory over the Adversary. In the interim, as in any game, it was moves and countermoves, until the Almighty made the ultimate move.

Sergei Lossky remained a dyed-in the-wool literatus, regardless of the absence of any teaching position or lecture podium from which to profess his views. He had come across an interesting pair of books by John Steinbeck: a 1948 *Russian Journal* relating the writer's forty-day tour of the post-war Soviet Union; and "an inspection of our whole nation and its citizens by a blowed-in-the-glass American," entitled *America and Americans*, published nearly two decades later in 1966. Since the literary comparison of his two countries had long been a salient concern of Sergei's, he was curious what light Steinbeck's two narratives might

shed on the matter, and the lavish photographic illustrations in both volumes only added to their interest. *A
Russian Journal* proved impossible to read without a thick
lens of irony, for while Steinbeck's narrative sketches of
Russian peoples and their cultures were both accurate and
sympathetic, the invisible glare of the Gulag Archipelago
shone ironically upon the hospitable scenes he described.
The tour had of course been planned and supervised by
the Stalinist regime, and Steinbeck seemed in awe of the
extraordinary devotion, even adoration, bestowed upon
Stalin by the Russian peoples. "Nothing in the Soviet
Union goes on outside the vision of the plaster, bronze,
painted or embroidered eye of Stalin." Even in their homes,
they all but worshipped him: "The stores sell millions and
millions of his face, and every house has at least one picture
of him." Moreover, the peoples' love of the Great Leader was
confirmed by every single Russian of whom he inquired. It
evidently escaped the American writer that this was what
the face of Terror looked like!

In the American book, Steinbeck was much more in his
element, producing an affectionate and sometimes humor-
ous portrait of his country, though not without bold
streaks of stern criticism shaped by reflective observation.
In his final chapter, "Americans and the Future," Steinbeck
arrived at dark considerations regarding the nation's destiny.
He wrote of a "subtle and deadly illness," a "creeping, evil
thing that is invading every cranny of our political, our
economic, our spiritual, and our psychic life." It is not
just "immorality," he says, struggling to define the illness
afflicting the nation, nor does "lack of integrity" exactly

describe it, nor "dishonesty" either. "What are we losing or have lost?" he asked, and his answer was *rules*. "The rules were not always obeyed but they were believed in, and breaking them was savagely punished." But this was where Steinbeck's argument veered toward the comic: "Early on to make the rules effective they were put out as the commands of a God and therefore not open to question." Implicit in that comment was that, of course, we now know that was all nonsense. What struck Sergei as *funny* was that Steinbeck saw no connection between the "creeping, evil" loss of respect for rules, on the one hand, and the dismissal of the belief that basic rules originate from a real God, on the other. But the punch line was Steinbeck's own theory of the origin of the "subtle and deadly illness." He wrote: "I believe it is because we have reached the end of a road and have no new path to take, no duty to carry out, and no purpose to fulfill." The natural purpose of humankind, in Steinbeck's view, had simply been survival, and with that goal accomplished by scientific technology, there was no reason to continue—since any *supernatural* purpose was *ruled out*! Sergei found it utterly uproarious.

Not so uproarious, by contrast, was the deteriorating security situation in Clarion County and around it, as the Adversary's culminating offensive began to be felt even within the prevailing strongholds of the American Republic, the Russian Federation, and a few remote autonomous regions. Still, Sergei loved riding for the Posse, and was proud to be in possession of one of the precious bot-killer slugs, loaded for the twenty-gauge shotgun he carried, a single-barrel with excellent accuracy at short range, as demonstrated by numerous practice rounds. He knew any attempt to stop a Goliath would most likely be at close range in the wooded areas he patrolled, and that the chance of success would be small, unless the bot were delayed or distracted somehow. In any case, he was in this fight to the End, as were they all. Several skirmishes were reported in Armstrong County just to the south, when Posse and Spec Ops patrols had encountered GEC teams moving north along the Allegheny River, and Butler County to the west logged the first Goliath sighting—all in the month of July. Fortunately, the bot had encountered a tank deployed by the military command and been blown to smithereens, but it was all too clear that the War was now close at hand. Thank God for the ADP!

The food outlook was also dire, as crop failures continued to reduce the farm's production, until Rosa announced that the family would have to curtail their own consumption in order to provide at least some produce to their customers and the military. Furthermore, she said, if time continued on into another winter, she didn't know *what* they would all eat. Disaster followed disaster. The new pullets all died, and when the mature birds went into summer molt, egg production plummeted. There had been a shortage of new calves, and half the ones they did get failed to thrive. Manuela's best nanny contracted severe mastitis and lost her milk.

At least, with less produce to handle, Rosa and Manuela had more time to spend in leisurely conversations, alternately sharing reminiscences of raising their two remarkable sets of twins, and consoling one another spiritually regarding the sorrows they both suffered. Opening their motherly hearts to one another, the two women found joy in a joint treasury of recollections, each surprisingly clear, and clad with the exact emotion that had animated its original—or so it seemed to them. Spiritually, Rosa had the fruits of her Evangelical and Catholic faith, and Manuela of her Catholic and Orthodox, to share in mutual consolations amid the darkness and the shadow of death gathering above and around all they held dear.

John, Chris and Sergei often sat together on the veranda those summer evenings, drinking John's dark, strong *starkbier* and talking about everything from the latest military intelligence to the most recent agricultural disaster, to the looming question, unavoidable now, of the imminence of the End. Maxim often joined these rustic symposia as well, whether he and Maria, with or without Magdalena, were driving back to the parsonage late, or whether they were staying overnight as they sometimes did. One evening in late July, the priest shared several passages from St. Gregory of Nyssa's *Dialogue on the Soul and the Resurrection*, which he had recently been rereading. Gregory's sister St. Macrina, had voiced in that dialogue the doctrine that "resurrection is the restoration of our nature to its original condition," and that "after the fire has consumed whatever is contrary to nature, then the nature of the redeemed will flourish and will ripen into fruit, receiving again the common form which was set upon us by God in the beginning, the archetypal beauty." This notion of what they would soon be facing, as the purification of created nature from the corruption spawned by the Fall, led to a thoughtful interchange between Maxim and Christopher to which their fathers listened with interest. Another evening several weeks later, after the four had downed about half of their allotted brew, Maxim pulled out an envelope addressed to himself and bearing a Louisiana postmark. Removing a folded slip of paper from the envelope, he read slowly and rhythmically:

> But Evangeline's heart was sustained by a vision, that faintly
> Floated before her eyes, and beckoned her on through the moonlight.
> Over them, vast and high, extended the cope of a cedar.
> Swinging from its great arms, the trumpet-flower and the grapevine
> Hung their ladder of ropes aloft, like the ladder of Jacob,
> On whose pendulous stairs the angels ascending, descending,
> Were the swift hummingbirds, that flitted from blossom to blossom.
> Such was the vision Evangeline saw, as she slumbered beneath it.
> Filled was her heart with love, and the dawn of an opening heaven
> Lighted her soul in sleep, with the glory of regions celestial.

"Longfellow!" Sergei exclaimed. As the voice of his son fell silent. "I'd know his hexameters anywhere." Christopher quietly added: "Lines from the poem for which she was named, and though enigmatic, signaling that she is well, and portending perhaps what is coming." Other such engaging evenings also transpired on the veranda that summer.

Maria was struggling with a surge of anxiety as the season wore on, not so much with regard to the general conditions of life in this seventh of the Darkening Years as by the specific fact reported by her intel sources: that the Man of Sin had very specific designs on her daughter. She knew they had the mobile ADP for protection, and that they could quickly flee to the farm if necessary, where the wider perimeter was deployed. Still, the very thought of that Satanic intention was loathsome and terrifying, and she needed constantly to take refuge in prayer, for spiritual fortitude, and frequently to distract her mind with her *History of the Apocalyptic War*. Maria had begun pondering some kind of coda to the sprawling narrative—something Thucydides had not lived to do for the war of which he was the historian—although she was not unaware of the irony of considering a coda to a history she could not possibly write to its end. The sole retrospective would be from Paradise, and the idea of writing history while dwelling in eternity made her smile—though after all, the saints in light would presumably enjoy modes of bliss according to their created characters, so anything was possible. Maybe Magdalena would be writing her romance there, too.

Meanwhile, as the year advanced into September, the

closest to a coda our historian could come was a summary of her assessment of the American Restoration as a key stratagem in the Apocalyptic War. The Descent into the darkness of global tyranny had nearly transpired forty years sooner, when it was interrupted by the presidential inauguration of January 2017, in conjunction with other events around the world. From that point, the first seven years had been devoted to a demonstration of national possibilities, and to multiple disclosures of operations inimical to those possibilities, so the real Eliatic flowering had amounted to little more than three decades—but what glorious decades! It seemed to our historian a fitting culmination of the American adventure, to have been one of the wings of the great Eagle, as the close of the Age drew near.

Maria was also conspiring with Sophie, keeping their mothers in the loop, to surprise Magdalena and David with a special party for their thirteenth birthday. The menfolk, too, were assigned roles to play in the simple courtly ceremony that was planned, which would include a series of clips of White Stone. The cousins had been born, as the reader may recall, on the Feast of the Holy Cross, September 14, which happened to fall that year on a Friday. Accordingly, it was arranged that Maria's family would stay over in the farmhouse cottage the night before, start the birthday festivities at breakfast, and continue intermittently through an early supper before driving down to New Bethlehem for the Divine Liturgy of the Holy Cross.

At precisely 3:00 AM that Friday morning, the entire family was awakened from sleep by the mellow sound of a horn, issuing from every aeviphone in the farmhouse and cottage. Checking their phones, everyone found the following text:

> RECALLED TO CELESTIAL BATTALION.
> PERIMETER DOWN.
> RIDE TO HILLTOP AND PRAY.
> HOI ANGELOI.

Maxim, in addition, received the following instructions:

> REMEMBER THE CIBORIUM.
> AT TRUMPET BLAST, POUR.

The priest had not returned the golden vessel to its compartment inside the Participator after activating the ADP. Instead, Max had committed it to Christopher's keeping in the cottage, where it was now quickly retrieved and stowed in a pouch belted about Maxim's waist. Dressing quickly but without panic, they all made their way to the stable, where the seven steeds were swiftly saddled while the assignment of riders was arranged. Since there were ten of the latter, it was decided that Alba would carry John and Rosa, Tolstoy Sergei and Manuela, and Samson David and Magdalena, with Chris and Sophie on Honeysuckle and Sable, respectively, and Max and Maria on Thunder and Dancer.

The night was pitch dark as they rode out of the farm-yard and onto the tractor path toward Christmas Tree Hill, the highest "hilltop" on the farm. Besides the fact that their mounts knew the way, however, their direction was also marked by a celestial sign. The Northern Cross of the starry Swan loomed large and blue in the northwest sky. Shining like sapphire through the thick nanoparticulate haze, its bottommost star, Albireo, marked the exact direction of their flight. David and Magdalena had been first to saddle up. Once mounted, and without waiting for instruction, they had assumed the lead, their stalwart mule stepping swiftly along the path while the rest fell into double file behind them. As all eyes adjusted to the darkness, the blue luminescence of the sideral Cross allowed them to distinguish major features of the landscape, and soon the Guardian Oaks were discerned, marking the entrance to the woodland. Suddenly, Samson snorted and drew up, just as David sighted the reason for the mule's alarm: standing athwart the path, barely ten yards away, was a GOL-1AΘ! The standing orders under which the massive warbot was operating were to destroy all personnel in its patrol area *except*—and this proved its fatal flaw—in the case of the two juveniles known as White Stone, who were to be captured alive (especially the female). David and Magdalena, fully informed of that order, shouted in unison, "We are White Stone!"

Our boy hero had already loaded his sling with the supermagnetic slug, and as the Goliath stepped toward them, leaning slightly forward for a closer look, he made his move. David could feel Magdalena's arms around his waist as he drew and aimed with the lightning speed years of practice had honed. The lethal slug found its target in the critical forehead sensor of the foe. The monstrous figure froze momentarily, then went slack and collapsed to the ground. Taking no pause for elaborate congratulations, the family quietly cheered their champion as they rode on into the woods, making their way toward the hilltop to which they had been directed by the angels.

Fortunately, John and Chris had cleared a path to the top, through the band of fallen evergreens wrought by the windstorm. When they reached the Mother Pine their view was unimpeded, as they looked down over the tops of the Guardian Oaks toward the farmstead. Immediately, they began singing and chanting psalms, hymns and spiritual canticles, which they continued with prayers interspersed. Just after 3:30 a glow flared up in the direction of New Bethlehem, indicating a major fire. As their devout incantations continued, other fires appeared in the night—neighboring farms aflame. Around 4:00, as they continued to pray for mercy and protection, their own house and buildings began to burn. At this range they could see the incendiary operatives at work, some of whom were beginning to examine the path the family had just taken. At that moment, Sophia looked around to the northwest, where the enormous blue Cross blazed in the hazy sky, and remarked that Albireo was about to touch the horizon, as if planting the celestial Cross on Earth. Refusing to watch the agents of doom approaching from below, she and several others kept an eye on the star until, just as it was setting—behold! The blast of a trumpet like none that ever before had shaken the atmosphere of Earth, resounding as if the air itself were brass. Whereupon Father Maxim, having maintained his presence of mind in prayer, immediately retrieved the golden ciborium from its pouch, removed the top, and poured out its shimmering contents upon the ground.

And so, dear reader, our *Romances* arrive at the End of Time. Accordingly, in a very real sense, the actions remaining to be described were essentially simultaneous, even though it is necessary to narrate them sequentially. As the gold fluid, poured out by Father Maxim, splashed on the ground, *in an instant, in the twinkling of an eye*, everything changed. A shaft of light pierced the night sky from east to west. They heard the Guardian Oaks and the other *trees of the wood shout for joy*, even as they proceeded to burst into flame, and at the same time everything else, including their physical bodies, *dissolved with fire* in one brief, excruciating flash. And yet they found themselves embodied still, and fully conscious, and now they were rising, and as they ascended they saw *the Son of Man coming in a cloud with power and great glory*. Mounted *on a white horse* rode the Child they knew so well, but now *His eyes were like a flame of fire, and on His head were many diadems. And the armies of heaven, arrayed in fine linen, white and pure, followed him on white horses*.

On all sides and to a great distance, our Metaphysicals could see others rising in their celestial bodies. Mounted angels were rounding them up and gathering them to the royal Child. Below, the surface of the old Earth seemed spread out flat into one great plain, except for one mountain to the east, which rose higher and higher. As it rose, they saw the holy City, New Jerusalem, *coming down out of heaven from God*, until it rested atop the great mountain. Converging with the others toward the radiant figure of their Savior, they *saw a great white throne and Him who sat upon it, and the dead, great and small, standing before the throne, and books were opened, and the dead were judged.*

EPILOGUE:
THE LAST JUDGMENT

I Poet, having proven a romancer,
Must henceforth ply my tale in rhyme and meter,
For only such a form may hope to answer

The call I now pursue. Assist me sweeter
To sing, O Holy Spirit, as I venture
To bring these characters before Saint Peter,

Or rather, before Christ. E'er having sent Your
Creative energies to aid my faithful thinking,
O send them now, as I bend this adventure

T'ward Paradise. Prevent my song from sinking
Beneath its theme, and help it voice the voices
Of these my characters, their viewpoints linking

Before the Lord. Ahead, my poem poises
To enter Heav'n, but first the final Judgment
Must be traversed, ere anyone rejoices

Around the Throne. And so they stand, their touch rent
From mortal flesh, now clothed afresh in bodies
Of living light, before Him who'd so much meant

To all of them. So will I stand, when God sees
Fit that it be—but now my voice must neighbor
Another voice, who more my tale embodies.

I Maxim, stand before the Lord my Savior,
My life an open book, clearly detailing
My inmost thoughts and my outmost behavior—

I am appalled! An open book, assailing
Any pretense to the prescribed perfection,
Any slight hope of possibly prevailing

By my own merit. But I see affection
In those bright eyes of flame, as they examine
My mortal life—this searing vivisection

Is done with love. Revealed is all my famine
For fantasies inflaming sexual passion,
Despite my best intentions, duly damnin'

Me by the law. More than I could imagine
My small hypocrisies appear expanded,
Larger than life—those times when I would fashion

Some little falsehood. Searing light so candid,
O Lord my Savior, cleanly cauterizes
My sinful soul, and I emerge rebranded

By my *logos* in Thee. But now arises
My lady, who is also undergoing
This Judgment, and as I voice its surprises,

So I Maria, stand before the knowing
Gaze of those eyes. My being is transparent
To His omniscience: He sees my pride, owing

To my achievements, and beholds my arrant
Failure to overcome that temperamental
Streak in my soul. My prowess as a parent,

Which largely rested on the transcendental
Endowments of my daughter, I have prided
Myself upon. It was God-given mental

Power that wrought my works, yet I abided
In self-esteem, and even felt superior
To certain peers. No misdeed is elided

Upon the pages of this book, as drearier
My record grows—but I reach out for mercy,
And He responds. His blazing eyes beam cheerier

Into my heart; I feel His grace immerse me,
Dissolving all my faults as fire already
Dissolved my mortal flesh—not to disperse me

But purify. And now, I spy the steady
Form of my brother, fixed in the unerring
Stare of the Lord; his voice is firm, if heady:

I Christopher, who long displayed such daring
In metaphysics, yet could never master
Flammable fury, raging anger, airing

Itself in words—now stand before the Pastor
Of all the sheep. Blasphemous phrases shouted
In dudgeon high—or uttered silently, the faster

To cover them—are now completely outed
In awful clarity. Oft I directed
Anger at others, although seldom touted

The feeling outwardly, my heart infected
Nevertheless. Therefore my condemnation
Is justified—and yet I am elected

By Him whose fiery eyes have observation
Of all I am. Sudden, I rediscover
Within those eyes my own predestination,

Foreknown eternally by Him, the Lover
Of humankind. A chorus of rejoicing
Sounds in my heart, my body seems to hover

In liquid light—now she, my love, is poising
Before the Throne. As I have made confession
In the clear Light, sincere contrition voicing,

So I Sophia, speaking in succession,
Behold thy burning eyes, my Lord, inspecting
My life minutely, and thine intercession

I humbly seek. I see thine eyes reflecting
My special taint, the envious resentment
Of good befalling others—and correcting

That mortal flaw. Where once I found contentment
Eluding me, because I was comparing
Myself with others, thy saving emendment

Hath made me whole. Incisive vision, paring
My very soul of the corruption and perversion
Wrought by the Fall—I thank Thee for so caring

To make me pure. Long have I known immersion
Within thy love, but now in resurrection
Body reformed, I joy in a new version

Of that affection. Like an intersection
Of sweet *amor* and brilliant light, cohering
Between my heart and thine, O Lord—affection

Divine and human. Lo! the light is clearing,
And here is my beloved son, the poet
And the musician—Hark! His voice I'm hearing:

I David, though my short life may not show it,
Was wicked in my way—just for example,
Throwing a rock where I knew not to throw it,

Or snitching cookies. Also, I would trample
Mud and manure in places where I shouldn't,
And several times I shot birds in the bramble,

Just for the practice. It was like I *couldn't*
Always be good, no matter how I wanted
To measure up—but sometimes I just *wouldn't*,

I don't know why. I constantly was haunted
By knowing You, my Lord, achieved obedience
In your lifetime; while I, despite my vaunted

Accomplishments, have failed in full allegiance
To follow You. Then too, my maturation
Made the sweet girl, whose love had shown me regions

Of high romance, into a fresh temptation
Born of the flesh. But You, my Lord, while playing
Your game with us, accomplished my salvation

And gave me peace. I am praising and praying
Your Name, O Lord—and look! I see her features
Who is my lady. List what she is saying:

I Magdalena, come before our Teacher's
Radiant face confessing mostly excess
Of human love, more focused upon creatures

Than You, Creator. To be really reckless,
One creature in particular, who always
Ruled in my heart—You know, my Lord!—nor sexless

Feelings I mean. My love could ne'er forestall praise
Of You, my Lord, and yet my girlhood lover
Often eclipsed your image, in the small maze

Of my heart's core. You know, my Lord! No cover
Do I attempt, but only plead your presence
Within my love for him, and beg You suffer

This presence still. Shall we not share your essence
In Paradise? For I surmise your sentence,
Merciful Lord: etched in the incandescence

Of your dear face, I see my full dependence
On grace fulfilled. Gone is the time of seeking,
For we are found in glad attendance

At your high court, my Lord, now peeking
T'ward Paradise—standing in sweet composure
While, far away, another voice is speaking:

I Poet, bring this Epilogue to closure
With these few observations: Six examples
Must serve to signify our Lord's disclosure

Of Judgement to His own—symbolic samples
Of His Salvation. I do not voice the voices
Of those who turned away—Nabal in shambles

Before the Lord, hearing the awful noises
Of all his victims, burning still with passions
He had embraced. Those whom the Lord annoyest,

Who hate His Word and spurn His great compassion,
I do not sing. But if the Holy Spirit aid me,
And the good angels, I shall seek to fashion

A song of Paradise, where serenade me
My Metaphysicals, as I imagine:
All to the glory of the Lord who made me.